"The Bai ~~MW01516208~~ novels get. ᴛᴀɴʏᴀ ɴɪᴄʜᴏʟs is able to achieve many different effects without appearing to try very hard, and therein lies much of the beauty of this achingly fine and wondrous creation. She made these characters come alive, and she made me care deeply about their fate. She's a wise and sure-handed writer. I loved her book."—**Steve Yarbrough**

"The Barber's Wife is a compelling story of love and loyalty set in rural America, but above all, it's a powerful and moving portrait of one woman's courage and competence in response to the acute human need she observes around her. A small town surgical nurse in 1930s Oklahoma, Mayme Holloway is gritty, smart, independent, and she is sometimes unexpectedly noble. She challenges traditional moral conventions and lives by her own evolving and authentic values—often at great risk. Tanya Nichols is a master storyteller, and this is a fabulous book."—**Corrinne Clegg Hales**

"In sparkling prose, Tanya Nichols has opened up a moment in history, reinventing several months in the life of notorious but beloved bank robber Pretty Boy Floyd through the lens of the fictional Mayme Holloway. The genius of this novel is the way Nichols keeps Floyd in the background, never borrowing significance and proving, as Yann Martel asserts," fiction is closer to the full experience of life." Mayme is wonderfully drawn, vibrantly alive on the page, smart, passionate, flawed. The supporting cast is equally vivid, and the dusty, quietly threatening atmosphere of 1932 in northeastern Oklahoma

1

accurately and subtly rendered. This is a graceful and compelling novel. That it is a first novel is enormously impressive."—**Liza Wieland**`

The Barber's Wife

Tanya Nichols

Alternative Book Press
2 Timber Lane
Suite 301
Marlboro, NJ 07746
www.alternativebookpress.com

2014 Paperback Edition
Copyright 2014 © Tanya Nichols
Cover Illustration by CL Smith
Book Design by Alternative Book Press
All rights reserved
Published in the United States of America by Alternative Book Press

Originally published in electronic form in the United States by Alternative Book Press.

Library of Congress Cataloging-in-Publication Data
(available on request)
Publication Data
Tanya, Nichols, [2014]
The Barber's Wife/ by Tanya Nichols—1st ed.
p. cm.
1. General (Fiction). I Title.
PS1-3576.T36N534   2014
813'.6—dc23

ISBN 978-1-940122-22-9
Printed in the United States of America
10 9 8 7 6 5 4 3 2 1

For Mary Kate

Contents

1.

Mayme dropped two glass vials into her dress pocket, locked the glass front cupboard, and quietly slipped out the side door without saying good-bye. It wasn't exactly stealing; she was simply taking some necessary items to another place, more like shifting things around than thievery.

She hummed an old lullaby as she tiptoed down the stone path, her soft voice charming the quiet half moon. She and the fading moon were both tired; it was time for them to rest. Most days, Mayme welcomed the early morning walk home just to get some fresh air into her lungs, to forget the foul odors of sick people and what it took to cure them. But tonight, her feet were on fire and her back ached like she'd been hauling bricks instead of bedpans and pills. She planned on taking Ernie Bell up on his offer for a ride down the hill, but by the time she got out the door, a rumbling snore buzzed from the back of his ambulance. Waking him from that deep a sleep just to carry her a couple of blocks seemed more than cruel. So she walked.

The road seemed treacherous in the dark, but she knew so well the only real dangers were stray stones and dips that could send her tumbling. Mayme licked her lips and closed her eyes, taking several steps blindly. She let her jaw drop and her mouth open as if her chin was the guide through darkness.

The damp morning air tasted cool enough to drink. She listened, testing her senses, imagining a world without vision. A band of crickets trilled sweetly in the tall grass, their spindly legs working furiously to fill the night with eerie music, their secret language. If Wilma were here, she would say they were celebrating the birth of a baby girl, but Mayme knew better. Those were the sounds of males, chirping and screeching a mating call to some lonely female cricket hiding in the tall rough weeds, listening, listening. The wooing songs will grow softer as the lady cricket draws near, as though he whispers and murmurs impossible promises. And like most foolish girls, she will believe every one of them. Within an hour the crooners' seductive pleas will be lost to the thrum of cicadas, but at the brink of dawn, it is the crickets' song that drifts through the trees, a serenade for lonely hearts and early risers. Mayme loved the sounds of darkness.

She opened her eyes and smiled at the thought of Wilma and her stories, old Cherokee myths that she believed in every bit as much as Mayme's grandmother had, as much as O.C. believed in his Bible. But how, she wondered, pondering the old legend, could anyone expect to tell the difference between a cricket singing a happy tune for a girl baby and a sad lament for the baby boy who might grow up and shoot the little bug? Their chirping just sounded like crickets, no happy or sad about it. And besides, the sex of a child was a simple case of chromosomes. But no matter how many times she explained the science to Wilma, Wilma said the crickets knew as much as any science book. Foolishness. But, still, Mayme had to admit, her friend was always right; there was no denying it.

When they were just scrawny girls sharing a desk at school, Wilma would stop whatever she was doing, lift her chin and listen hard to a screeching insect, and a slight smile would spread across her face. She'd lean over and whisper to Mayme, "oh, I bet Mrs. So and So just had a new baby girl" or "uh-oh little cricket, it's a boy been born, better watch out."

Whatever tune those crickets were singing this morning, Mayme knew for a fact that the newest baby in town was a girl because she had been there when Alice Grant delivered her only a few hours ago. It was the one bright spot of a long night of emptying foul-smelling vomit basins and bedpans. She was there, wiping the new mother's forehead with a cool cloth, holding her hand, whispering words of encouragement through the long hours of painful labor. She wiped tears from the mother's cheeks as her body stretched and cramped to pass the tiny body through a dark narrow passage. Before the night ended, she witnessed the dark patch of crowning head, then purplish shoulders slip from the warm safety of a watery womb. Under a glaring light, the baby gagged and choked on the first breath that filled her tiny lungs with air. All that struggle, all that pain, over in one breath. Sometimes, it was beautiful.

Mayme had taken the wet and wriggling newborn from the hands of Doc Mooney, the same man who had pulled her into the world nearly thirty years before. She held the baby tight while he cut the slick umbilical cord, then wiped her clean and wrapped her in a soft flannel blanket. Odd, she thought, that she, a childless woman, was the first person to actually cuddle the little girl, her mother still chloroform groggy, gazing at her new child through half-closed eyes. It felt better then good to hold such a fresh bundle of life, a perfect weight in the crook of her arm; the sweet smell of blood and birth even better then the smell of rain in August. That was what the crickets really knew. Their whistling and screeching pierced the blackest night with lovely mystery.

Over the low water bridge and down College Avenue she walked, her polished white shoes gathering dust along the way. She watched her feet, counted to ten slowly, then looked up. How far had she traveled in ten seconds? These were her rituals of the night, feigned blindness, then the counting of footsteps.

A yellow light glowed on the second floor of Dr. Stern's house. She could just barely make out the Masonic symbol mounted just below the roofline, a remnant from the days of Judge Hardy. Thirty some odd years earlier, before Mayme was even born, the judge had built the big house for his wife, Sarah, and their black dog, Chester, hoping to fill the rooms with a bunch of perfect children that never came. Mayme was working the night they brought the old man in, his skin shiny like wet dough, spittle drooling down the side of his face, everything stiff and frozen on the left side of his body. She took one look and knew he'd had a stroke. It didn't take a medical degree to see that. He was dead by morning, and it wasn't long before Mrs. Hardy sold the big old house and nearly everything in it to the newest doctor in town. Mayme didn't know if Dr. Stern was a Mason; but she doubted it. He didn't seem to have time or inclination for any sort of Masonic ritual nonsense. Doc Mooney was slowing down, turning more and more of his patients over to the younger man. That's what Doc called him, the younger man. From what Mayme could tell, this younger man worked most all the time. Besides seeing patients at the hospital and in his home office, where he treated everything from pinworms to polio, he made regular visits to the children's home before calling it a day. And that was if there was no emergency that called him into the hospital during the night. No matter how frantic the day, he kept a quiet way about him. At first Mayme thought he might be snooty, like so many of the doctors had been during her time at nursing school, but she changed her mind about that after one late night in the operating room picking gallstones out of Helen McKinney's gut, one by one.

Exhausted and hungry, once Helen was back in the ward, they had sat at the small table on the upstairs sleeping porch. Though they were almost too tired to eat, they shared the fried chicken sandwich she'd brought for her dinner and a pot of warmed-up coffee left over from the morning. It was so easy, sitting with him, eating and talking about patients, their various illnesses and new treatments he'd been reading about.

"Lester Hokes has me somewhat puzzled," he'd said. "He's had an epileptic seizure every week for the past month. If I give him any more phenobarbital, he'll be a walking comatose fool. What do you think, Mrs. Holloway? You have any ideas?"

What did she think? For a moment, Mayme was dumb struck. It wasn't that she wasn't used to chiming in with her opinions, but being invited to actually offer them by someone like Dr. Stern, a doctor from New York, caused her typical wit to stumble.

"Oh, Lord, I don't know, maybe . . ." She paused to take a sip of cold coffee, not wanting to say something foolish. Her gaze lingered over the porch railing into the tallest branches of the black locust tree that offered cool shade to feverish patients on the second floor. "Well, I think it's interesting that he seems to have more seizures in the spring and summer, fewer in the winter. It could be the cold chills his brain, keeps it from misfiring, and the heat speeds it up." She sipped again at the cold coffee, pleased with her contribution to the conversation, even if it was not a theory found in any medical journal. Dr. Stern had no comment; he seemed to be lost in contemplation. She wanted to add more, something smarter than the weather.

She closed her eyes for a moment and really considered Lester. What was different about Lester as opposed to some other seizure patient? She'd known him all her life, like she knew most everybody in town. "You know, his wife mentioned he's been working two jobs lately. He's up half the night cleaning offices over at the college, then works all day over at Hulbert's cotton gin. I've heard fatigue can trigger a seizure. Maybe he should simply get more sleep. Especially with all that phenobarb running through him."

11

"You're right," Dr. Stern said, turning to look directly at her. "About fatigue. Maybe I can convince him to cut back to one job, see if that helps, and start him on a ketogenic diet while I'm at it."

"I thought that was just for little kids."

"It is, but it's worth a try. And good for you for knowing that." He smiled and nodded his head in admiration.

The small compliment revived her sense of humor and endless need to charm her audience. "Well if you're trying diet, my grandmother would have had him eating bread baked with a little placenta mixed in. Next time we deliver a baby, I could run home and do a little baking for him." She lifted her eyebrows and grinned, knowing how silly the old lady's folk medicine must sound to someone like him, but also knowing there were plenty of folks who preferred the placenta bread to the shots and pills they offered at the hospital.

Dr. Stern had laughed at that idea, but not in a scoffing, uppity way that she'd imagined. He actually scrunched his eyebrows a little, as if he might be thinking past the old-timey foolishness, considering the possibility and potential science in the homespun medicine of hill folk. Mayme had a hunch that he was going to be special somehow. She liked him, and she really liked sitting there with him, talking about treatments and cures, just enjoying each other's company for a change, not just passing instruments and wiping his brow during surgery.

There were rumors around town that the new doctor was sick himself, he was so thin, but Mayme thought he was probably just worn out by supper time and if there wasn't someone there to offer him half her chicken sandwich, he might just skip eating altogether. And, she figured, he probably didn't get enough rest with the hours he seemed to keep. No matter what shift she worked, night or day, he showed up there at some point. He needed to take a night off and find himself a wife, someone really

12

smart like him, maybe one of those college girls from Northeastern.

In front of the Jensen's big house, a yellow cat crept out from under a mulberry tree, studied Mayme with two glowing green eyes, then dashed across the yard and up the trunk of a hackberry tree, a streak of gold in the dim light, the hunter in search of some wild prey.

"Scat," she whispered, even though the cat was already long gone to some unseen hiding place.

Mayme trudged on. She knew how tired felt as much as anybody, particularly after two weeks straight of twelve twelve-hour shifts and nearly every bed full, but she also knew how hard it was for the folks who didn't have any work at all. They were tired in a whole different kind of way, and she thought their hungry weariness might be worse then her own aching feet and heavy eyes. She saw it too many times. She wasn't a doctor, but most of the hill folk knew her from way back when and trusted her. They also knew she wouldn't want any money, that she wouldn't take it even if they had it to offer. Lord knows she'd delivered more than a few babies in old shacks out in the woods for nothing more than a handful of wild greens or maybe a couple of freshly laid brown eggs. She didn't need the food and hated to take it, but there was such joyful pride in the offering, she couldn't refuse. And then there were those folks who called on her because she knew how to do more then patch them up; she knew how to keep a secret. She let those folks pay all they wanted. That payment wasn't out of any sense of pride, and it sure wasn't a handful of greens or a sack of eggs. It was cash.

Past Delaware, Keetoowah and Choctaw Streets. Ten steps more. She finally looked up to see a dim yellow light glowing from the bedroom window of her small white clapboard house on Chickasaw Street. The earth began to glow with the promise of a pretty day. She wouldn't see it if she was lucky. Her days were mostly lost to sleeping in a dark room, the oversized shades drawn tight to shield her from any hint of daylight.

Mayme didn't hurry in. She sat on the porch steps listening to the last of the cricket serenade, slowly unraveling her plaited and twisted-up hair, dropping the bobby pins into her cap. She was waiting on the sun, just one glimpse of the morning sky before going to bed where she would dream in colors brighter than any she'd ever known.

Her head ached from the pinch of the knot she had coiled at the nape of her neck, the lumpy bun worn just below the rim of the white cap. O.C. had cut it off short for her a few months back, showed her how to put a nice wave to it with pin curls, even bought her a hair waver; but before she knew it, her limp yellow hair was hanging down past her shoulders, needing to be braided to stay in a bun. The fancy hair waver sat in a drawer unused. He kept telling her to come to the shop and get it trimmed up, but she hadn't made the time. It was just as easy to pin it up she told him; no one really saw it anyway. He seemed disappointed, even offered to cut it on the back porch some afternoon, but she resisted. She hated to admit even to herself that she liked it long enough to pull a strand of hair through the small gap in two of her teeth, a tiny place where bits of food lodged and made her crazy until she could get it out of there. She tried to remember to stick a piece of thread in her pocket, but it never seemed to be there when she needed it. A strand of hair was always there. She just hoped no one ever saw her do such a nasty thing.

As the sun inched higher, Mayme sat and massaged her scalp, letting the pain in her head, back, and feet melt away. She closed her eyes and imagined a spindly male cricket, crouching in the tall grass, trilling softly, his fragile legs scraping and rubbing together, anxious for romance. She listened carefully, motionless, certain by the softening tones that a female was close by.

Inside the small house, O.C. was beginning his day as hers came to an end. Right about now, he would be shaving, expertly running the straight-edge razor down his neck and along the jaw line, always following the grain of his beard. He'd hold a hot towel over his face, letting the steamy heat seep into his pores to remove any trace of lather before splashing on a dose of his homemade aftershave, a concoction of spring water, a splash of moonshine, sprigs of mountain mint and dried lavender. By the time he came out of the bathroom, he would be sweet smelling, his hair combed slick, his white shirt tucked neatly into his grey wool slacks. After taking a close look at himself in the mirror, a silly smile would stretch across his boyish face, pleased with the good-looking man he'd see there.

There was a time, not so many years ago, that she would hurry home from working a night shift, slip into the house quietly, leave her white dress and shoes dropped on the kitchen floor and slide into bed, naked as a jaybird. O.C. would be lying there, waiting for her, ready. He didn't mind skipping breakfast on those days, and she didn't mind missing a peek at the morning sun, but that's when they were first married, when they were still getting used to each other's parts and the feel of naked skin rubbing up against another. Now, it seemed one of them was always heading in the door while the other was heading out. He no longer lingered in the early morning hours of darkness, waiting for her, and she didn't scurry home breathless or drop her uniform on the kitchen floor. The last time she'd hurried home and snuggled up against him, he just patted her on the back of the head and kissed her on the forehead before crawling out of bed.

It wasn't just them, she told herself. Everyone these days had to work three times as hard for half the money, if they even had work to do. She and O.C. were lucky to have good jobs and that ate up all their time and sapped their energy. Still, Mayme thought, it didn't cost anything to roll around naked and trembling in the shimmery early morning darkness, and she couldn't think of a nicer way to drift off to sleep then laying in someone's arms. It might even be nicer than the feel of the first rays of daylight

15

falling across her face. But, to tell the truth, she couldn't remember what it was like. Before. Before what, she wasn't sure; just before.

Mayme filled her lungs and let out a loud, heavy sigh. All O.C. wants, she thought, was for her to get off her bony butt and fix him a little breakfast, fried eggs with runny yokes, drop biscuits, and coffee. Other wives cooked for their men who were headed off to work, even packed them nice little sandwiches and cookies in a lunch box. But those women hadn't been up all night holding a bedpan under Clarence Lawler's rear end and a basin under his chin when everything rushed out of both ends at once. They hadn't had to restrain Wanda Duggans, who was always a little delirious, even when she didn't have a drainage tube coming out of her abdomen. It had been a long night. Mayme was bone bone-weary tired, and in no hurry to move anywhere, so she sat quietly and clung to the fading darkness, feeling invisible, free and alive in the cool morning air.

A dark-colored car was moving fast when it turned off Muskogee Avenue onto Chickasaw Street. A sharp left turn into the narrow driveway showered the lawn with a spray of gravel and dust as the wheels crunched and churned down the rocky strip of ground. Mayme jumped to her feet, spilling the lap full of hair pins as the driver squeezed his shiny black vehicle past their old truck to take it all the way around back, where he parked behind an ancient dogwood tree, maneuvering the car nicely between a skinny red bud and a big-leafed hydrangea. She lunged for the front door. They'd done this once before, shown up at the crack of dawn and parked out back, hidden from view.

"O.C.," she called, her heavy feet stumbling over the threshold, "O.C., get up; we got company."

He was sitting at the kitchen table, bent over, rubbing a square of flannel over the toes of his shoes, wiping off the dust and talc of the day before, giving his black wingtips a soft shine. He looked up and smiled. "Hey, Darlin', I was just . . ."

"We got company," she repeated, her voice tight with urgency, her finger pointing toward the back yard as she scurried up behind him, pressing him to get up out of his seat. "Didn't you hear the car? Drove in with the lights off and parked out back. It's gotta be Charley. Ain't no one else'd drive in like that."

O.C. flung the kitchen door open wide and watched eagerly for the man and woman to climb out of the shiny Coupe, a long-nosed box on wheels.

"What y'all doin' out here so early in the morning?" he whispered, grinning all over, happy to see this unexpected company. His light eyes swept across the landscape, checking for any unwanted visitors that might be close behind his friends. "Well, I'll be. Choc, old buddy, ain't you a sight for sore eyes."

After closing the car door quietly, the young couple moved quickly toward the house, the woman high stepping through the tall grass. "Need a haircut and a clean shave, what ya think?" Charley held one arm tightly around his wife's waist as he climbed the narrow wooden steps, his other hand reaching out for O.C. Sporting a grey felt fedora and a navy pinstriped suit, he looked like a big city businessman until you noticed the heavy beard and dark circles under his eyes. Alongside him was Ruby, looking pretty in her soft green dress, an ivory satin collar draping her shoulders and neck. The skirt was gored at the front and the back so that it clung gently to her waist and hips, then it swirled and flowed loose below her knees. A brandy-colored hat hid most of her dark wavy hair and shadowed her face. Charley let go of her as they passed through the door; Mayme could see he was moving slower than usual, his grin clenched tight with pain. With one look she knew why he was really here, and this time it wasn't for any old shave and haircut.

"I swan," Mayme said, her arms opening wide to greet her friend. "Ruby, I was just thinking about you,

17

wondering how y'all were getting along." The two women embraced, then stood back and examined each other, Mayme's face filled with concern, Ruby's with a blank kind of sadness. "My Lord, don't you look beautiful in that color, and with the brown hat, well, it's just like a walking stalk of fresh corn or somethin'. Real pretty. Not many can wear green, you know."

"Oh, thank you," Ruby said, smoothing her hands over the front of her thighs, removing any wrinkles that might have appeared during a long car journey. "Charley got it for me." She grinned when she turned to glance at her good-looking husband. "Over in St. Louis, I think. Isn't that what you said, Honey? St. Louis?"

Charley answered with a sly smile, never committing to the detail of his whereabouts in front of folks, even his dearest friends.

"Well, he did a fine job a pickin' it out," Mayme said. "It fits you like it was made just for you and nobody else."

She squeezed behind O.C. and Charley, who stood there slapping each other on the back, shuffling around like two boxers in a ring. Before settling in for a visit, she peered out the window, then pulled the small blue-checkered curtains together.

"I guess y'all heard the latest bit of trouble Charley run into," Ruby said. She looked softly at her husband as she spoke and lifted her left hand out to light gently on Charley's forearm. He gave her a long look, his grey eyes slowly moving from her face down to her thin fingers.

Just watching them made Mayme's heart swell. She turned away from their sad yearning, knowing full well the trouble Ruby spoke of and what it would mean to their chances at ever having any kind of real life together. She quickly scooted around and held a kitchen chair out, first for Charley and then another for Ruby, then used her fingers to smooth her mess of stringy hair back behind her ears, wishing she hadn't been so quick to yank out her braided knot.

18

"Well, just get in here and sit yourselves down, make yourself at home. Charley," she said, "go on and sit. I can tell you're hurtin', so don't say it's nothin'."

Mayme fussed over her friends and filled the air with endless chatter, her way of making folks feel at home. "I was just fixin' to make O.C. some biscuits and eggs; how about a little breakfast to get the day started?" She flashed a toothy smile and wide eyes to her husband, both of them knowing full well that if it weren't for the appearance of Charley and Ruby Floyd, he'd be eating a stale biscuit left over from the night before with a bit of jam his mother made. And the only coffee he'd get is the cup he would buy at the diner next door to his shop.

"Eggs sound good," Charley said. "We been driving around most the night. I could stand to eat a little somethin'."

O. C. nodded, a silly grin still plastered on his shiny face. "I could eat a egg or three."

"Let me help," Ruby said, already scooting her chair back to stand.

"Oh no you don't. Not in that beautiful dress, you're not," Mayme said.

"Just give me one of your aprons and it'll be fine. Besides, I can see you just got off work and probably are 'bout ready to drop, ain't ya?" Ruby's fingers swept along the back of her husband's shoulders as she passed by and he reached up, grabbed her hand and kissed her fingers loudly, making a spectacle of his affection. She smiled and bent down to plant a light kiss on the top of his head.

Mayme examined her rumpled uniform and laughed. "I do look a fright, don't I?" She shrugged her shoulders; it wasn't the first time they'd seen her looking a mess and it wouldn't be the last she hoped. The contrast between O.C.'s finicky ways and her messiness had been a longstanding source of humor for the four of them.

"Well," she said to Ruby, "if you insist, how 'bout you make the biscuits; yours are so much better then mine. I'll take care of the coffee and eggs." She rolled up her sleeves as she talked, then took two clean aprons from a narrow cupboard, giving Ruby the nicer one that slipped over her head and covered nearly every inch of the front part of her pretty dress. "I don't know why I even bother with an apron since this old uniform's going straight to the wash pile."

"Mayme, you'd look good in a flour sack. You don't even need a girdle or nothing, so hush." Ruby pulled her hat off and handed it to her husband before tying on the apron, her sad look gone for the time being.

Just seeing Charley and Ruby Floyd shot a bolt of energy straight through Mayme Holloway. They were dangerous and romantic. Scared and nervous half the time, but they had a way of setting sparks off one another that made the fine hair on her arms stand on end. She pulled a canister of flour from a low shelf by the window and handed it to Ruby. The two women went to work, elbow to elbow, filling the small kitchen with the clamor of skillets and mixing bowls. All those wistful thoughts of chirping crickets and her aching feet were easily forgotten.

"How's Dempsey?" Mayme asked. "He must be getting bigger ever' day."

"Oh, he's good, real good." Ruby's face lit up when she talked about her boy. "He just misses Charley somethin' awful." She measured out a spoonful of baking powder and dumped it into a big yellow bowl of white flour. She didn't need a recipe for biscuits; she'd been making them since she was a young girl helping her mama in the kitchen.

"That's rough." Mayme turned the burner up on the coffee pot, then stood back and wiped her hands on her apron, ready to move on to the next task. "What about you? How are you doin' with everything? I mean now that . . . " She didn't finish the sentence, just turned and opened the ice box and took out the bowl of eggs her mother-in-law had delivered the day before.

20

"It's not easy, that's for sure, but we make do. We find ways to all be together now and again. Even when it's for just a little bit."

"Well, where's Dempsey today? With your momma?"

"No, he's over in Boynton with Jess. We left him there late last night and drove out to the river for a while and then over here. There's a dance over in Dustin tonight, and Charley wanted to get some new shoes from Herman and get his hair cut . . . and see you about a couple things . . . so's we thought we might as well see if you all'd want to come to the dance with us. Be like old times." She reached up and used the back side of her wrist to scratch her cheek, and a fine sprinkle of flour drifted down, dotting the collar of her dress.

With a dry dishcloth, Mayme reached over and brushed away the white powder from her friend's satin collar, then glanced over her shoulder to her husband. "Hey, O.C., did you hear that?" she asked loudly, stealing his attention away from whatever Charley was saying.

"What's that, Darlin?" He had leaned his chair back so that it balanced on two legs and rested back against the wall. With his long legs dangling in front of him and his hands clasped in front of his flat belly, he resembled an overgrown child anxiously waiting to be served. Normally, that look would annoy his wife to no end, but today she found it rather endearing.

"There's a dance tonight over at Dustin, and Charley and Ruby are goin'. Wanna go?"

She already knew the answer. The one thing that shook O.C. from his Baptist roots and probably kept him from being a preacher himself was his love for shuffling around a dance hall any chance he got. O.C. loved to dance. And he was good at it. Really good. Mayme always felt special when they skimmed and skittered around a salty dance floor, O.C. always thinking of the next move, his strong arms showing her the way.

"Yeah, O.C." Charley said, "let's kick up some dust, Son."

21

"Don't you have to work?" he asked his wife, letting his chair drop with a thud to all four legs. "I'd heard about that dance, the Virginia Ravens of Hannibal is playin', but I didn't bother to mention it, just figured you'd be workin' all night again."

"No, Mrs. Daniels gets back today, so we're not so shorthanded. And I think we're finally getting through with all those flu patients." She turned to Ruby and said, "We've been having a bit of an epidemic with some kind of flu or virus for the past week. Nothin' serious, just lots of nasty work. To top it off, Mrs. Daniels been gone, visiting her sister back east, so I've been working every night. Twelve-hour shifts usually." She spun back around to face O.C. and Charley. "Anyway, I don't have to be back to the hospital till Monday afternoon. What do you say O.C., wanna go?"

"Shoot, yeah, I wanna go. We ain't been dancing in, Lord, I don't know how long; too long, I guess." He puckered his thick lips and eyebrows, thinking, planning ahead. "I gotta keep the shop open till 6:30 today, but we can go any old time after that." He slapped his knee three times and shuffled his feet under the table, already hearing the beat of a two-four rhythm, the hum of a fiddle. He stopped abruptly and sat up straight. "Hey, what about your foot? I thought you were injured. The papers said . . ."

"I can't walk, but, hell, I can dance - if Ruby leads." He looked over at his wife and winked. "Besides, we'll rest up today while you're working and I'll be fine. Maybe Mayme can give me a little somethin' to make it feel better." He ducked his head a bit and turned his hooded eyes to his friend's wife, hopeful she'd have some relief tucked away in her bag or at least a bottle of something back on a shelf. Something. Mayme always had something.

Mayme cracked an egg and tossed the shell into the sink. "Soon's you eat somethin', I'll take a look at ya, see what I can do." She reached down and patted the front of her pocket, making sure the small glass bottles were still there. Maybe she was like Mama Holloway; maybe she had hunches too. She'd taken those vials on a whim after stocking the shelf with a new supply, never knowing when she'd get a call and maybe need something stronger then a shot of corn whiskey.

Ruby and Mayme went on with fixing breakfast, now talking about nothing more then the price of eggs and milk, Ruby's new haircut, the funny waves and kinks in Mayme's hair after being in braids all night, reminiscing about some of the times they'd had last fall in Ft. Smith when Charley and Ruby were Mr. and Mrs. Jack Hamilton, living together like a normal family, eating dinner together every night, Charley making them all his famous spaghetti and meatballs. Those were fun days.

The men sat at the kitchen table and for a time they did nothing more then watch their wives, each quietly enjoying the other's company. Finally, Charley shook his head from side to side and said, "Hmmm, hmm, hmmm. Ain't that a sight?"

O.C. grinned. "Well, friend, let me tell you, it's not somethin' I see a lot of – Mayme in an apron, cooking I mean."

"Yeah, but she's a working woman, O.C. She's got better things to do'n sit around worrying about whether or not you got somethin' to eat. You may not know it, but that woman's got a reputation, a good one." He held a book of matches in his hand, tapping them on the table, a slow and steady rhythm.

"Yeh, she keeps busy; that's for sure. I don't even want to think about the things she sees over at that hospital, turns my stomach just to think about all that stuff, so she keeps quiet about most her doings."

"That's why she got that good reputation." He pulled off his coat and rolled up his sleeve to show off his tattoo, the one they'd seen many times. "That's why I got her picture tattooed on my arm. Looky there, O.C., ain't she purty?"

O.C looked at the large-busted Red Cross nurse inked on Charley's arm and laughed. It was a favorite joke of Charley's that the likeness was Mayme, though he'd had the artwork done long before he even met his friend's wife. Mayme was a nurse, but she sure didn't have the curves and volume of the buxom beauty on Charley's forearm.

O. C. Holloway and Charley Floyd had been friends since they were small boys. Many summer days were devoted to running through the woods, braving ticks, all manner of snakes and dense patches of poison ivy just to find the best swimming hole in all of eastern Oklahoma. They ran for their lives, hopped freight trains and rode from Sallisaw to Watts and back again, smoking cigarettes they stole from O.C.'s daddy. On Sundays they sat together in church, exchanging elbow nudges and side glances at the sight of Emma Jean Jacobs, the prettiest girl in the sixth grade, the one they were both going to marry one day. And after church, they begged their parents to let one or the other come home for Sunday dinner, not wanting to spend even one afternoon apart. Back then, they were inseparable.

When O.C.'s family moved away from Sallisaw to open a hardware store in Ft. Smith, their lives moved in different directions. Charley stayed in the hills and learned to make corn whiskey and Choctaw beer when he wasn't pushing a plow in a wheat field or tearing up his fingers picking cotton. While Charley mastered the trade of bootlegging, O.C. went to barber college and learned to cut hair and shave another man's face.

Back in Sallisaw, Charley fell in love with Ruby, a long-legged Cherokee beauty. He married her on a warm day in June and by Christmas, they had a baby, a boy he loved more than he thought he could love anybody, Charles Dempsey Floyd. Charley gave him his name and the name of his idol: prize fighter Jack Dempsey. After struggling to make some kind of living in Sallisaw, Charley headed east to St. Louis to look for something better then working as a harvest hand. What he found was someone

24

to help him rob an armored car of the Kroger payroll, a job that would cost him nearly four years in prison. He and Ruby weren't really married anymore - she divorced him while he was doing time at Jeff City – but they were in love, maybe more so then before he went away. They were better then married.

O.C.'s life was everything Charley's wasn't. The only excitement he ever wanted to find was in a dance hall on a Saturday night. He met Mayme at Skeeter's in Ft. Smith, where she was studying to be a nurse at Sparks Memorial Hospital. She was scrawny, but cute, and smarter then any girl he'd ever met and so full of energy he christened her "the sparkplug of Sparks." O.C. was good looking and always smelled like a sweet meadow of goldenrod or a summer night in June, and there didn't seem to be an ounce of meanness in him. No matter what she'd seen that day at the hospital, he made her think the whole world was beautiful. She only agreed to marry him when he said he would follow her home to Tahlequah, her hometown, where she already had a job as a nurse at the hospital there working with the doctor who paid for her to go to nursing school, the one who practically raised her. She wanted to take care of the folks she knew, she told him. More than once she fantasized about moving away and starting over where no one knew anything about her, but deep down, she just couldn't imagine living for good any place else. Whenever loneliness grabbed hold of her, she longed to be back home where she knew the houses, streets and hills as well as she knew her own name. And, when she really pondered the whole idea of marrying someone, she couldn't really imagine loving any one person more than she loved all her other friends, no matter how good that someone smelled.

So, Mayme and O.C. married, moved to Tahlequah, and before too long, O.C.'s mama moved there too. After all, there was no reason for the old woman to stay in Ft. Smith if O.C. wasn't there.

25

Charley found O.C. by chance one afternoon when he'd wandered into a Ft. Smith barbershop after a hard night, needing a quick shave and cut before heading back home to Ruby over in Sallisaw. The two old friends hadn't seen each other in more than ten years but knew each other instantly.   For O.C., it was like finding his lost brother; he loved his old friend.   Since then, whenever Charley got a chance, he liked to visit O.C., sometimes for nothing more than a quick shave.   They would talk non-stop about old times, the days before Charley was a wanted man, when they ran free and wild, wanting nothing more than a chance to camp out along the river so they could sleep on the cool damp soil and feel the stars on their skin.

"Charley," O.C. finally said, pressing in close, his voice hushed and low. "Is it true, what they said in the papers? Did you really kill that old boy?"

Charley studied the scattered freckles on the back of his hands while he opened and closed his fist, slowly, as if searching for something to hold onto. "O.C., you know I wouldn't hurt nobody if I didn't have to."   He met his friend's steady gaze as he spoke, telling the story his own way. "He was shooting at me; hell, he shot me. A bunch of times.   And Ruby and Dempsey was right there in the house. There wasn't nothin' I could do."

"I heard you got hit," O.C. said, nodding his head slowly, his eyebrows narrowing and lips tightening in imagined pain. "When I seen you limping in here I figured it was true.   He get you in the leg or something?"   His smooth face now drooped low in concern, his lower lip jutting out, ready for more sorrowful news.

Charley chuckled low, then said, "Yeah, he got me in the legs and . . ." he paused, wiped his hand across his mouth, and whispered, "shit, O.C., he got me in the balls." His face grimaced in painful laughter, the corners of his mouth drawn tight, his eyes closed at the memory.

"He got you in the what?" O.C.'s mouth dropped open in disbelief. He scooted his chair closer. "Serious? You

26

took one in your..." he lowered his voice and looked over his shoulder to the ladies, "in your bags?"

"Well, he got me in the ankle too, that's the one that hurts like hell, and he hit my gun and bent the darn thing. But, yeah, one of them bullets went right through my legs and took a piece of my manhood right along with it. Son of a bitch asked for it." His smile was gone and the corner of his mouth twitched nervously. "Wasn't nothin' I could do," he said again, his voice as rough as sandpaper.

"Lord Almighty," O.C. said, his thin shoulders sinking into his chest. "Sweet Lord Almighty."

After breakfast, O.C. left for the Normal Club Barbershop with a promise to call home just before closing time to let Charley know when to pay him a visit. He'd also stop in to see Herman, pick up a pair of new shoes for his friend. Herman always kept a nice pair on hand in Charley's narrow size for just such an occasion. Later in the day, Charley would drive O.C's old truck the short distance to the shop, not that fancy thing parked out back. O. C. would then lock the front door and treat his old friend to a nice haircut and shave in private before they made their way out to Dustin for a rare night of dancing and fun times.

With the shades drawn, the small house was dark and quiet. Mayme sent Charley and Ruby to the bedroom while she gathered together what she would need: scissors, hydrogen peroxide, bandage rolls, strips of flannel and gauze, a clean bowl. She kept a medical cabinet fully stocked on her service porch and an emergency bag up high in her closet, all of it carried home from Holland Hospital in the pockets of her uniform or buried in the bottom of a knitting bag beneath skeins of yarn and half knit sweaters. No one would ever remember seeing her with knitting needles in her hand or wearing a scarf or sweater of her own making. She wouldn't know a knit from a purl to save her life, but the big bag of yarn came in handy for hiding misappropriated goods.

27

Charley took off his shirt and pants, stretched out on the four-poster bed Mayme shared with O.C., and closed his eyes. Ruby hung his clothes on a hanger and sat next to him. She lightly scratched his chest, his forearm, his shoulder, and his left ear, knowing that her touch relaxed him. She watched Mayme take the black doctor's bag down from the top shelf of her closet, then watched her remove a glass syringe and fill it with clear liquid from a small glass bottle she pulled from her pocket.

"I sure like this furniture, Mayme. Cherry wood, isn't it? The pine cones are so fancy," Ruby said.

"Sears catalog," Mayme answered, never taking her eyes off the syringe. "You know you can get anything at all out of the Sears catalog." Needles tended to make most folks a little unhinged, so she had learned to make small talk while she prepared injections. Today she talked of bedposts and lace doilies; sometimes it was Babe Ruth or the crooks on Wall Street. Talking about her pretty things, for some reason, caused Mayme a twinge of guilt. She felt bad for having a home and a few nice things while someone nice as Ruby spent most of her time in an old shack behind her mama's place or on the run, sleeping God knows where.

"Charley," she said with a grin, "roll on over there; I'm gonna stick this one in your back side." She held the needle up and tapped the side to force any air bubbles up to the top of the barrel, then pushed on the plunger to release a small stream of the precious liquid into the air. Charley did as she said, groaning as he shifted his weight, reaching over to grab Ruby's thigh for leverage. He pressed his face against his wife's hip and she held the back of his head, knowing how he hated laying there hurt and vulnerable in front of her. Mayme squeezed the upper quadrant of his left buttock with one hand, then jabbed the needle into the fleshy middle to inject him with a small dose of morphine. It was probably stronger medicine than what he needed at this point, but it would give him some real relief - for a little while anyway. He rolled back over

28

onto his back and smiled, the pain fleeting with just the thought of what the drug would soon do.

"I need to take a look at some of those wounds, make sure they're not infected. Especially that one." She pointed to his crotch, and all three of them chuckled at the thought of Mayme carefully examining Charley's battered scrotum.

"Let Ruby do it," he said. "I can tell you she takes good care of that particular part of my anatomy." He winked at his wife, lifted himself up on his elbows and peered down toward his genitals.

"Ruby didn't go to nursing school. Besides, no matter what you think, you ain't got nothin' I haven't seen a hundred and fifty-eight times already. Tell ya what, though, I'll start with your ankle and work my way up."

Mayme dropped the dirty syringe into a metal bowl and took Charley's ankle into her hands, careful and slow. She pursed her lips, narrowed her eyes, her whole face a tight knot of concern. "I guess your friend down south couldn't get that bullet outta there, huh?" she asked, gently pulling away a dirty strip of old bandage.

"No, not then anyway. It's sure not pleasant though, I gotta tell you; that ankle hurts like a son of a bitch." Mayme tugged the last bit of bandage away. "Fuck," he gasped, when her probing finger found the spot of lead, then offered his apologies. "Sorry, Mayme, Ruby." Charley laid back, pointed his chin toward the ceiling, and let the drug carry him away while Mayme continued to examine his damaged leg.

A large bruise that spread from his calf down to cover most of his foot was fading from black and purple to various shades of green and yellow. The ankle was puffy and swollen, and a black crusty wound about the size of a fifty-cent piece was oozing a small amount of dark blood and puss. She poured a small drizzle of hydrogen peroxide directly onto the ankle, then used a square of soft flannel to wipe up the dripping excess, careful not to apply too much pressure where the small ball of lead remained embedded in the talus bone. Oxygen gas bubbled and fizzed as it sterilized the open wound. She wished she could take him over to the hospital and get Dr. Stern to fix the wound up proper, but Mrs. Daniels would throw a ring-tail fit if she waltzed in there with the infamous Charley Floyd. She had a feeling Dr. Stern would help her out no matter who it was, but not Mrs. Daniels, and in the end, it was her hospital. Mayme would have to patch him up the best she could with the few provisions she had on hand. Charley's body was growing limp and his eyes were drooping. The morphine had taken hold. By the time Mayme finished wrapping a neat clean bandage around the ankle and foot, he was snoring softly.

"He's exhausted," Ruby finally said. "He needs some rest. Some real rest, not just a hour or two here and there like he does his self most the time."

"Well, he sure didn't pick a line of work that lets him rest too easy no matter where he is – there's probably always someone lookin' for him."

Mayme tugged on the elastic band of Charley's underwear to get them down below his butt, then slid them down his legs and dropped them on the floor. "Hope you don't mind, Ruby, but there's really no other way to do this. It'll be easier with him knocked out."

"You're not the first one to get a look at Charley's pecker," she said, a crooked smile crossing her face. "You need some help?"

"No, I got it." She lifted his right leg and moved it further right and then moved his left so that his legs formed a V-shape. It was only then that she got a good look at his wounded scrotum. "Lawsy," she said, gently lifting the two sacs of flesh into one hand, "another inch and he wouldn't have a pecker at all. Lawsy."

Ruby laughed. "I don't know if that should make me laugh or cry." Her laughter faded quickly. "I truly don't know. Shoot, half the time I want to shoot his old pecker off myself."

Mayme took a fresh swatch of the flannel and rested the injured scrotum on the soft cloth in the palm of her hand as she doused the dirty wound with the hydrogen peroxide. "Lawsy," she whispered under her breath this time, gently dabbing the antiseptic that leaked away, wiping away bits of dried blood and dirt, watching the fizz and bubbles do their job. As she wiped a drizzle of antiseptic from his inner thigh, a creamy white discharge dripped from Charley's penis onto the back of her hand. She used a clean bit of the cloth to wipe away the ooze, tossed the dirty rag aside to make sure it would not be reused, and lifted her eyes to meet Ruby's hard gaze.

"I know; he's got the clap," Ruby said. "He nearly cries ever time he pees, it burns so bad."

Mayme finished cleaning Charley's wounds, then stood and gathered up her bandages and medicine bottles. She'd heard about Charley and his other woman, the one who started the whole Pretty Boy thing. Everyone had. "What about you?" she asked. "You got any kinda discharge down there? Burning sensation when you void? When you pee?"

"Me? No, I'm fine. Well, with that bullet wound and all, and since that whole mess in Tulsa, we ain't, uh . . . Well, it's been a while since we done anything much intimate like that." Her pale cheeks reddened below her dark eyes, and her lips seemed to tremble when she spoke. "I know he sees that Beulah woman. I hear things. That's where that come from."

"Well, women don't always know they got something like this, not for a while anyway." She'd have to remember to tell Charley later on that Beulah Baird needed to get some treatment too or he'd just be in for more stinging pee and a dripping pecker. And she didn't want to take any chances with Ruby either. "Just to be safe, make sure you wash yourself real good down there, lots of soap and hot water, especially if you have any contact, even if it's just touching, you hear?" She threw a cotton sheet over

Charley and made a mental note to boil the linens after they'd gone.

Ruby nodded, her eyes fixed on some unseen spot in the corner, as though she wished she could make herself disappear in that small patch of nothing. Mayme could tell her friend was embarrassed, a little shamed even. She moved closer, spoke softly. "It's gonna be fine, really. Later this afternoon, I'm gonna go get you both a little something – nothing bad, just a little ointment for you, a bit more for Charley." She grimaced at the thought of the treatment he would need, an odd sort of justice, she mused. "Meanwhile, you get some rest. I'll be right out here."

"Hey, Mayme," Ruby said, already unbuttoning her green dress.

"Yes," Mayme answered, turning back to watch her friend.

"I been meaning to ask you." She paused and smiled. "Why do you say Lawsy all the time now? That some new word or something?"

Mayme shrugged. "It's just a nice way to say Lord so that it doesn't seem like I'm taking his name in vain. O.C. hates for folks to swear and Mrs. Daniels don't allow no profanity at the hospital whatsoever, not even shoot, so somewhere along the way I just made up my own words. But I guess the good Lord knows what I'm doing, so it doesn't really matter to him." She shrugged her shoulders at her own foolishness.

"What's I swan supposed to mean?"

She laughed. "Means I swear, which is really dumb because if I did, and I guess I do, then I wouldn't say I swan, I'd just swear. But sometimes you just need a little bad talk to get through it all, even if nobody but me knows what I mean." She stopped and thought about what she'd said and added, "Probably better that way."

"Thank you, Mayme," Ruby said. "For everything. You're a good woman."

Mayme looked over at her gentle friend, standing there barefoot in her ivory-colored slip, a small patch of lace just below her cleavage, her handsome bank robbin' husband snoring away in a morphine dream behind her, a bullet stuck in his ankle, suffering from the clap, wanted by every lawman in the country, the poor man's hero. She thought they were both pretty. "Get some rest."

Charley and Ruby would sleep in Mayme and O.C.'s fancy new bed while Mayme slept on the living room sofa. She would dream of crickets and newborn babies wrapped in flannel and smelling of fresh life. She didn't know what Charley and Ruby would dream or if they even dared. For them, it was probably enough just to sleep with their bodies wrapped around each other, Ruby's head resting on his shoulder, her green dress hanging on the back of the door.

2.

It was Saturday, the busiest day of the week at the Normal Club Barber Shop. From the moment O.C. unlocked the door, it seemed someone or his cousin was waiting for a turn in his chair. O.C. was glad for it, eager for the day to pass quickly, happy for every quarter that landed in his till, money he could use treating Choc and the girls to refreshments at the dance. He hummed and whistled as he lathered and shaved, cut and styled a steady flow of heads, pausing only to sweep up the wisps of hair and talc that gathered on the floor, then swish around a grip of razors and combs in a blue swirl of antiseptic.

One after another, folks filed into the barbershop on Muskogee Avenue. Little boys who had to sit on a board laid across the padded arms of his hydraulic chair. College boys getting spiffed up for a Saturday night on the town. Businessmen struggling to maintain a successful appearance despite their dwindling bank accounts. Even a couple of young girls came in with their daddies looking to get their bangs trimmed up. O.C. treated each one of them like they were something special, slipping the young ones a couple of pieces of gum from the yellow box of Chiclets he kept by the register. At a nickel a box, he could afford to keep at least a dozen of them hidden behind the counter. It was only when Grover Bishop showed up at the end of the day that O.C.'s pulse quickened and a rush of moths darted through his belly.

"Morning, Sheriff," he said.

The tall man strolled through the door looking irritable even as he offered his famous half smile, nod and wink to whoever might be present in any room he entered. "Morning? Why, it's nearly supper time, O.C. Don't you even know what time it is?" The sheriff took off his white hat and tossed it on the row of red vinyl chairs along the wall.

"Shoo me," O.C. laughed, shaking his head in disbelief. "It's been so busy today, I plum lost track of all time. There's some kind of party going on over at the college." He motioned toward the empty chair. "But now that you mentioned supper, come to think of it, I'm so hungry I could eat a horse and chase the rider, so get on up here so's I can close up and go home."

The big man rubbed his palm against the top of his head, messing up what little hair he still had. "And I ain't officially sheriff, yet, O.C. Still the undersheriff."

"Not for long, sir, not for long." O.C. stretched one arm out gallantly toward the barber's chair and bowed slightly.

Grover hitched his pants up a bit and watched himself move toward the long mirrored back wall. "Well, there's not so much to take off the top, you mowed it so short last time, but I'd like a nice clean curve around back and up 'round my ears." He slid back in the chair, his boots thudding heavily on the metal footrest and ran one rough hand across the top of his head, still gazing at himself in the mirror, one eye squinting at his stern reflection, an unlit cigar clenched in his teeth. "You know I used to do some barbering myself once up on a time, in the early twenties."

"Yessir, I do believe you may have mentioned it a time or two." He paused while Grover fidgeted around, maneuvering the bulky gun belt along the arms of the chair, getting comfortable for his short break from keeping the peace.

"You know, Grover," O.C. said with all the sincerity he could muster, "folks around here talk about your eagle eyes, but there's one thing I see that you will never see. Know what that is?" O.C. shook out a clean white apron with a flourish, draped it over the sheriff's long torso and snapped it around the steely lawman's neck.

"Oh, go on, tell it again if it'll make you feel better." He pulled the cigar from his mouth, reached under the drape and stowed it away in his shirt pocket.

"The back of your head." O.C. chuckled at the same old joke he'd been telling since he first started cutting Grover Bishop's hair. Today, he was particularly proud of himself for keeping his wits about him, laughing and carrying on as if it was just a normal Saturday. He'd been careful not to tell anyone about his plans to go to the dance in Dustin, though he sometimes found himself nodding his head or swaying to the endless tune that played in his head. He picked up a long black comb with his left hand and his sharpest shears in his right, both steady as could be. The sheriff closed his eyes.

O.C. pulled his comb through the lawman's fine hair. There wasn't hardly anything there to take off, and the former barber could shave his own face just fine, but sitting in the barber chair fed a man's spirit ever bit as much as sitting in a pew on Sunday morning, so sometimes a trip to the barber was more about the ritual than the haircut. O.C. began to snip tiny bits of hair that he combed up straight between his fingers, the blades of the shears whistling as they sliced through the air. His heart pounded and his mouth felt dry, but his hands moved expertly. He couldn't help but feel a bit of a thrill knowing that the next man to sit in this chair would be his old friend, one of the most wanted men in the whole country, a man with a thousand dollar price on his head. The brush with danger from both sides of the law again stirred the moths to flight, but his hands stayed steady.

O.C. used electric clippers to shave the back of the sheriff's head and above his large pink ears. As he worked, he lowered his face close enough to smell the man's sweat and a hint of the peppermint candy he had crunched in his teeth like rocks just before walking through the door of the barbershop. O.C. stood so close he could almost taste the fear of the unfortunate souls who had faced the weapon that hung at the big man's side or, even worse, the submachine gun carried in the patrol car parked out front. A nudge closer still and he breathed in the stench of righteous pride that swelled with every villain captured or killed by the lawman's own hand.

O.C. reached back for the lather and brush and covered the lower half of Bishop's face in thick white foam, leaving his bushy eyebrows and warm eyes to shine above the lathery beard. He dropped the brush back into the cup before taking up the straight-edge razor, already sharpened to a fine edge on the new metallic strop Mayme had ordered from the Sears catalog. She warned him to be careful since it would make his razor as sharp as the scalpels they used over at the hospital. Sharp as a scalpel – he liked that.

Slowly, carefully, he tipped the sheriff's head back, holding his jaw with just one fingertip while he ran the smooth blade up along the front of his neck, over the jugular vein, the Adam's apple, and that tender spot just below the jaw. He began to hum his favorite hymn, "Shall We Gather at the River," to turn his mind to Jesus for a spell, but there was a moment when he caught a glimpse of himself in the mirror, the pearl-handled blade in his right hand, the trusting lawman below him, his neck stretched back and waiting, eyes closed, so vulnerable. He stopped humming and shuddered at how easy it would be for him to kill a man, even this strong man, to feel the warm blood spill from his throat through O.C.'s own trembling fingers down to the dusty floor, where it would not be swept up, but would pool and stain.

A powerful heat ran through O.C.'s body at the gruesome image, such evil thoughts pouring from some dark place deep down inside him. Where did such evil come from? Forgive me, Lord. Sweet Jesus in heaven, forgive me, he silently prayed, pleading for mercy, begging for such horror to be forever removed from his imagination. He stiffened his spine, breathed in deep and focused on making the tall fearful man clean and handsome, even beautiful. Glory, he thought, Glory. How on earth does Charley do it?

"That's a good one," Bishop said.

"What's that?" O.C. was startled by the question, the familiar voice of authority interrupting his prayer.

"That song. I like the way those Lewis Sisters do it."

"Yessir, they have that family harmony. Nothing beats that," he said softly. "No sir." He finished shaving the sheriff and laid a hot towel over the clean face.

No one could possibly know how much he loved the look and feel of a man's clean face, the sting of pleasure when he would massage a tonic deep into a scalp, the magic of drawing another's tension out through his own fingers. Folks knew he seemed to love the work he did so well, but they could never know how much.

"You got any of that fancy smelling aftershave on hand?" The sheriff pulled off the hand towel, opened his eyes and raised one eyebrow at the barber. "When I was a barber, I usually had a little something special on hand for certain customers."

"The Burma-Shave?" O.C. asked, knowing full well what Grover Bishop was talking about. "I got plenty of that."

"No, I was thinking more along the lines of that one I heard about from Jim Lauderback, some concoction you make yourself."

"Oh, I might have a little bit of that on hand," O.C. said. He'd heard about the sheriff picking up Lauderback with a jug of sour mash not long ago, and it was no secret that O.C. used a little shine in his homemade aftershave. No doubt Lauderback told him he was just delivering a batch to the barber, though O.C. wouldn't need any replenishment for a good while. But a little hooch was the least of his worries. All he cared about at the moment was getting the lawman out the door before Charley Floyd showed up. He knew Grover Bishop wasn't after his bit of shine used only for splashing on faces with the likes of Charley Floyd, Ford Bradshaw, and a dozen or more outlaws running through the hills, especially since Erv Kelley had been shot and killed not far from there.

O.C. opened the small cupboard and lifted the pale green bottle from the top shelf. He splashed some on his hands, then slapped it onto the sheriff's face and waited for the wide eyed gasp that would follow as the stinging burn seeped into the tender skin. Beautiful.

Grover Bishop pushed himself out of the chair and pressed his face to within two inches of the mirror for a close inspection of O.C.'s work. "I couldn't a done a better job myself, Mr. Holloway." He dropped two quarters and a nickel into O.C.'s palm, returned the unlit cigar to the clench between his teeth, and grabbed his white Stetson. "Give my regards to Mrs. Holloway," he said, carefully placing the hat on his head, studying his appearance as he spoke. "And tell her I said thank you for taking such good care of my Aunt Annie last week – she was in overnight with that flu bug I guess. Sang Mayme's praises."

"Will do. And you keep care of yourself. Don't get in front of any fast -moving bullets." He tossed a fake salute to the sheriff, then grabbed a broom and started sweeping, removing the hair of Grover Bishop from the floor beneath the chair, again humming an old time dance tune. It wouldn't be long now.

3.

The sun was slowly easing down on a color pallet of spring. The dogwood tree in the backyard was in full bloom, its branches heavy with soft blossoms of the palest pink and white, like a swarm of fluttering butterflies. The blue sky streaked bright pink and silvery grey while the late afternoon shadows softened the shaggy yard of crabgrass and dandelion weeds. Mayme pulled her housedress tight around her and peered over at the shiny black car, its rear end sticking out like a large animal hiding its head in a tangle of wild ivy. Any minute the phone would ring and O.C. would tell her he was just waiting for Charley. She planned on being ready so she could catch a ride and save a bit of time. She needed to do something special with her damp hair that wouldn't take too much effort, put on a nice dress for a change, and figure out something to feed everybody, hopefully something that wouldn't require a run to the market. O.C. didn't much mind eating fried egg sandwiches or cans of soup, but it didn't seem right to open a can of Campbell's chicken noodle for company, even if they were more like family than proper company, even if they did show up unannounced.

Ruby shuffled into the kitchen, yawning and buttoning up the front of her dress. "I can't believe how hard I slept," she said. "Charley's still snoring like a bear."

"You hungry?" Mayme was staring into the pantry, considering spaghetti, a Charley Floyd favorite. Back in Ft. Smith, he would have them over for his special spaghetti

40

and meatballs dinner and they would eat like fools. A quick inventory satisfied her. Noodles, onions and a couple of jars of tomatoes left from last summer were on the tiny shelf. And she was sure O.C. had bought a little ground round when he'd done the shopping this week. Seems like he'd said something about sticking something or other in the refrigerator.

"A little. I guess we should . . ."

Both women stopped short at the sound of a loud persistent knock on the front door. Mayme motioned for Ruby to go back in the bedroom and stay out of sight. It wasn't unusual for folks to come to her door, but there wasn't any reason for anyone to know there were guests in the house, especially these guests. She would simply send whoever it was away or do whatever the situation called for, but when she peeked out the front window, all worry and caution faded away. Mama Holloway stood on the porch, her old black dress hanging so long it almost reached her toes, a large basket covered with a white dishtowel in her hands.

"I had a hunch you'd be needing a little something extra tonight," she said and handed the basket to Mayme. Her milky eyes blinked and squinted, as she peered into the dark house, searching around the corner as if she knew she might find something or someone hiding behind her skinny daughter-in-law. Mama often had good hunches. "If I'm wrong, you can just eat on it tomorrow."

"Mama, you like to scared me half to death. Come on in here." She opened the door wide to let her stout mother-in-law pass, then closed it behind her. "Ruby, come on out; it's just O.C.'s mama." She lifted the white dishtowel up from the basket. "What you got in here, Mama? Oh my goodness, fried chicken, and enough to feed a small army - O.C's gonna love that."

"And cornbread too. Prob'ly still warm, I imagine." She smoothed the towel back down over the basket and held it out to Mayme.

41

"I won't even ask how you knew we'd be needing this," Mayme mumbled as she carried their dinner to the kitchen, knowing Mama wouldn't hear a word she said. "It's plain spooky. Gives me the willies."

Mayme had long ago given up on trying to figure out how the old woman just seemed to know things were going to happen before they happened. Ever once in a while, Mama would stay home from church service to cook a big dinner, enough for two families to feast on. She'd mash potatoes, bake pies, fry a couple chickens and a mess of okra. When company showed up at the door uninvited and unannounced, she would have the meal already prepared, even have the table set with the right amount of plates. Or she'd send a fresh chocolate sheet cake to someone's house for no reason at all only to learn the next day that that someone was sick or going through some hard patch and the cake was a true blessing. Everyone knew she had a special way with food, and her unexpected way of feeding folks in their time of need was what she did best.

Ruby was fully dressed and had her hair combed nice when she stepped out of the bedroom to greet Mama Holloway. "Ruth," she said, bending down to kiss the old woman's cheek, "we were hoping we'd get to see you."

Mama never smiled, but she wasn't scowling when she nodded in approval at the sight of Ruby Floyd. "Well, then I guess it's a good thing I come to visit then, ain't it?" She tugged at the folds of her old-fashioned ankle-length skirt and planted herself in the big tapestry chair Mayme had bought last Christmas, the same time she bought the pretty cherry wood bedroom set. Though Mama had scoffed at such an extravagant purchase during such hard times in the country, she never sat anywhere else when she came to visit.

Mama Holloway rested her feet on the matching ottoman, folded her hands together and rested them across her round belly, just like O.C. did when he sat in the big chair, though he lacked her round paunch to use as a resting place.   She was ready to receive visitors.   And though the devout woman would never admit it at her Bible reading group, she was proud to know Charley Floyd, to have known him when his crimes were nothing more serious then tipping over outhouses or sneaking a piece of penny candy from the jar at their old store, even prouder to know he still called her Mama.   She loved Charley almost as if he was one of her own.

"You two sit and visit a minute," Mayme said.   "I got to get dressed and do something with this wet hair so's O.C. won't be ashamed of me."   She turned to her mother-in-law to fill her in on their plans so she wouldn't get too comfortable and think she was there for the entire evening. "O.C.'s gonna call in a bit for Charley to come down to the shop for a haircut and I'm gonna catch a ride with him. I got a couple things I need to get in town," she explained. "Then after supper we're all goin' to a dance tonight over in Dustin.   So you can sit here and keep Ruby company while me and Charley are gone, but then we'll be running off quick like."

"Well, don't you worry, I won't stay. I'll just get supper on the table for y'all and then I'll get out of your way."   She scowled, but Mayme didn't seem to notice.   She was watching Charley stroll out of the bedroom, sleepy-eyed, barefoot and hobbling on his bad leg.

"Mornin' sunshine," Mayme said.   "Look who's here to see ya."

He smiled a big toothy grin, ran his long fingers through his thick dark hair, then felt the stubble around his chin.   "I thought I heard an angel," he said.   "Figured maybe I'd died in my sleep or somethin', but it's just my second Mama."   He took her hand and kissed it like she was royalty, then leaned down and gave her another peck on her high forehead.

"Charley Floyd, you stop that," she said, pulling away and waving her hand at him as if he were a pesky fly. Though she tried to give her best sour face, her pale eyes twinkled and one corner of her mouth turned up, if only briefly, but they all saw it. "Angels, my foot. You better get your life right with the Lord, Son, you want to hear angels."

"I hate to interrupt you two," Mayme said, "but I'd like Charley to go take a hot bath before we go. He's got a few scrapes that could use a good soak." She looked at him and raised one eyebrow to let him know she was talking about one specific ailment. "And Ruby, you should get yourself a hot bath too, but make sure you scrub that tub good before you get in it. There's some disinfectant in there in a green jar under the sink. Wouldn't want you to bathe in any of Charley's germs."

"What happened to you?" Mama asked.

"Oh, some old boy shot me in my ankle," he said. "It was just a crazy accident. We was coon hunting down there by Park Hill and uh, you know, it was dark."

"Uh-huh," she said, "I heard somethin' about you getting shot, but it wasn't no coon hunting accident. Don't add lying to your trespasses, Charley Floyd, not to me." She paused to frown at him, a look he would remember from long ago. When she spoke again, her voice had thinned to the fragile point of nearly cracking. "I didn't want to believe it." Mama's gaze drifted downward as she shook her head from side to side; her sagging face drained of the little color she had as though she'd just heard the worst news of her life. Mayme knew she had heard the whole story about Charley shooting Erv Kelley. Killing a lawman was hard news for the old woman to take in; she knew what that meant for this man she had loved since he was a barefoot boy catching grass snakes and fireflies.

"Ruth," Ruby said, "why don't I make us a cup of coffee while those two get ready to go. You can tell me some of those old stories about Charley and O.C. back in Sallisaw. I want to hear more about the time they switched all those babies around during that revival meeting. That musta been something else."

Mama shed herself of the mournful scowl, the corners of her mouth lifting into a tight-lipped grin. "Oh, that was a good one," she said, moaning a bit as she pushed herself out of the comfy chair to follow Ruby into the kitchen, only too happy to tell the same old stories again and again. "All those mothers going home with someone else's child in the back of their buggy. You never heard so much weepin' and wailin' in all your days. Specially that Celia Cantrell. You'd a thought somebody had died, the way she carried on."

Ruby pulled a kitchen chair out for Mama to sit on. "You still have that purdy baby doll in your dresser drawer? Dempsey still talks about the time you let him peep in at her."

"Oh yes, I'm saving her for when I have a grandbaby to give her to." She turned to frown a little at Mayme, but her childless daughter-in-law had already disappeared into the dark bedroom.

Charley and Mayme left the house just as the sun was setting. The evening sky was now streaked with shades of orange and pink to the west of town and a stretch of purple to the east. A fading light filtered through the leaves of the budding magnolia trees. A few Saturday shoppers were straggling home, and most businesses were already closed and locked up for the night. Charley sat behind the wheel of O.C.'s old truck, his hat tipped low to shade his face from any gawkers. Folks around here were generally friendly to his kind, but there was a $1,000 reward for his capture and times were harder than hard and, of course, the sheriff was one of the best in Oklahoma. Ever since the Kelley ordeal, it seemed every lawman and his kin wanted Charley Floyd captured or dead, and they wanted it bad.

"Drop me off up here on the corner," Mayme said, pointing ahead. "I need to see Dr. Stern and get a few things for your little peter problem down there." She winked at him and nodded toward his crotch.

Charley shook his head and leaned away from her. "I don't know how O.C. puts up with you; you're downright mean sometimes for such a scrawny girl."

45

"Oh, O.C.'s happy as a hog in sunshine. Don't you worry 'bout him."

"You want I should wait for you?" Charley pulled the truck over to the side of the road and took a moment to look up and down the street before shifting the gear to neutral. "Or come back or something?"

"No, you go on; O.C.'s waiting on you at the shop." She pulled the handle, pushed her weight against the creaking door and slid her legs out. Her fancy dress was slippery against the worn seats and caught on a small crack at the edge. "Dagnabbit," she said, feeling the pull of the dress on her backside, fearing it would rip and ruin her careful plan.

"What's wrong?" Charley asked.

"Oh, this skirt is hung up on the seat, but I can get it." She moved slowly and carefully, using her fingers to release the snag of fabric before hopping out onto the side of the road like a nimble sprite freed from a magic carriage. She slammed the heavy door shut and scooted quickly around to the driver's side then leaned through the open window. "Tell O.C. I'll be back as soon as I can. Y'all go on and eat supper without me if I'm late; don't wait. I can chew on something later."

Charley nodded and touched one finger to his hat. She stood and watched the old rusty truck slowly pull away from her, gears grinding, engine sputtering, the back of Charley's head bouncing along. He'll be the one to break O.C.'s heart one day, she thought, as the truck turned left and disappeared into the purple shadows of Keetoowah Street.

A crazy patchwork path of red brick led to the massive front door. She knew he was home; every light in the house seemed to be on and she could hear the strains of lively music drifting through an open window. Before knocking, she reached up and felt the silky ribs of the black grosgrain ribbon trim on her turban hat, made sure no loose hairs were peeking out, then tugged on her jacket sleeves and ran one nervous hand across her backside

46

making sure she hadn't ripped her skirt on the old seat. Standing there on the porch, she suddenly felt like some cheap dime store floozy showing up on the doctor's doorstep in her shimmery black and white chiffon party dress, asking for medicine to treat a bad case of the clap. For a friend. The things she did for other people surprised even her sometimes.

"May . . . Mrs. Holloway, what a pleasant surprise," Dr. Stern said as he opened the door wide and the music grew louder. Band music.

"Evenin', Dr. Stern. Do you mind if I come in for a minute? I need to talk to you about something. In private," she added.

In both hands, she gripped a large black satin purse in front of her stomach as though it were a shield for battle. Now that she was at the doorway of Dr. Stern's house, she wished she had taken the time to travel the extra three miles out of town to Dr. Mooney instead. He was older, knew these parts, these folks. He was one of them. He would understand what she wanted and wouldn't ask a bunch of questions, but she hesitated to let the old man know all that she did. And besides, there just wasn't time for the long trek.

The doctor stepped back and waved his long arm in a welcoming gesture. "Of course, come in, come in. What can I do for you?"

Mayme stepped through the door and caught a healthy whiff of whiskey on the doctor's breath as she brushed close to him. She knew that woody smell all too well. He led her into a small parlor off the dining room, a room that looked like it was rarely used, reserved for receiving guests like her - unannounced.

Heavy dark green brocade draperies hung from floor to ceiling, gracefully tied back in thick gold braids, letting in what little light remained of the fading evening. A small gold damask sofa with carved wooden legs and graceful sweeping arms looked as though no one had ever sat on its perfect cushions. A side chair to match rested in the

47

corner alongside an empty white birdcage. He turned on a brass floor lamp, and the room seemed to glow soft and warm. Mayme sat on the edge of the chair and looked up at him, anxious and uncertain of how to begin.

"You look awful pretty tonight," he said, his eyes moving from her face all the way down to her shiny black shoes.

Mayme felt a warm flush rise across her cheeks. "Thank you. O.C. and I are going out later," she explained. "You know I haven't had a night off in a while, so we're gonna kick up our heels a bit. I mean, we're going dancing."

"Good for you," he said, once again focused on her face. "I know how hard you've been working lately." He remained standing, his shirtsleeves rolled up to the elbow, shoeless. "Can I get you something, Mrs. Holloway? A glass of water or I can make some coffee real quick if you can wait a bit." He seemed eager to serve her something, glad for a bit of company, she supposed.

"No, nothing for me, thank you. And please, call me Mayme." She rested her bag in the seat beside her, smoothed the skirt of her dress and waited for him to sit down before going on. In this light he seemed softer then he did at the hospital, less angular, more like a thick fluid crossing the hardwood floor in his stocking feet, weightless and loose. His hair seemed longer then usual and natural curls drooped over his ears, as though he'd rolled them in big round curlers like she sometimes did for special occasions. The top buttons of his shirt were undone and a small patch of chest hair was peeking through, dark and curly.

"Okay, Mayme, but only if you call me Joseph, or even better, call me Joe. No one here calls me Joe. Even Doc Moody calls me Joseph."

Mayme nodded in agreement. "Fine, Joe." She smiled and nervously looked around the room, her wide eyes moving from top to bottom, examining every corner. She always wanted a house with a room like this, tall ceilings,

48

carved molding around the ceiling, bold yet quaint and inviting, everything flowing in one direction. Though the curves and lines of Mrs. Hardy's abandoned furnishings were pretty, they seemed wrong for him. It was all a bit old fashioned and too feminine for him, a bachelor.

She took a breath, ready to ask if he planned to fill the empty birdcage, and turned her gaze on him again. He sat perched on the edge of the sofa, watching her, his legs bouncing gently to the sounds of an orchestra and a gravelly voice.

"That's real nice music, Joe," she said, desperately trying not to stare at his open shirt collar and curling hairs that peeked out along the neckline. Her cheeks felt warm and her heart raced just at the thought of the conversation she was about to have; she didn't need to think about what he looked like under his shirt.

"Oh, it's the end of the Billy Barnes Show. The radio."

Mayme nodded as if she already knew that.

"I was fixing myself a little supper, listening to the news and the music came on." He paused, grinned slightly, his chin lifted high. "I confess, I'm an avid listener of radio dramas. The Phantom of Crestwood is on tonight, right after Billy."

"Oh, I like that one too," Mayme said. "Though I've only heard it once or twice. I'm usually at the hospital this time of night."

"Well, I don't know if you've heard, but they're making a movie of the show. The last episode won't be on the radio; it will only be in the movie."

"Really? That sounds exciting."

"I think so, but I love listening to those mystery shows, detective stories especially."

Mayme smiled, thinking her life was sometimes too much like some of those melodramas; she didn't need to listen to the radio to feel that rush of excitement. All she had to do some days was crawl out of bed and it was waiting for her.

Joe listened to the music closely for a moment, his right ear pointed toward the doorway. "That's Louis Armstrong, 'All of Me,' his brand new one. I've got the record, probably played it a dozen times already. Do you like him?"

"I'm afraid I don't know much about him, but I like what I'm hearing just fine. I bet O.C.'d like it too. He's the music lover in our house."

She wondered why the sight of a few stray chest hairs peeking out from under white buttons made her blush; a few hours ago she'd been swabbing pus from Charley Floyd's penis and hadn't batted an eye. She knew more about the look of most folks' body parts then they did, but suddenly she felt peculiar, a little shy even.

"Are you hungry?" he asked and was halfway off the sofa before she could answer. "I have some . . ."

She raised her right hand to stop him from rushing off to the kitchen. "No, really, I just need to talk to you for a quick minute. I don't want to keep you from your supper, besides I have . . ."

"Oh, it's nothing that won't keep," he interrupted. "One of my patients, Mrs. Henry, you know her?"

"Sure, they have the dairy." Mayme nodded and crossed her ankles, careful not to catch her new stockings on her heel, eager to move the conversation around to her needs, her reason for showing up on his doorstep at the dinner hour in her best dress.

"That's right. She brought over some kind of cheesy looking casserole this afternoon and all I have to do is stick it in the oven. I think she's trying to fatten me up." His hands fluttered in a nervous gesture at the reference to his shrinking body weight.

Mayme smiled, letting his odd insecurities lessen her own. "I have a mother-in-law who does that for me. Only I don't think she's so worried about me wasting away so much as O.C."

They both smiled. "Oh yes," he said, nodding his head, his lower lip jutting out, "I know Ruth Holloway well.

50

She's something else, kind of cranky at times, but a fine cook. I've had her apple pie more than once when I've gone on house calls."

"She brought a basket of fried chicken and cornbread over tonight. Saved O.C. from eating another fried egg sandwich." She reached up to brush back her hair and remembered how she had taken the time to wave the sides with the Antoinette waver, like O.C. had taught her, then pinned the back up in a low coiled bun, all carefully tucked under her new hat. Not a single hair was out of place. Outside a car rumbled down the road, honking its horn as it passed, a blast of greeting or farewell, or a warning to some stray dog trotting in the roadway. The room grew still as Hoagy Carmichael played "Stardust" in the background, a tune even Mayme knew.

An awkward pause spread between them in the unfamiliar atmosphere of brocade and chiffon and the doctor in his stocking feet. They were accustomed to closeness, spending long hours side by side under a bright light in the operating room, discussing instruments, diseased livers and gallstones, the latest surgical techniques, or even small talk in the hospital kitchen, but not sitting alone on a Saturday evening in Doctor Stern's sitting room. "I imagine you're glad to see Mrs. Daniels back in town," he finally said.

"You have no idea how happy I am. Well, I guess you do. You've been there as much as me. Of course," she paused, pressed her palms against the tops of her knees and willed herself to begin the discussion that brought her to his door. "But to be truthful, if she wasn't back, I probably wouldn't be here." Her eyes met his, watched him closely, prepared for confusion, anger, or shame. But there was none of that. He sat patiently, calmly, waiting for her to tell him more.

They sat quietly, listening to a high-pitched trio sing the wonders of Colgate toothpaste, while Mayme measured carefully her choice of words. Joe spoke first, encouraging her to expose the hidden need she carried through his

51

door. "So, you're not here to eat. And you're obviously on your way to a party or dance or something fun . . . you're all dressed up." He settled back in his seat, rested one bony elbow in the palm of his left hand and wiped the smile on his face off with the right as though he removed a masquerade mask. He seemed disappointed to let the familiar look of concern and worries replace the eager grin he'd shown at the door. This was the man she knew, the one she was used to seeing in a white coat, a stethoscope wrapped around his neck, eyes narrowed and fixed on a chart. "What can I do for you, Mrs. Holloway?" he asked, his voice steady and controlled as though she was a new patient seeking his help for some mysterious ailment.

"You know," Mayme stalled, reaching for her throat and faking a small cough. "I might take a little something, just oh, whatever it was you were drinking." She met his gaze again, opened her eyes just a bit wider and dipped her chin, inviting him to read her thoughts. "Something to clear the phlegm maybe."

"Let me presume you're not referring to a cup of coffee."

She didn't answer other than to simply smile and shake her head.

"Uh-huh," he murmured as he passed by her. He returned moments later with two small crystal glasses filled with an amber liquid.

Mayme held the small glass up and studied its rich color. "You don't get this from around here, do you? And this isn't the stuff they let doctors prescribe either."

"No, unfortunately. I have a distant cousin in Kansas City who gets this for me. He has, uh, connections. When I run low, I have to pay him a visit. Seems I see quite a lot of him since moving here."

She sipped from the small glass and felt the liquid burn all the way down. It was a warm burn, like an oak fire spreading in her belly, not the sharp edge of Lauderback's moonshine that made her face twist and left her gasping for air. O.C. always kept a bottle for his aftershave recipe, and occasionally she would sneak a quick nip after a long night at work. It helped her sleep without dreams, erasing the memories of blood and stink. Mayme licked her lips, took a second sip then wiped her mouth with the tips of her fingers. It was pure danger, she decided, able to destroy any demons that haunted her. If she had stuff like this around, she'd never have another nightmare again.

Revived by the shot of whiskey, she looked directly at him when she spoke, prepared for any reaction. "I need some medicine for a friend. And I can't go to Mrs. Daniels for it. She'd have questions I don't care to answer."

"Uh huh." His eyes were unflinching, dark and intense in this small room. He sipped his whiskey slowly, his eyes fixed on Mayme. "Go on."

"I need some Argyrol and Protargol." She lifted her chin when she spoke and straightened her spine, ready for any blow that might come her way.

One dark eyebrow lifted, questioning, knowing. "Can I assume this medication is intended to treat a case of gonorrhea?"

"Yes, sir, it is." She didn't flinch a single muscle, but she felt the hair on her arms stand on end, felt her heart beating hard in her chest.

"Why doesn't this person simply come to my office? Or visit Dr. Mooney? You know this is no simple treatment; it takes several weeks of care. Specialized care. From a physician." He paused for a moment, considering his next words, holding his glass out in front of him as though he offered it to himself. "Or why don't you simply get this medication as you do the others?"

Mayme sat unmoving, numbed by a sense of overwhelming dread. Her hands and feet began to tingle as her intestines twisted and rolled deep inside her. Lightheaded with a sensation of falling, she set her whiskey down to grip the sides of the damask chair and gaze out the long window. Darkness had settled in for the night. The wind was picking up, scattering the seeds of dandelions and jewelweed along the winding bank of Bear Creek, from one end of town to the other. A few blocks away, her husband was shaving the face of Pretty Boy Floyd, one of the most wanted men in the country, while her mother-in-law sat at Mayme's kitchen table swapping recipes with Pretty Boy's wife. She wished now more than anything that she had simply let the handsome sagebrush bandit suffer the consequences of his own philandering and that she was the one there in her kitchen learning how to bake a choke cherry pie like Mama Holloway. When she spoke, her voice was little more then a hoarse whisper, "I'm afraid I'm not quite sure what you mean, Dr. Stern."

"Mayme," he said softly, as though he were comforting a small child, "I know." He paused then repeated, "I know. Not everything, but I know a lot more than you think I do."

She watched him carefully as if he was a dangerous animal, wounded and hungry for blood. She reached again for her glass and took a large swallow to wash away any shadow of weakness or fear.

"Listen," he started again. "I treat people out in the hills too. They talk to me, tell me how good you are. One old man, in fact, wouldn't let me near him at first, only wanted you."

She nodded but remained silent, knowing that in times like these it was usually better to let someone else do most of the talking, see what more they had to say before sticking your neck right into the noose offered with a smile.

He smiled and leaned closer, as if he was taking her into his confidence, inviting himself into hers. "Don't be nervous; I think what you do is remarkable. Truly. I watch you at the hospital all the time, the way you talk to patients, and ..."

"You watch me?" she asked, interrupting him, her choked voice raising an octave higher, strained and tight.

"Yes, I do," he said, confidently, almost proud. "You fascinate me. One minute you're telling Clement Gill to shush up because he doesn't know his rear end from a hole in the ground and the next you're scrubbed up

54

standing next to me in the operating room, cool as a cucumber while we pick gunshot out of Willie Pennebaker's buttocks, knowing what I'm going to need before I even do. Sometimes you sound like a country girl that never wore shoes or finished primary school and sometimes you sound like you're the one with the medical degree, calculating solutions by metric weight and tending the most grotesque wounds with absolute calm. No offense is intended by watching you; I just think you're the most interesting person I've met in this town. Maybe ever."

Blood rushed to her face. Changing the way she talked to folks was just being polite, her way of making them feel comfortable, no matter how difficult the situation. She didn't want to seem snooty. It never occurred to her that anyone was paying attention. "Thank you," she said. "I just wish I knew the way to talk right now."

He stretched and arched back, then planted his stocking feet on top of the black lacquer coffee table that rested between the davenport and his chair. In an easy voice, he told her a story, one he seemed to enjoy recalling. "There was this time, oh, I don't know, about four or five months ago, I believe, when Mrs. Daniels noticed some ether was missing from the inventory. She asked me if I'd taken it without recording it in her logbook. At first I thought perhaps I had, and worried that I was tired and becoming careless, but when it happened again, I started to pay attention. I started checking things out, you might say, curious if someone was helping themselves to a few things. It didn't take long for me to figure out it had to be you with that big bag you carry around. I kept my eyes open, listened to what folks had to say. I know what you do, Mayme."

He paused for a moment and simply looked at her and offered a soft smile, soft eyes. "So now, if something is missing and she notices, I simply tell her I took it for the children's home, and then she doesn't mind at all. Just tells me to try to be more conscientious about my record keeping." He raised his eyebrows, dropped his feet, shrugged his shoulders and downed the last of his whiskey. "I've even logged a few things out when I know you've walked off with them. I believe a bit of morphine might have wandered off this very morning."

Mayme sat in disbelief, stunned that anyone had the slightest inkling about her occasional pilfering. She'd been so careful. So careful. "Thank you," she said again. Before going on, she cleared her throat and willed the pounding in her chest and the tremor in her knees to calm themselves. "Why? Why would you do that for me? You barely know me."

"I don't know. I guess I liked being a part of some secret operation of yours somehow." He leisurely crossed one long leg over the other and grabbed hold of his right ankle that rested on his left knee and massaged his foot. "I knew you weren't using it yourself, that it was going to some good use, or I wouldn't do it. Believe me, I've seen nurses and doctors who get a taste for some of the pharmaceuticals. I wouldn't help you with any of that."

"Part of what?" she asked, her worried mind stuck back on what he had said he liked. "I just do a little midwifery and first aid now and again. It's nothing like a, what'd you call it? Secret operation?" Mayme shook her head in amusement, feigned a small laugh, smoothed her flowing skirt across her thighs and studied her long shadow stretching across the floor and onto Joseph's crossed legs. "I swan, Dr. Stern, the things you think are plain . . ."

He cut her dramatic speech off. "Oh, I don't think removing an appendix on a kitchen table is just a little midwifery or first aid either." His sly smile appeared once more and this time he winked at her. He winked at her.

Mayme's green eyes flashed alarm and her right hand slowly reached to cover her heart, protecting it from this surgeon slowly slicing her open, revealing secrets that no one should know. She'd only done that procedure on her own once. Just once. Ralph Covey. He'd been hiding out

56

at the Bradshaw place when he took sick. She took one look at him and knew that appendix had to come out fast. There had barely been enough time for her to drive back to town to get the ether from the supply cabinet. No one knew about that but the Bradshaws and Ralph. As far as she knew anyway. She hadn't even mentioned it to O.C. She never told anybody anything. Ever. If Ralph Covey told, she could be in all kinds of trouble. Last she heard, Ralph Covey had been caught and was doing time over at Jeff City. If he talked... oh, the very thought made her shiver.

"How do you know? Who told you?"

"Lucy Bradshaw brought her new baby in with whooping cough; started asking me about being a nurse and learning how to operate on people. When I told her nurses didn't do surgery, she told me about you and how you saved some boy's life right there on their kitchen table. You know Lucy, don't you?"

"Lucy," Mayme repeated. She'd been there that night, hovering around, ready to pop with another baby, her third one and not yet twenty years old. "Well, that was an unusual circumstance; it was an emergency and there just wasn't time to get that man to a proper hospital. He needed medical attention no matter what he'd been accused of."

"Mayme, who needs the Argyrol?" Joe asked, suddenly turning the conversation back to the matter that brought her to his door on a Saturday night, not in a nurse's uniform, but all dressed up for a night of dancing. "I know it's not O.C. and it's certainly not for you. And if it was just some old boy around town or out in the hills, you'd send him to either me or Conrad to take care of the problem. You wouldn't want to fool with that yourself for just anybody. And you certainly don't need Protargol for, what'd you say? A little midwifery? Who are you shopping for tonight, Mayme Holloway?"

Mayme rose to her feet and stood as straight and tall as she could stretch herself. It was time to leave, time to abandon this foolish errand before things went too far south for her to find a way out. "I'm sorry I bothered you, Dr. Stern. You're absolutely right; I think I will send this fellow to your office after all.   He was just a little embarrassed was all." She picked up her bag and turned for the door. "It's getting late and O. C. and I are going to that dance tonight . . ."

"Mayme, please sit down." His tone had turned sober, a man accustomed to giving orders to people who would not question or disregard his instruction.   "I told you; you've nothing to worry about.   Trust me, I know more about this situation than you think I do.   And I know what's at stake. Please, sit down for just a bit more."

"Really, Dr. Stern . . ."

"Joe, remember?"   He moved toward her, stood close and touched her elbow gently. She could feel the warmth of his touch through the thin crepe of her jacket.

"Joe, I really can't stay here." She turned and looked up at him, shifting her arm away from his touch.   "I shouldn't have come and you shouldn't get involved. You really have no idea what you're liable to get mixed up with, so I best be going."

"It's a criminal, isn't it? Maybe one of those infamous bank robbers we read about in the newspapers? I hear these hills are full of them."

This time she flinched visibly, the soft hairs on her arm standing on end.   A wave of nausea or lightheadedness caused her knees to weaken, but she wouldn't fall. She stood frozen to hear what more this man had to say, to hear how much he really knew or thought he knew about her life outside the hospital. "What? Where would you get a fool idea like that?"

"I told you, I hear things. For example, I hear Pretty Boy Floyd shows up around town every now and again, that he has old friends here.   A particular barber is supposedly a close friend." One eyebrow lifted on the word friend. "And Ford Bradshaw's got family he likes to visit all over the place, we both know that's true. I believe Lucy is a

58

cousin if I'm not mistaken. And that Jim Benge fellow lives somewhere close by too. But, everybody seems to have a story about Charley Floyd in particular. Heck, everybody loves him. They don't care if he robs every bank in the country; he's their hero. And most of them, I don't believe anyway, care much about him killing poor Officer Kelly." He shoved his hands in his pockets and jingled some coins nervously. "Most of them aren't interested in the reward money and that, for your information, includes me."

He paused, waiting for her to interject, to offer a lengthy argument as she so often did, but Mayme remained silent. She simply watched him, listened to what he had to say, paying close attention to every word and every movement, but offering nothing in reply. The unfamiliar silence was difficult and slowly suffocating the two of them. Eventually, he spoke, hoping to earn the slight woman's favor and trust.

"I was treating one of the deputies the other day, and he told me to keep a watch out for someone coming around with a bullet or two in him, that Kelly had shot Pretty Boy Floyd that night. He'd seen a lot of blood out at the scene and it wasn't all Kelly's. Of course, this isn't about treating any bullet wounds, but if it was, I want you to know that I would be . . ."

"Joe," Mayme interrupted. Her eyes were fixed on his, intense and unwavering. "I don't have any doubt you hear things. The things folks talk about when they're sick or even when they're sitting in O.C.'s barber chair never cease to amaze me, but just knowing about something won't send you to prison. Acting on it will. And for as many folks who love Charley Floyd, don't be fooled; there's just as many would love to see him dead or locked up somewhere. Grover Bishop for one, and he's not someone to mess with. And there's plenty could use that thousand dollars reward to feed their family. They care more 'bout that than some crazy outlaw they hardly know. Haven't you heard? There's a depression going on. This isn't one of your radio mysteries you like so well. Your imagination is working overtime here. Really."

He nodded slowly, giving the handful of coins in his pocket a final roll. "I see," he said then rested one palm on her back and gently maneuvered her back toward the comfortable chair. She didn't even try to resist, allowing his touch to guide her as if she was simply entering a strange and foreign room with him leading the way. Somehow she was certain her secrets were safe with this man. Dr. Joseph Stern wasn't going to do anything to hurt her, not now, not ever. She felt it deep in her bones. From the other room, she could hear the unseen radio, a breathless woman, seductive and alluring, asking a gentleman for a light, eerie organ music playing in the background, a creaking door. She wasn't afraid.

"Sit," Joe said, softly guiding her back down into the pretty damask chair by the empty birdcage. "Just rest a moment, and I'll get you what you need and write out the instructions and send you on your way. I never meant to upset you or make you worry. Trust me, that's the last thing I intended to do." He turned away, then paused, then looked her way once more. "I don't suppose you have a urethroscope on hand, do you?"

She shook her head and watched him slowly move toward the doorway, his bony shoulders slumped down in rejection, his thin arms and wrists dangling from his rolled up shirtsleeves. There was something sad about him, like a scrawny kid that no one wanted on their team no matter what they were playing. How, she wondered, could she pity this man, a doctor, living in a fine home, surrounded by such beautiful things? But she did. He was lonely, and she knew lonely. As quickly as the blanket of fear had fallen over her just moments before, it was replaced by the comfortable memory of a shared chicken sandwich after a long night in the operating theater. There was a reason she felt safe enough to come here in the first place; she liked him.

"No," she said. "No urethroscope, but I have a Janet syringe and a velvet eye catheter. That would work, wouldn't it?" Her smile was teasing and proud. Not many folks could say they had their very own Janet syringe and she knew it.

He stopped, and this time turned around to fully face her. "You have a Janet syringe? Where the heck did you . . .?" He grinned, shook his mop of curly hair, and lifted one hand as if to stop her. "I don't even want to know where you got one of those. Yes, that will work, but it would be better for the Argyrol and Protargol irrigation to use a Keyes Instillator."

"Oh, I don't have one of those either, but if you'll loan me yours, I promise to return it sterilized and ready to go."

He drifted back toward her, studying her sudden change of mood. Standing in a pool of yellow light, he seemed curious, as if he questioned the experience they both knew she had, his words a subtle offer to share in the ordeal. "You do know that Argyrol is a horrible thing to deal with, don't you? It's filthy and stains absolutely everything, but it's not as irritating as the Protargol."

"Oh, I know what a mess it is. I've ruined more than one apron with that solution." She paused, held one finger up to him, bidding him to stay, then picked up her glass to swallow the last of the smoothest whiskey she'd ever swallowed. "Can I ask you something personal?"

"Certainly." He leaned against the paneled wall, pale and lean, badly in need of a haircut, comfortable in her presence without shoes and his shirt collar unbuttoned. Messy hair didn't bother him in the least.

"Why? You lead a charmed life, Joe. You got this nice house, nicer than most folks round here could even dream of, you're a doctor, people love you, respect you, you're a nice man. So, for crying out loud, why on earth would you want to get messed up with all this nonsense? Why don't you just go find a nice girl and get married? You're not from around here; you don't owe these old boys anything, and you certainly don't need their money. So why bother?"

She held the empty glass tenderly in her hands, wishing there was just one more swallow swishing in the bottom of the delicate cup, wishing he'd offer a refill.

Joe breathed in deep, the air whistling through his nose, puffing his narrow chest outward, jingled the coins in his pockets one more time, and shook his head, puzzled. "I don't know. It all seems rather exciting, but that's not it. Truly. There's plenty of excitement around here without looking for it." He blinked slowly, his eyes closed while he considered his words. "When I watch you work, listen to you talk to some of your patients, or when I hear people talk about what you do, something in my gut tells me I want to help you, no matter what the risk. It sounds corny, but I believe that everybody should be able to have proper medical care, even the ones that can't pay anything, and even the so-called bad guys." He ended his speech with one last dip of his head, a quick flinch of his eyebrows and a flutter of dark lashes.

"I guess that's as fair an answer as any. Half the time I haven't a clue why I find myself riding down a dirt road looking for an old shack in the woods, but still I keep going." She gazed into the empty glass, turning it side to side watching the dance of lights through the fine cut crystal.

"So, will you let me be of some help to you in your, shall we say, endeavors?" He swallowed hard; Mayme watched his Adam's apple roll up and down his throat.

"Well, I'm here, aren't I? This is helping. You're giving me something I need, and I'm more than grateful. Why don't you get me those things and let me think about all this for a minute or two. It's been a lot to take in."

Joe nodded in agreement, tapped the wall two times with his knuckles and slipped out of the room. His office was at the back of his house, two rooms he could access through a side door he had built into the kitchen after he bought the place from the judge's widow. Patients entered through a separate door at the rear of the house, never getting past the small examining room and into his private residence. He could come and go without anyone knowing if he slipped away to use the bathroom or made a quick exit out the front door.

By the time Joe returned with a black alligator bag filled with bottles, syringes, tubes and instruments, Mayme had studied the situation and devised a simple plan for the time being; if it would grow into more than this one time, she couldn't begin to know.

She pawed through the contents of the doctor's bag, held up a glass pipette and rubber tubing, then read the label on a large green bottle. "Lord, look at all the instruments you need just to treat the clap. Excuse me, I mean gonorrhea."

"You might not need everything there, but if it's a chronic case, treatment might take a while, anywhere from seven to ten days at a minimum. I want you to prepared for whatever you might need."

"I bet it won't be long before there's an easier fix for this, seeing as how so many men have to put up with all the agony. Someday, mark my words, Dr. Stern, there will be some drug that cures you with one shot in the gluteus maximus."

"Oh, I know you're right. It's on its way; already out there in some laboratory being tested; but for now, this is what we have. Shall I explain it all, or do you know what to do with all of this?"

"A little refresher course wouldn't hurt. It's been a while since I assisted with one of these procedures."

"Start with the Argyrol and then move on to the Protargol. You'll want to irrigate the meatus fully, and hold it in there for at least sixty seconds before releasing it."

"Hmmm-hmmm." She listened carefully, an eager student visualizing every detail. "That's what I was planning to do, give him both medicines, so I'm glad to hear it from you. How do you feel about mixing that treatment with a dose of herbs?" she asked. There were few people she could talk to about medicine outside of the hospital. Mrs. Daniels was an excellent nurse, knew all kinds of tricks from her days in the war, but she would never jeopardize the hospital with the kind of help Mayme usually needed. She had turned to folk medicine cures more than once when she couldn't get her hands on the necessary pharmaceuticals.

"What do you mean?"

"My friend, Wilma, I don't know if you know her, Wilma Hummingbird?"

He shook his head no.

"Wilma swears that sandalwood oil is the best thing for curing the clap. That and a mixture of eucalyptus, wintergreen and kava-kava. Her grandfather was a medicine man and taught her everything he knew; we argue over treatments all the time. But, I don't see how any of that could hurt, and if it helps even a little bit, seems like a good idea to add that in."

"Well, that's not only Cherokee medicine. Herbs and teas can be very beneficial in many things, even, as you say, the clap. The main thing is, no matter what your ailing friend thinks, he shouldn't drink any alcohol, not even beer while he's being treated. Tell him to stick to the tea and lots of water."

"Oh, well, I doubt he'll follow that kind of advice, but I'll pass it along." This time she winked at him, but he didn't seem to notice.

"I still think it would be better if he could come here once a day for the next seven days. And I know the risk, Mayme. I'm well aware of what is at stake. I also would be willing to make a house call if he'd prefer not going out in public. This procedure is more complicated than it seems, and it can be pretty painful. It's not that I don't think you're capable; it's just I might have acquired better skill during my years in medical school, and that skill could save this fellow some anguish in some vital areas. You talk to your friend and let me know tomorrow." His head dipped to one side and his shoulders lifted and lowered. No commitment. No demand.

64

"Thank you, Joe, but I don't much think this fellow will like the idea of hanging around town too long with Grover Bishop trying to prove he's the best lawman in Oklahoma. Just getting him to stay in one place for seven days might take all the convincing I have in me. Adding you in the mix might be impossible."

Mayme returned the contents to the bag, and snapped it shut. "But, to tell you the truth, I was thinking that maybe it would be better if you gave me a hand on this one. I've seen this treatment done, assisted a time or two, but never actually done it completely by myself. And I don't want to be the one to destroy this particular fellow's manhood."

"No," he laughed, "I wouldn't recommend that."

"I was thinking that I could put him up somewhere, out of town a ways, and if he's agreeable to the whole idea, and only then, maybe you could go with me at least once and let me observe. After that, I'm pretty sure I can handle it myself. The thing is, he has a couple of other injuries that I'd like you to take a look at as well, but I don't want to go into that just yet. Not until I've had a chance to talk to the patient."

"Other injuries?" He dipped his chin, met her gaze, but didn't press for the details of those injuries. "Where would you take him? Somewhere close enough to visit every day I hope."

Mayme took hold of the black bag and stood up. She knew when it was time to end a conversation. "It's best if I just keep that information to myself for now," she said. "I have the next couple of days off; I don't go on duty till Monday afternoon, so I pretty much have all day tomorrow to get this all set up if that's what our patient wants. What about you? Do you have any time tomorrow if he should agree to you taking a look at him?"

"Tomorrow's Sunday. I'm not seeing patients other than at the hospital early in the morning. You name the time and I'll be ready . . . to see our patient."

She grinned, recognizing her own slip of the tongue. "I'll call you after I get it all arranged, and if he agrees, then I'll come and get you. We'll ride out there in O.C.'s truck and then I'll bring you on home. A rusty old T won't draw any attention out on those back roads, but your new Chevy might. How's that sound?" Mayme liked spinning the tables, taking her turn at giving the orders for a change.

"Sounds good. You're a smart girl, Mayme Holloway. I mean that."

Mayme smiled. It was nice to hear him say she was smart. And she could tell he meant it, the way he studied her face, watching her all the time and listening to her every word. She lifted the bag a nudge higher. "If you don't mind, I'm gonna go ahead and take all this with me, in case my friend doesn't like my little plan, in which case I'll just go it alone."

Joe again touched the small of her back as he led her to the door, just the tips of his fingers resting tenderly at the curve of the base of her spine. He pulled the door open wide and lingered in the buttery light of the hallway to watch her stroll down the winding brick path, her black heels clicking and scuffing along in the dark. When she turned to walk on down the street, he called after her. "You're not walking home in the dark, are you?"

She turned back around and waved him back inside. "Don't worry, I'm used to it."

"I'm sure you are, but wouldn't you rather have a ride? It's late and besides, you have a dance to get to." He was already closing the door behind him, his broad smile hidden in the shadows.

"It's only a couple of blocks; I'll be fine."

"I'll drive you," he said, ignoring her protests, pulling keys from his pocket, running across the grass in his stocking feet for the pale blue car parked in the small lot behind his house. "Wait right there; I'll come and get you."

4.

While O.C. gave Ruby a turn on the dance floor, Mayme sat with Charley at a small round table tucked in a dark corner. Together, they watched their partners glide along in each other's arms, one long line of motion in perfect rhythm and grace.

"Look at them," Mayme said, "I don't know which one's prettier."

"Oh, I may not know much, but I know my Ruby is not only prettier than O.C., she's prettier than every woman here." He looked at Mayme, lifted his crossed arms and ducked his head ready for a punch. "Present company not included in that remark, Miss Mayme dear. You look mighty nice tonight too."

Mayme laughed and waved her hand at him, shooing away his efforts to compliment her. She watched O.C. twirl Ruby around, then come back together with her, his feet never missing a beat. "Thank you," she said. "And I have to say O.C. did a fine job slicking you up for the night. You smell good enough to drink."

Charley grinned at her. "I'll never understand why that boy wastes good shine on that fire water splash of his. Why doesn't he just buy some Burma-Shave or Bay Rum and give his customers a drink? They'd be happier with that than feeling like they'd been slapped in the face. By God, that stuff has a burn to it."

"Well, don't convince him to change his recipe. I doubt he'd offer to contribute to anyone's sinful ways, and I need a bit of that shine ever once in a while. He only buys it for his special recipe, never touches a drop hisself. In fact," she paused and leaned close, holding her palm open to him, "I could use a bit right now, so hand it over – I know you got a flask in that pocket. Come on, give it up." When he didn't move, she reached under the table and grabbed his knee, then moved her hand a couple of inches higher, and higher still, her fierce grip slowly making its way up to his painful testicles.

"Stop it," he said, trying not to laugh and draw attention to the two of them. He pushed her hand away and reached into his coat pocket. "Know what you are, Mayme Holloway? You're too damn fresh. And impertinent, too. O.C. ought to carry you out behind the woodshed and take a switch to your scrawny butt. Christ Almighty, it's a wonder he doesn't drink his aftershave."

Mayme smiled her sweetest smile, took the silver flask below the table edge and poured a bit into her empty coffee cup. She swallowed the clear liquid in one fast gulp, prepared for the burn that always made her eyes water. "Shoot, Charley, I think you're drinking the aftershave. God damn," she said as she wiped the corner of her mouth with the back of her hand and coughed loudly.

"What happened to all that Lawsy stuff?" He laughed at his friend's wife, took a quick swallow himself, then slipped the flask back into his pocket, his eyes never leaving the dance floor and the sight of his wife, spinning about in her pretty green dress. "Shit, girl, I knew you hadn't give up on talkin' like a dirty sailor."

"So, Charley," Mayme said, pressing in close, nudging him in the shoulder like he was her older brother. She was anxious to finally have some private time to share her plan and getting him in a happy mood might make the talk easier. "I got a little something almost all worked out for you for the next few days to try and get your peter fixed. But just so you know, I'm only doing this for Ruby, not any other Beulahs or Ginnies or Mary Lous you got on the side. They're the ones got you in this mess in the first place.

And you know, if you get all cleared up and whoever she was doesn't, you'll be pissing fire just like before."

She hadn't planned to mention the other girls; it just came out. The day had left her feeling giddy, and maybe a little tipsy, she realized. She had sneaked a couple nips of the aftershave shine before they left, and she'd had that wonderful drink at Dr. Stern's, the good stuff, and now a plug of Charley's flask. She felt good was all.

Charley dipped his chin low and glared up at her, a toothpick sticking out of one corner of his mouth. He ignored the Beulah remark, to Mayme's surprise. "What ya got in mind?" he asked. The way they sat pressed together in a shared whisper looked more like a pair of secret lovers then a nurse discussing a painful treatment with a patient.

"Well, I still have to check the place out with Wilma - you remember her, don't you? But I know it won't be a problem." She waved to O.C. and Ruby, laughed out loud for no reason and nudged Charley, who chuckled in reply, as if she'd willed him to laugh. She'd been told on more than one occasion that she could make a deaf mule laugh if she wanted to, and O.C. and Ruby ought to believe the two of them were just sitting on the side having a grand old time. "Anyway," she said, returning to her serious tone, "Wilma has this old cabin out in the woods, her granddad's old place. I think they use it for hunting ever once in a while, but it mostly just sits empty. It's out near Horseshoe Bend. You know where that is?"

"Sure do." He nodded and took the toothpick from his mouth and studied the gnawed up end.

"If you can take a week or so being isolated out there with your purty wife, so long as you keep your drawers on, my friend, Dr. Stern - you can trust him, I swear - he said he'd go and treat you, at least once. I can take over from there or, if you want, you can have him come back. He's willing to do it."

Charley's face grew dark, his eyes narrowed and tight, his jaw hard and fixed. It was a look Mayme'd only seen once before, the night he'd shown up telling them that the cops had arrested Ruby and Dempsey up in Tulsa trying to get to him. He was ready to kill every one of those bastard cops, he'd said. He sat up straight, looked over his shoulder nervously, then grabbed her by the arm, just above the elbow, pulling her face to just an inch from his own and whispered, his words spitting out like sharp pebbles, his breath rank as kerosene. "I don't know no Dr. Stern. Does he know who he'd be treating? What exactly'd you tell him, Mayme?"

Mayme struggled and tried to pull her arm free, but he only gripped tighter. "Charley, damn it, stop it right now. You're hurting me." He lessened his grip, dropped her arm and glanced over to the dance floor again and smiled and waved to Ruby while Mayme talked. "You know I wouldn't do nothin' that'd put you in harm's way. And if you don't want the doctor, I'll do it myself. 'Sides, the only one who's in any danger right now is me, for Pete's sake, just for trying to make you well again."

She sniffed loudly and crossed her arms indignantly, but her heart was still racing. It was always dangerous to pet a wild dog, especially if he was hurt and trapped. Maybe it would be better to keep Dr. Stern, Joe, she reminded herself, out of this one, no matter what he said. Charley was one of the nice ones. He was her friend. This side of him was a reminder of what it took to survive in his world, what hard years in a place like Jeff City could do to a man. There was a darkness under that handsome face and that darkness fueled those men who lived on adrenalin and fear. She shuddered to think what would happen if the likes of Ford Bradshaw or Charlie Underwood got riled up about something, or if one of them got caught and spilled the beans about her fixing them up now and again. She'd lose more than her job; she'd end up behind bars like the rest of them.

They kept talking while the Virginia Ravens filled the hall with a swinging four-count rhythm that O.C. and Ruby followed with ease, dipping and swaying like a couple of movie stars. Mayme shared with Charley all the details of her conversation with Joe, even the part about him knowing she lifted a bit of medication and supplies now and then. She made sure he knew she could do the procedure alone, but it wasn't necessarily her strong point and it was a tender area she'd be working on. Time and again she reminded him that she had nearly as much to lose as he did. Of course, she wouldn't face the electric chair, but she might as well, considering how she could never work again, and the very thought of being locked up in a cage made her want to lay down and die.

"You got that part right anyway," Charley said, agreeing with her pronounced preference to throwing herself under a freight train to spending her life behind bars. "I'm never going back, no how, no way."

By the time the Ravens announced the last waltz of the evening, it was agreed. Mayme would lead Charley out to Wilma's place near Horseshoe Bend, then head on back for the doctor in O.C.'s truck. The doctor was to be blindfolded once they got past old Cooley's place, just to be safe. Ruby and O.C. would know only that Charley was somewhere getting a much deserved rest. It would mean a whole lot of road time for Mayme, but it promised Charley a measure of comfort for his ongoing freedom.

For the last dance of the evening, O.C. and Charley danced with their wives. Mayme felt lightheaded with excitement and anticipation as O.C. spun her around effortlessly, before taking her back in his arms. She looked up only to see him watching their friends who clung together tightly, gently swaying to the lonely melody, neither one of them wanting to move from their stolen moment together.

A deep purple sky dripped heavy with stars. Mayme sat in the passenger seat while O.C. drove the handsome car, murmuring endlessly about the smooth ride, so unlike his cranky old truck. He was nervous as a cat about driving the thing, knowing without a doubt that its rightful owner was probably somewhere near Tulsa spitting nails about his car being stolen, cursing himself for leaving the

71

key in the ignition. In the back seat were Charley and Ruby, sitting so close they looked like one person, her dark head tucked under his chin, the sound of her man's heart beating steadily in her ear. Occasionally, you'd hear a rustle of shifting arms and legs, a soft whisper, a wet kiss.

Charley had told O.C. to drive to Henrietta, and slid into the rear seat with his wife. He would leave her there to catch a bus home, not knowing when or if he'd see her again. His heart would ache at the sight of his love going, wishing he could go with her, go home to his boy, his own mama, another life. It wasn't ever supposed to be like it had turned out, him always on the run, being blamed for every bank robbery whether he was anywhere near the place or not. Still, he often wondered if he could go back and do it all differently if he would.

As soon as Ruby was safe in the depot, Charley opened the driver's door and signaled for O.C. to scoot over. "Nothin' like driving fast on dark roads to clear my head," he said as he took the wheel.

Alone in the back seat, Mayme stretched out to grab the little sleep she would need. As she drifted away, she listened to the boys ramble on about nothing and everything in the front seat.

"What's your favorite Bible verse, O.C.?" Charley asked.

"Oh, that's an easy one. I've always been partial to John 15:13. 'Greater love hath no man than this, that a man lay down his life for his friends'."

"That's a good one. I'll have to lay that one there on old George. He's a fan of the good book, reads out loud while we're driving, makes me nutty half the time."

The car bounced over a dip in the road, and Mayme nearly rolled off to the floorboard. "Hey, Charley," she yelled, "don't forget you got a lady in this here car." She slapped the back of his seat and felt the steel of his homemade bullet proofing. He'd had this car for a while.

O.C. looked back over his shoulder at her, his eyes shining brighter than the North Star. "Hang on, Darlin'.

72

This man here sure don't spare the horses. No sir." He reached across the seat and grabbed his friend by the scruff of his neck. "No sir."

"Amen, Brother," Charley said, pressing on the accelerator, pushing the sleek steel box to its limit down the empty gravel highway, the wheels spinning and spewing a cloud of dust lost in the night.

"Lawsy," Mayme said, curling up tight on the narrow seat. A slice of moonlight was just visible out the small square window above her. She closed her eyes and prayed they would make it back home without crashing into the Illinois River or sliding into someone's fence post along the way.

It would be nearly dawn when Charley parked the car back behind the small house on Chickasaw Street. Mayme would make a quick change of clothes, happy by then to shed the slinky dress and uncomfortable shoes. Joe's alligator bag was waiting for her on the kitchen table packed with the instruments and antiseptics he'd given her plus the extra supplies she anticipated they would need once he got a look at Charley's other wounds. She had chuckled a little when she added the vials of morphine she had borrowed that morning, thinking of Joe trailing behind her, secretly protecting her from getting caught. She would pack provisions for several days into the empty crates she saved for such occasions, then lead Charley out to Horseshoe Bend before the sun came up. As soon as she got him settled, she'd turn right around and go back for Joe. Somewhere along the way, she had to stop by Wilma's to make sure there'd be no uninvited guests for a few days. She didn't want to trust the telephone, not knowing who might be listening in on the line. O.C. would rest a spell, then clean up nice and walk to Sunday morning service at the First Baptist Church where he would sit on the aisle in the third row next to his Mama. No one would even wonder where his wife was.

73

"Take care, my friend," Charley said as he headed out their back door, pausing to slap his old pal on the back a couple of times.

"No greater love hath no man," O.C. said, "no man."

"No sir, no man."

O.C. stood at the doorway and watched his friend drive away, his own wife leading the way to some secret place, a safe place. And for that, he was grateful.

5.

"I feel a bit foolish," Joe said, "and maybe more than a little nervous, too." He reached up and touched the strip of worn cotton tied around his eyes, a strip of pale green floral feed sack Mayme had found in the hospital store room and set aside for Mama Holloway's quilt making.

"Well, just hold on tight, you don't have to stay in the dark too long, just a turn or two more." The old truck bounced hard along the ruts and crags of the narrow dirt trail that led to the small cabin. Only fifty yards off the main road, the one room shack could not be seen through the dense curtain of greenery that lined the road. If you didn't know where to look, when the highway dipped around and curved to the right, you wouldn't know to turn left down a rutted path that looked more like an old gulley through the hickory woods than a driveway.

"They sure didn't prepare me for anything like this in medical school." He turned toward her when he spoke, though Mayme was sure he couldn't see her or anything more than a slight line of his own lap through the lower edge of the blindfold.

"Yeah, well there's a lot in this world you just can't prepare for, Joe. All you can do is grit your teeth, hang on and keep moving till you get there or fall down trying."

She took advantage of his blindness and stole an extra long glance at him sitting there beside her, his eyes covered with the pretty cloth, hanging on for dear life to the door frame with one hand and the dashboard with the

75

other, his body a rigid twist of elbows and knees. She didn't want to let on that she was more than a little nervous about carrying him out to meet Charley. Bringing someone she worked with, especially a respectable doctor, into this shadowy world of secrets and a fair share of danger was risky for both of them, but she had to admit she welcomed the company. More than once she would have loved to just have another body there for the drive home, a witness to some of the peculiar demands and predicaments of folks who live in hiding.

After bumping and bouncing over the dirt and gravel road, the truck shuddered and let out a final cough when Mayme brought it to a halt. "This is it," she said and reached over to tug the blindfold down from Joe's eyes. He blinked twice, adjusting to the light, then turned to meet her steady gaze. "You ready?" she asked.

Joe ducked his head to peer out through the dirty windshield. "Oh my," he said, taking in the scene around him, swallowing hard. "I guess I'd better be."

"It ain't much, but it'll have to do." Mayme could sense his apprehension at meeting the mystery patient inside.

The small cabin of hand-cut logs had been standing there for more than forty years, worn with age, dirty from neglect, but it was solid. An old water pump at the side of the house provided sweet spring water all year round, even now when there was little to no water just a hundred miles to the west. The old privy was gone, but a nice new one was standing not far from the back door. Wilma's husband, Matthew, decided it was a worthwhile investment of his time to build a replacement when the old one nearly collapsed on him last year while he sat perched over the dark hole, his pants around his ankles.

Wilma told her how he'd carefully drawn up plans, mapping out the cabin clearing, making sure to measure a safe distance from the water pump before digging his new hole in the ground. He hauled lumber and tools out and spent an entire weekend shoveling dirt, sawing boards and pounding nails. He installed screened vents under the roof line to allow for ventilation and even put a toilet paper holder on the wall and a small window up high on the door to let some light in. Wilma complained about the window feature, an invasion of her privacy, but Mayme liked the idea of extra light in there. The few times she had to use an outhouse, she worried so much about snakes and bugs coming up to bite her in the butt she could hardly pee. Most times, when she was out somewhere like this, she just slipped behind a tree. At least then she could see if something or someone was coming to bite her in the ass.

Joe and Mayme exchanged a quick nod of the head, a signal of preparedness they always shared in the operating theater just before Joe made a clean cut into some poor soul's belly.

Standing on opposite sides of the truck, they both took a moment to look around the area, ready for some sign of greeting, some sign of life, but the only sound was the endless buzz of cicadas. There didn't appear to be anyone around, certainly no sign of Charley's touring car. Mayme leaned her weight against the truck door, easing it closed as quietly as possible. Joe watched her and did the same.

"It doesn't look like anyone is here," he said, squinting his eyes and peering into the clumps of trees that surrounded them, even looking directly overhead into the cloudless blue sky.

"I think that's the whole idea of hiding, Joe."

He returned her smirking grin and followed her up the single step to a narrow covered porch, the roof held up by four hickory logs, the stubs of sawed off branches still jabbing out from the trunk. Mayme tapped lightly on the door lightly, then walked on in without waiting for an answer.

Black-and and-white checkered curtains covered two dirty windows on the eastern side. The only light in the small room was what leaked in through the open door, making a square patch of fragile light on the dusty floor.

Mayme went directly to the kitchen table where an old kerosene lamp stood ready for use, a large box of stick matches at its side. She carefully lifted the glass globe from the metal clips, struck the match and lit the wick before turning the key to lift the flame high for a brighter light.

"Is that the only light we have?" Joe asked. He was already examining his workspace, his clean hands braced on his narrow hips as he took in every inch of the single room.

"No, there's a couple more of these lamps up on that shelf over the sink there." It was Charley talking, leaning in through the doorway, a gun hanging loose in one hand, his hat in the other. "Hey there, Mayme," he said, slipping the revolver back in a holster he wore around his shoulders, the gun snug against his ribcage, close to his heart.

"Damn it, Charley, you like to scared me half to death," she answered, wiping her hands on the front of her cotton dress.

"Just making sure who my company was 'fore I show my face is all."

Joe spun around to face his new patient, to discover at last who he would be treating in this rustic hideaway. As soon as he'd heard Mayme say the name, Charley, it was clear that he'd been right all along. Pretty Boy Floyd. He dropped his bag on the floor and extended his right hand and took two awkward steps forwards, his feet heavy as lead.

"Mr. Floyd," he said, "it's a pleasure to meet you, sir."

Charley lifted his chin and moved closer, meeting Joe's outstretched hand with his own. The outlaw dipped his head to one side and stared at Joe with an intensity that made even Mayme dither.

"How do," Charley said. "Now, if you don't mind, I'm gonna have to check you out, make sure you ain't hiding no gun, thinking you can pull a fast one."

"I don't have any guns," Joe said. He shook his head from side to side and patted his own chest and thighs.

"No offense, but I'm the one that does the patting down."

"Of course, of course." Joe raised his arms out to his side, moved his feet farther apart, and offered himself up for a full search.

"Charley," Mayme said, "I promise you, he's okay."

"He better be," Charley said as he felt along Joe's sides, down his bag, along his legs, around his ankles. "He's skinny as a rail fence, that's for sure."

"I am that," Joe said. "Skinny, I mean, not a fence."

Mayme could tell Joe was now feeling more skittish then he'd imagined about treating an outlaw holding a loaded gun. She wished Charley would calm down some, but she also knew how hard it was for him with a big price on his head, moving around all the time.

"Well, to tell the truth," Mayme added, "none of us three'd cast much a shadow." She used her banter to lighten the heaviness in the air. "Good thing I brought along the rest of Mama Holloway's chicken and biscuits for later, after we get through workin' or we might just blow away, all of us."

Charley picked up the doctor's bag and peeked inside. He picked up a long instrument and eyed it curiously, his face a dark scowl. "I'm not sure I like the looks of this thing, Doc. Considering what it is you're here for." His eyes narrowed as he gave Joe a hard stare, his grey eyes fierce and cold.

Joe reached over and took the bag and set it on the table and returned the urethroscope to its contents before closing it up. "I won't lie to you, Charley, it's not a pleasant treatment, but then again, it's not a pleasant disease." He coughed, cleared his throat and continued. "I have some medication to help with the pain, so you just need to take a few days to relax, do the treatments and you'll be fine in a week or so." This was advice he would give any patient that visited his office, words he could rattle off while scratching notes in a chart and planning his evening, but when he spoke to Charley Floyd, he struggled to maintain his natural composure, his voice cracking and weaker than usual.

"Where's your car, Charley?" Mayme asked.

"Oh, I tucked it away somewheres safe till I'm ready to move on." He wandered to the window, took a peek out through the curtains.

Mayme nodded her head. Even now, if the law managed to find them out there eating fried chicken in Wilma's old cabin, they wouldn't so much as take a breath before shooting a hundred bullets through him and probably her and Joe too while they were at it. Poor Joe seemed to just now be realizing what he had put himself at risk for. She wondered if he'd ever come back again, if he'd still be willing to cover up her small transgressions at the hospital, if he would still be her friend. "Well, just don't forget where you put it, like that time last summer. Remember?"

Charley laughed out loud. "Hell, yes, I remember. Shoot, Mayme, you know too damn much. Too damn much."

Mayme didn't respond other than to smile at him sweetly, knowing he was right. She knew a lot about this man and most of it she liked just fine.

"Joe," she said, turning her attention to the business that brought them to their hideaway in the woods, "if you wouldn't mind, I brought some clean sheets and towels and a few other things; they're out in the truck. Can you carry those in for me while I get this stove going and heat some water? And Charley, you might want to go relieve yourself before we get started."

"She means I'm supposed to go take a piss in that fancy outhouse," Charley said, tossing his hat and coat onto the foot of an old iron bed, "and in case you ain't figured it out, Doc, when Mayme Holloway says frog, you best jump." He limped out the door, pausing long enough to scan the clumps of trees surrounding the small yard,

80

and headed toward the new privy with the toilet paper holder, where last year's Sherman Seed and Grain calendar featuring a picture of a healthy wheat field under big red numbers, 1931, hung on the wall.

The friendly banter between Mayme and Charley began to ease Joe's anxiety so that he could almost forget that his patient was a bank robber suffering from a venereal disease and, from what he could tell, some painful leg or foot injuries as well. He seemed eager to get to work, to see what was causing that painful limp, to treat the gonococcus, and to ease the man's physical pain.

As long as Joe was busy doing something, no matter what it was, he was sure footed, so hauling supplies or moving furniture around was fine with him. There were plenty of doctors that would, as Mayme would say, get their bowels in an uproar, if someone asked them to lug in supplies, but not Joe. He hummed as he carried in the baskets Mayme had hauled in the back of her old Model T. She knew precisely what they'd need once they got here, things he never would have even thought to ask for. Linens, hand soap, Mercurochrome, rubber gloves, carbolic acid, hydrogen peroxide, gauze strips and what looked to be a good-sized bottle of moonshine, judging by the lack of any type of label.

Mayme plucked the unlabeled bottle out of the basket and quickly stashed it inside a cupboard, behind a dinted can of Folgers coffee. "O.C. will be fit to be tied when he learns I absconded with his shave shine," she said and chuckled to herself. "Let's not tell Charley about this or he'll get into it."

"Let's not tell Charley 'bout what?" He stood in the doorway again, smirking.

"Damn it, Charley, are you walking around in your socks?"

"It's my Cherokee blood," he said as he ambled over to the kitchen area and opened the cupboard. He scooted the coffee can aside and looked up at the bottle, but didn't take it out, just smiled and closed the small pine door.

81

"That's not for you, Mister. I just figured I'd leave a little something for Matthew to thank him for the use of his cabin. You're not to be drinking spirits while you're getting treated."

"She's right," Joe added. "You shouldn't drink alcohol for a few days. You need lots of water and tea if we have it."

"Whatever you say, Doc," he said, taking a seat at the kitchen table. "I don't plan on this being a long-term situation out here anyways."

It didn't take more than a couple of seconds for Mayme to take a quick inventory of her surroundings. It was much like it had been the last time she was here, before she'd gone away to nursing school. She and Wilma had spent a long weekend in the woods, smoking cigarettes and planning their lives. Wilma was going to marry Matthew Hummingbird and have lots of babies. Mayme was going to be a nurse and be the one to cure all those babies when they were sick and take care of their mother like Doctor Moody had done for them.

The small cabin had only one room, but Wilma's granddad had managed to arrange things so that there were distinct living areas. One corner was taken up by a sagging double bed, an old bureau with four big drawers at its side. A cane back rocking chair sat in another corner, facing the cold fireplace, along with an old sofa that had holes eaten through by some hungry critter. She prayed there wasn't a nest of mice sleeping down in the soft piling. One half of the cabin seemed to be taken up by the kitchen. A wood-burning stove was covered in soot, but there was a good sink and waterspout that gushed fresh cool water when Mayme pumped the handle. And best of all, there was a good-sized sturdy table with four solid chairs. Mayme'd turned a kitchen table into a hospital bed more than once, saving the bed for a clean resting place when the messy work was done.

Before she and Joe could even begin to think about pulling out the sounds and scopes they'd need, she would have to give the place a quick once over with a broom and a dust rag, put clean linens on the bed and cover the table with a clean white sheet. No need to contaminate poor Charley any worse than he already was.

"This place is an absolute fright," she announced, grabbing a bucket and an old flannel cloth from the corner, swiping at a thin layer of dust along the counter top, then scowled at the sight of a rising cloud of dust. "I'm gonna need to clean things up around here a bit, so why don't you two just have a sit and get to know each other while I do some housekeeping. It won't take long. I just sure wish they had electricity in here so's I could see better."

The two men dragged a couple of the high-backed chairs out to the porch, leaving Mayme to transform the dingy hunting cabin into a sterile examination room, or at least a cleaner version of the hideaway where no one usually bothered much with things like clean sheets or table cloths.

"Where ya from, Doc?" Charley asked, plucking a toothpick from his vest pocket and sticking it in his mouth, resting his foot on one of the branch stubs along the porch posts.

"New York. Upstate New York, Buffalo, actually." Joe flicked the back of his hand against the top of his thigh, slapping away invisible lint, then gripped his knees, and cleared his throat, covered his mouth with a sideways fist and coughed a dry cough that sounded a bit like a choking engine.

"Sounds to me like you might be comin' down with that lung crud." Charley pulled the toothpick from his mouth and examined the end, growled and spit an ugly wad of phlegm out into the dirt. He flipped the toothpick around before sticking it back in his mouth. "Lung crud. You probably call it somethin' fancy, but that's what it is."

"No," Joe said, "I'm fine, it's a nervous habit, clearing my throat. Just so you know, Mayme didn't tell me who our patient was before we got here, but I guessed it was you. I'd heard you and Mr. Holloway are old friends, so I

83

just assumed." He shrugged his shoulders and watched for Charley's reaction. "Guess I'm just getting used to it all."

"Yep. Me and O.C. been friends longer'n I can remember and Mayme's his wife, so I ain't gonna let anything happen to her if I can help it. So as long as you don't do something stupid, you'll be fine too." Charley fixed his gaze at some point beyond the clearing, as if his vision could pierce the dense growth of trees and vines and reach the gravel road below.

"Oh, don't worry if you mean tell the sheriff, oh no, no, no. I'm not interested in any reward money. It's really no concern of mine what you've done. I'm just here to provide medical care, not judge your crimes." Joe felt his words spilling out in a perfunctory way that irritated even him. "Pardon me, I'm rambling like a fool."

"Well, if you don't calm down some, there's no way in hell you're gettin' near my pecker with that metal rod you packed in that bag." Charley cast a sideways glance in Joe's direction with a quick dip of the head, his grey eyes soft in the cool afternoon shadows.

"You know," Charley added, "if I'd done half the things they say I done, I wouldn't have to do nothin' ever again 'cept spend all that money. I'd have Ruby and Dempsey with me and we'd be livin' the high life somewhere."

"Ruby and Dempsey? Is that your family?"

"Yep. Ruby's my wife and Dempsey's my boy. He's seven now." Charley's face softened into a natural grin at the mention of his son's name, his age, as if he could see the boy's smiling face before him.

"A son. I'd like to have a son one day." It was as if the idea had never before crossed his mind, his words revealing some desire secret even to himself, catching him off guard. "Or a daughter. A daughter would be good."

"Well, hopefully you'll have yourself a boy and a girl both and be able to watch 'em grow. This ain't no way to be a family." The smile faded and again Charley's focus turned to the road beyond the tops of the hickory and oak trees that surrounded them.

The air grew heavy and still with the lull of conversation. Cicadas buzzed fiercely from the surrounding shadows while a colorful pair of tanagers fluttered through the tall branches, a flash of red and yellow feathers on the fly. The two men sat silent for a time, both staring off into the dense woods, looking for some unbidden prize, an answer for the unspoken troubles that plagued them.

"Why'd you come out here for anyway? To Oklahoma," Charley asked, breaking their silent reverie. "It's a long way from New York and there sure ain't much going on around these parts. Most folks are headin' west, not settling here."

"I wanted the job." His thin shoulders shrugged in simple resignation. "My mother has a couple of apartment buildings in Buffalo. Mrs. Daniels, the head of the hospital, lived there for a while after the war. She and my mother had worked together and become good friends, still are. She wrote to my mother, told her they were looking for a new doctor, wondered if I might be interested. So, here I am."

"Your mama a nurse too?"

"She was, until she married my father. He was a doctor."

Mayme paused to listen to Joe talk about his family, where he'd come from, how he knew Mrs. Daniels. In the past few hours, he had become more than the nice new doctor in town who was easy to talk to. She liked him, liked being around him, liked how she felt around him. If she was a single woman, she'd say she was smitten; the way she felt so light and fluttery she might tumble off with a drift of leaves on a stiff breeze.

"A doctor for a daddy," Charley mused, his tongue clicking with this new bit of information, pondering the news before saying more. "Well, I'm sure he'd be proud to know his son followed in his footsteps."

85

"That's what he wanted." Joe's gaze held hard to the tops of the trees, to the river beyond.

Mayme felt a pang of sadness in Joe's falling words, that's what he wanted. What did Joe want? Didn't he want to be a doctor too? Or, did he simply mean it was something his father never got to realize, that he died before seeing all that Joe had become? She peeked out through the open door and studied his somber face, the long line of his jaw, the gentle curve of his nose, his brown eyes fixed on the horizon, an unknown future. As if he could feel her gaze upon him, he turned his head toward her and smiled. It startled her, his eyes meeting hers, resting there as if he would never look at another thing again. Eyes can speak a silent language that Mayme knew well so she was the one to blink, to finally look away.

The afternoon sun warmed the small clearing in the middle of a hickory and oak forest where two strangers shared enough to brew a measure of trust between them. Charley told him about taking Dempsey to see Frankenstein, how the little boy loved to sit in the dark theater and hold his father's clammy hand. Joe told him how much he missed his own father and mother, how he'd written to his mother and asked her to come and live with him in the big house he'd bought, but she didn't want to leave her home, her friends, her properties.

"If you ever find yourself in New York, look her up," Joe said. "She'll fix you a grand meal and put you up for a night or two. And for what it's worth, some of her places are furnished if you need to stay a while, away from these hills. And if you're a friend of mine, that's all she needs to know. She's a good woman."

"You never know," Charley said, "I might find myself in Buffalo one day, things get too hot 'round here."

"You never know," Joe agreed.

Mayme finally stepped out on the porch and tossed a pail of dirty water out into the dirt. "Okay, boys, I think we'd better get to work while the light's still good."

Charley nodded his head, his lips pressed tight together. He threw his head back to view Mayme standing in the door, an empty bucket in one hand, the other braced on her bony hip. "You bring some of that hooch you shot me with yesterday?"

Mayme wasn't surprised to see the trace of a smile cross Joe's lips smile since he'd known about her morphine stealing all along. "As a matter of fact, I did," Mayme answered, "but not much. I'm gonna need to stock up after your visit."

"This procedure doesn't require morphine," Joe countered, rising to his feet. "It's a bit uncomfortable, but not unbearable."

"You stick that thing up your own member and tell me you don't need a little something extra," Charley said, stepping directly in front of him, tilting his chin up to meet Joe's serious eyes with a hard stare that seemed forced.

"Touché, Charley."

"What?" Charley turned to follow the tall skinny doctor inside.

"He means you get the hooch," Mayme said, stepping aside to make room for them to pass. She felt a little smug explaining Joe's meaning to Charley, remembering the first time she'd heard Doc Mooney say the strange word long ago when she was just a young girl, how she'd looked at him puzzled, and how he had jabbed at her as if he was fencing and said "touché" again before offering its meaning.

The room was changed completely. White sheets covered the kitchen table, and a small makeshift instrument table was made from two chairs and two of the supply crates she'd brought from home. The curtains were tied back with bits of fishing line to let the available light shine through the freshly cleaned windows. Lamps burned on the stove and one hung from a hook in the ceiling above the table. There were three pans filled with water that had been heated on the stove. The bed had fresh sheets, the covers turned back and ready for Charley to climb in. It even smelled clean, the floor freshly mopped with the lemon-scented cleaner O.C. used in his shop.

"Charley," Joe said, "why don't you remove your trousers and hop up there on the table. And if you need to void, uh pee, again, you should do that now."

"Naw, I'm dry as a bone."

Mayme turned her back while Charley undressed. While she didn't mind examining every inch of a body, she felt it improper to watch someone disrobe. She pulled on a clean white apron and a pair of rubber gloves while Joe went to the sink and washed his hands, dipping them into the warm water before scrubbing them with the green soap borrowed from the hospital dressing room, rinsing them with cool water from the pump. When he was finished, Mayme handed him a pair of sterilized rubber gloves fresh from a muslin wrap.

"You've thought of everything," he said, tugging the gloves onto his clean hands.

"It's not my first time; I just don't usually have any help."

"I guess out here, you're the boss."

Mayme flashed a quick grin, but deep inside, a warmth spread through her belly. She had taken extra care, bringing far more supplies than if she'd come alone, eager to impress him with her abilities.

"Don't worry; I have a gown for you too," she said, lifting the clean white robe from the basket on the floor. "No need to stain your pretty clothes."

"Thank you, again."

Mayme held the gown up while he slipped his arms through the sleeves, then tied it behind him, breathing in the clean smell of him, noticing the damp curls of hair at the nape of his neck. She liked the smell of plain soap and a little sweat without any whiff of flowery aftershave. Sometimes O.C. put his shave on so thick, she'd start sneezing the minute she walked in the door.

"Lord, help me now," Charley said when Joe picked up the syringe that would be inserted into the tip of his penis.

"Well, I'm not anybody's lord, but I'll do my best," Joe offered.

"Much obliged, but, first, I believe Miss Mayme there was gonna give me a jab of that happy juice."

For the second time in two days, Mayme stuck a hypodermic needle into Charley Floyd's buttock, sending him to a floating dreamscape where he could sleep without listening for the sound of tires on a gravel road, knowing that he was in safe hands in a corner of the world where no one would find him. He lay back on the table and closed his eyes as Mayme injected the small dose of stolen morphine and let it carry him away. She knew he hadn't slept at all the night before and wasn't surprised when the drug sent him into a sudden sleep.

"He really needs to know how to do this part himself," Joe said. "Then he can keep treating if he has to leave suddenly." As he spoke, he lifted the outlaw's injured ankle and probed at the bullet wound. "This will be a challenge."

Mayme lifted the limp penis with one finger and examined the bullet wound along his scrotum before she began to cleanse the area with hydrogen peroxide. "Here's where one bullet passed through, just missed taking his penis off altogether." She used a cotton ball to again cleanse the wound and genital area, taking care not to reopen the sensitive skin that was beginning to heal. There would be a scar there, a private reminder of a very close call.

Joe reached over and touched the wound, palpating the area surrounding. "It's healing nicely," he said. "Let's get him irrigated and then I'll take a closer look at that ankle, see if we can't do something there too. In a couple of hours, he'll be awake and I'll irrigate him again."

"Twice in one day?"

"Yes, I'm going to use a repressive method since it seems he's had this for more than a day or two. We'll irrigate the anterior urethra twice a day for two or three days, then once a day, then every other day, increasing the strength of the Protargol from two percent to five. I hope he can stick around for a couple of weeks."

Mayme nodded to acknowledge her understanding, eager to absorb the new techniques, but she doubted seriously that Charley would plant himself there for two weeks. She didn't think he could take that much alone time, no friends around, let alone the danger of sitting still.

"I'll see if I can't get Ruby out here to keep him company. He'd like that."

Mayme watched Joe insert the tip of the syringe into the red meatus to inject the Protargol solution. "You want to hold it in here for about three minutes," he told her. She liked that he trusted her to take over this care, assuming she would be the one to follow up with the prescribed care during the days to follow.

"You really think he could do this himself?" she asked.

"Sure. Lots of men do. I'm surprised you don't know more about this treatment. You seem to know more than most residents."

"Well, Doc Moody is old fashioned about some things. He takes care of this type of illness in his office privately, and I've always worked at the hospital since I got out of nursing school."

"What Tahlequah needs is a public health center, a place where folks can go for preventative care." He still held the tip of Charley's penis in his fingers while he talked.

"That something you plan on starting?" she asked.

"I'd like to. There's this hospital down south that this doctor started based on socialism." He paused to look at her briefly, then turned his attention back to his patient as he explained. "The community owns the hospital; everyone paid a little money to get it going. That's the type of thing I'd like to see everywhere. Of course, the Medical Society is not too keen on such things."

He simply nodded and Mayme knew to step in, ready with a thick pad of gauze wrapping. "I like that idea," she said, "the people owning the hospital, but I don't really know much about socialism."

"Something tells me you will," Joe muttered to himself without looking at her.

Mayme wiped up the draining fluid and covered Charley's torso and upper thighs with a clean white sheet while they moved down to look at his ankle. There was nothing Joe could do in the primitive workspace other then clean the area and bandage it up again.

"If I could get him into the hospital, we could fix that up proper, but he'd have to be under general anesthesia, and the conditions would have to be far more sterile than this. And he'd be off his feet for a few weeks."

"That would never work for him," Mayme said, a touch of sadness in her voice. She knew he would have to live with the pain, his body slowly adjusting and compensating for the injury, but never healing."

Together they moved Charley to the clean bed. He stumbled across the short patch of floor, one arm around Joe, the other across Mayme's thin shoulders, until his body dropped like a heavy sack onto the soft bed where he would sleep for several hours. Mayme knew it was one of the rare occasions he would sleep soundly.

"I brought a little something myself," Joe said. He and Mayme had taken over the two chairs on the porch, leaving their patient to rest quietly inside. The afternoon light was filtered by the approach of promising clouds so that the clearing was washed in soft shadows. A gentle breeze whispered through the dense leaves of the hickory and oak surrounding them while a faint scent of the Illinois' winding flow of dark green water drifted up from the shady cove just down the road.

"It wouldn't be a fishing pole, would it?" She turned to him and smiled big. "I know where there's a little rowboat and a river full of crappie. Ain't nothing like it, Dr. Joe." She was comfortable switching to her common speech, the one she'd used her whole life, personal and rank with charm and bad grammar. It was as much a part of her as her left big toe, but she knew how to tuck it away when she had to, a trick she'd picked up at Sparks Hospital, where she learned more then how to change a bandage or fill a syringe.

"No fishing pole, but I do have a flask of that whiskey you seemed to enjoy." He fished the pretty silver bottle from his pocket and held it up between two fingers. "This might not be as fun as fishin' but, as you might say, it's better than a poke in the eye with a sharp stick."

"Oh, aren't you turning into the good country doctor, treating outlaws in the woods, talking like you was born and raised 'round here."

"I call it Maymespeak," he said. "You have a way of saying things like nobody else I know."

She took the bottle, grinning at the high praise, and sipped it slowly. After a second hit on the bottle, she handed it to Joe.

"Now if I only had a couple of those chicken sandwiches of yours," he said in a forced southern twang imitating her, "we'd be sitting in tall cotton." He offered a twisted grin at his second offering of his version of Maymespeak, then added, "I'm starving."

Mayme didn't say a word in reply, just jumped up from her seat and slipped quietly into the cabin. She came out with a couple of biscuits stacked on her outstretched hand. "Gnaw on one of these," she said. "Don't worry, I didn't make 'em."

"Let me guess, your mother-in-law."

"You got it. Even a day old, they're pretty good." She took a bite, wiping the falling crumbs from her mouth. "Follow me," she said, taking his sleeve to lead him down the single step. "I know a shortcut down to the water. Let's go have some fun while Charley's sleepin'."

In single file, with Mayme leading the way, eating their dry biscuits as they walked, they ducked through tangles of branches and stumbled over thick coiling roots out to the highway where a narrow path cut in off the road. They could smell the water, the musty lure of a cool riverbank. The old boat was where it always was, looking like it had been there forever, but sound, Mayme promised, pushing it out of the shrubbery to rest at the water's edge, perched for launching.

"Hop in," Mayme ordered, handing him a paddle. "I'll push us off; just give me a minute."

She turned her back to him while she reached up under her dress to unhook her good mesh stockings, giggling as she struggled to free the back two hooks, her hands reaching back through her legs. She had worn them out to the dance, all last night, then all day long. She slipped one down and then the other, skillfully removing the shoe and stocking together to avoid standing in the dirt in her stocking feet. The cool air tickled Mayme's bare skin, and she dug her stubby toes into the damp earth and smiled at her daring moves as she pulled the bodice of her dress higher, so that the hemline rose several inches above her bony knees, and bloused the loose fabric up over her belt into a self-made swimming dress.

Feeling like a ten year old kid on the first day of summer, Mayme splashed through the cold water, her tender feet gripping against the floor of small slippery stones, and shoved the small boat away from the shoreline. In one swift leap, she was over the edge and in the boat, her bare legs slick with water, her strong calf muscles taut and shining in the falling sunlight.

"You never cease to amaze me," Joe said, wiping the splash of water from his face before taking up the one paddle to row them out to the middle of the cove, his eyes scanning the whole of her. "Look at you."

"You ought to see me hop a freight train." She was pleased with herself and it showed, the light in her eyes burning bright.

Mayme stretched her body long, resting her upper body on her forearms, her head flung back so that her face could soak up the heat of the afternoon sun. She pushed her wet legs forward, maneuvering them under Joe's bent knees and closed her eyes. "What a day," she said. "What a couple a days, really. I'm exhausted." With eyes still closed, she grinned to no one and added, "I mean, I'm plum tuckered out."

"Now that, Mrs. Holloway, is an understatement." He shook his head in disbelief at all that had transpired since she had knocked on his door. He dragged the paddle through the water on the left, lifted it clumsily and sent a spray of water into the air that splashed Mayme in the face.

She laughed out loud, letting her voice lift high into the tops of the trees. She watched the sky over her, as if she could see her laughter drifting away like feathery clouds. By the time she lowered her eyes to look at Joe, her smile was lost to curiosity and genuine concern.

"Tell me," she said quietly, "how are you really doing with all this? I don't need to tell you what could happen to you if the law showed up. The two of us would be locked up just like Charley. Maybe not as long, but we wouldn't be paddling in a lake for quite a while, and you might never be able to open that clinic you dream of. It's o.k. if this one day is enough for you."

"I know," he answered. There was no sign of folksy humor now, no attempt to sound like one of the hill folk. "I thought about it all last night and the whole way out here. I almost backed out, but something kept me going. Despite the risk, it seemed like the right thing to do somehow." He pulled the paddle in and leaned back, stretching his legs out to rest alongside Mayme's. They sat quietly, letting the current carry them where it would around the small inlet. "Besides," he added with a broad smile, "think of the story I can tell when I'm an old man – I stuck a needle into Pretty Boy Floyd's willie."

Mayme laughed loud again. "Did you say 'willie'? Lord Almighty, did they teach you that term in medical school?"

"No, that's a remnant from Simon Goldstein, fellow camper at Camp Cobbossee, fourth grade."

"Camp whatchahoosee?" She giggled softly, again gazing at the sky, resting the back of her head on the rough edge of the boat, her braided bun serving as a small pillow. She felt the warmth of his legs touching her own and considered moving them, but never did.

"Camp Cobbossee. In Maine. My folks would send me there for two weeks each summer. It was great fun."

They drifted along, neither one of them feeling any need to say anything as the gentle rocking of the boat lulled them into their own private sky-gazing dreams.

"Do you and O.C. come out here often?" he finally asked, breaking the silence, sitting up to face her.

"Oh, Lord, no," she said. "O.C. stays busy with the shop and his club - he's president of the Barber's Association. And you know how busy I am at the hospital and running around these hills now and then. He doesn't really care much for fishing anymore, if he ever did." Mayme pulled herself up, shifted her weight and peered over the edge of the boat, down into the wet darkness. She dragged her fingers through the cool water, disturbing the still surface.

"Too bad. It's beautiful here."

"You ain't telling me nothin' I don't already know. My friend Wilma and I used to come out here ever chance we got when we were kids." Mayme smiled at the memory of her and Wilma swimming in their step-ins and undershirts after a long morning of fishing for black bass or crappie. Nothing tasted any better than a fish just out of the river, cooked over an open fire. They'd end the day sitting on the cabin porch, smoking stale cigarettes, planning their futures, imagining lives filled with exciting adventures and handsome men. She rested her chin on her forearm, methodically dragging her fingers through the water, as if she petted a small animal hiding just below the surface.

"So you grew up here?"

"I did."

95

"Do you have family here? I don't believe I've ever heard you mention anyone like your mother, father, a sister."

Mayme pulled herself away from the edge of the boat and wiped her fingers on the edge of her skirt, offering Joe a wistful smile. It hadn't occurred to her that he was one of the few people in town who didn't know everything about her and everybody else.

"Well, I guess that depends on what you mean by family," she said. "Wilma, her family, Doc Moody, even Mrs. Daniels. I think of lots of folks around here as family. My own people are gone." Her eyes scanned the landscape as she spoke, her words composed and steady as she shared a piece of her history with him. "Did you ever hear about the tornado up in Peggs? Back in 1920?"

He shook his head no, his eyes narrowed and focused, the doctor listening to his patient carefully, the new man in town learning a little local history, a man discovering more about a woman he liked more than he should.

"I was just thirteen then. My family was all from Peggs. My mama was up there visiting her folks, taking care of her own mother. My grandmother, Grammy we called her, she had fallen and broken her foot and needed her to be there while she couldn't get around, so I stayed home with my dad, to help him with chores Mama usually did. We lived outside of town then and had a cow that needed milking and a few chickens that had to be fed. Anyway, Mama was in Peggs when the storm hit. My grandparents had a storm cellar, but I guess they just didn't get there in time, prob'ly cause of Grammy's foot. When we got there, after the storm, their house looked like a pile of broken matchsticks, scattered all over the countryside." Her voice trailed off.

"I'm sorry, Mayme," he said softly. "I know how hard it is to lose a parent. I lost my own father some years back. What about your dad? Where's he?"

"Oh, Daddy tried to make it on his own, well, with just me I should say. But before long he met a woman, a secretary over at the college. He had a job there doing construction. Eventually they got married and moved out to California. She wanted to get him away from all the bad memories here. Guess I was part of that so they left me to finish school. I was fifteen by then and Daddy figured I would be better off staying behind till they got settled in."

"Where did you live? You couldn't have been on your own at fifteen, could you?"

"Well, I was, pretty much. First I had a room with this great old lady, Mrs. Hixon. She died a couple years back, poor thing, got pneumonia and couldn't breathe. For a while I had a job workin' for Doc Moody, cleaning his house, running errands to the hospital, filing some. That's how I got to know Mrs. Daniels, and she gave me work too. I loved being at the hospital, seeing her take care of everybody, and watching her boss people around too. You know how she does."

Joe nodded, grinned. "Don't I," he said.

"When I wasn't workin', I spent most of my time with Wilma's family. Wilma and I have been best friends since we were babies, so I practically lived with them until I went away to nursing school. That's pretty much it." She flashed a quick grin, her lower lip jutting out, and flinched her thin shoulders. "Daddy's still out in California, but I haven't seen him since he left here. I keep meaning to pay him a visit. Maybe next Christmas."

"Hey, what do you call that bird there?" Joe asked, changing the subject. He looked over her shoulder and pointed toward the shore, where the dense wood surrounded the watery cove.

Mayme shifted her gaze, searching the patches of dappled light near the highest branches where the wind made the leaves quiver and dance. "Where?" she asked.

"There, the bright red one, in that bushy tree."

The same pair of pretty tanagers that had fluttered near the cabin earlier now sat perched on a low branch of a hickory tree, a heavy swatch of ruby red feathers guarding his pale yellow mate.

"Oh, I don't know," she said. "The red one's the male, the lemony one's the female. That much I know."

"How do you know that?"

"The male's always the pretty one. Think about ducks, the male all shiny with his dark green head leading the pack and the female, just a drabby old brown, paddling behind."

"You're right," he said. "I'm just not sure the red is prettier then the yellow. Funny, though, how with birds the male is usually prettier, so different than with humans."

"Oh, not always. Everybody knows O.C.'s the pretty one in our house," she said, aimlessly flicking a spray of water into the air, the drops falling like broken bits of glass into the dark water.

"What are you talking about?" Joe shook his head in disbelief. "I wouldn't be watching you all the time if you weren't so easy on the eyes. And to tell you the truth, I don't think I ever gave O.C. so much as a second glance."

"You're just being nice," she said, embarrassed by the flattery, but nonetheless a warm glow spread across her cheeks. Hearing Dr. Stern say nice things to her made her feel slightly queasy, but in a nice way. She hadn't felt that way since before she got married.

"No, I'm being truthful. I honestly don't understand how O.C. lets you run around out here by yourself. Treating dangerous men off in secret hideaways." He paused, waiting to catch her eye, "or rowing around in a little boat with them either." Joe picked up the paddle and began rowing, turning the boat back toward shore, sneaking a sideways glance at her before looking back over his own shoulder.

"To tell you the truth," she said, "I don't think he gives it much thought. I don't ever tell him what I do or who I do it with, and he doesn't ask." She thought of his endless knack for empty conversation, a skill that served him well as a barber, polite dabs of humor and small talk that he could prattle on for hours.

98

"How come? You do some incredible things. You should tell him; I know he'd be impressed."

"Oh, O.C. says all that blood and gore makes his stomach turn, so as far as he's concerned, I just wear a white dress and shoes and hand out pills." One corner of her mouth turned up as her head softly moved from side to side, as if her own life was impossible for even her to understand. Whenever she tried to share some excitement she'd drug home with her, O.C. found a way to snuff it out without ever saying one mean thing. He had a way about him that she couldn't explain so she didn't even try. She'd simply grown accustomed to keeping most things she did or saw to herself, knowing he wasn't interested in her world.

"I'm sorry," Joe said. "I know how lonely it can be, not having someone to share your day with. I've been thinking of getting a dog just so I have someone to talk to at night, someone to tell about my crazy days, or even my crazy dreams."

"You can talk to me," she said.

"I'd like that."

"You know they say if you share your dreams before breakfast they come true, so if you dream something really good, hold off on eating till you tell me."

"Does coffee count?"

Mayme tilted her head to one side, gave the question careful consideration. "Coffee counts, unless you're having coffee with the person you're telling about the dream. Then it doesn't count."

It was such a simple thing, a plan to be friends, to talk about what they'd seen and heard, to share how they felt, even their dreams. Mayme sat and watched Joe paddle them back to shore, to the line of red earth and dark trees waiting for them. She wished the journey would be much longer, that they could float in the tiny boat for a long, long time.

Joe stopped rowing, again pulled the oar to rest alongside him and pulled the silver flask from his pocket.

He placed it in her open hand, wrapping her fingers around the small bottle, then covered her smaller hand with both of his. "We forgot to have a drink," he said, still cupping her hand.

It startled her, the way he took her hand into his own, the way he held it there. She looked toward her hand as if it belonged to another and thought it was beautiful, the curve of his fingers around her own, protective and intimate too. She raised her eyes to meet his gaze, her thoughts flickering briefly to the cricket hiding in the weeds, waiting, wanting. She didn't rush to drink from the bottle, didn't say a word, and didn't free her hand from his gentle hold. A knowing silence swelled between them, stealing their easy speech, willing them to only look at the other, to hear only the slap of the green water against the rocking boat, to feel the closeness of the other.

"Your hands are soft," he finally said, releasing his grasp and softly running one finger along the back of her smooth hand as she finally took up the flask.

Mayme breathed deeply, filling her lungs with air, but still she didn't drink. She lingered in the unspoken hint of intimacy, realizing this moment had been a long time coming. Perhaps, she thought, she willed it unconsciously from that first private conversation months ago when they shared a late night supper under the stars. Alone with him in a small boat in a sheltered cove, it was easy to drift, to be carried away by the current, down unfamiliar tributaries and streams, down deep to an underwater spring that would gush fresh water into some dark patch of earth. So many people were thirsty these days, their lands parched and barren. They prayed for just a taste of sweet spring water. Mayme wanted more than a taste; she wanted to drown in it.

"Just one little sip," she finally said, reaching out to him, touching him lightly on the forearm. She looked at his empty hands, resting between his knees, the hands she had watched handle a scalpel with such tender precision, hands she had gloved, passed instruments to, such perfect

100

hands. "We still have work to do," she said, then took one quick swallow.

Joe nodded and took up the paddle. "To shore," he said.

As they made their way through the winding path back to the cabin, they only talked of plants that grew in the area, plants that Mayme used for homemade medicine in the old folk recipes she'd collected over the years, some Cherokee, some not. As she chattered on about jewelweed relieving the sting of poison ivy, she was inwardly chastising herself that she had overreacted to the hands and the flask business, that he was just being curious and friendlier than they had been in the past. All they had done was touch hands and there was no harm in touching hands. What she was guilty of was a very active imagination and maybe a little starved for affection the way she fantasized about crickets and the feel of another body against her own. Surely if anything untoward had been on Joe's mind, he would have kissed her or tried to hold her hand again out in the cover of the woods, but he didn't. He just followed behind her asking if she'd ever used a horsetail as a bandage like his father had done during the war. He didn't act like anything unusual had happened between them at all. Mayme was almost embarrassed to think how foolish she was to believe for one minute that someone like Joe Stern would be flirting with her, an old skinny married woman. Perhaps she was more tired than she realized, not to mention that being around Charley and Ruby always gave her romantic notions the way they pawed at each other all the time. Foolish. She was just foolish.

Charley was awake, sitting on the edge of the bed, the white sheet wrapped loosely around his waist. He looked half drunk sitting there, still morphine groggy and nearly naked, clutching the edge of the sheet in one hand, rubbing the dark stubble on his chin with the other. When

101

Mayme walked through the door, he pulled the sheet tighter.

"Where the hell did you two take off to?" he asked, grimacing with the effort of speech.

Mayme avoided his gaze and hurried to pull the apron on over her head, to busy herself. "I took Dr. Stern out to the cove there. We paddled around in Matthew's old boat for a bit, let you rest a while."

Joe shifted his weight, right foot to left foot to right foot, as though he might be nervous at the notion of a slightly irritated Charley Floyd. He made his way to the table, again draped with a clean white sheet, ready to be used as an examination table, and straightened the linen cloth so that it hung evenly on all four sides. Before they'd wandered off to the river, Mayme had bagged up the dirty linens and covered the table with the new one. She had also boiled the contaminated instruments, leaving them to soak in a solution of carbolic acid.

"What's going on with you two?" Charley asked. "You're actin' funny, buzzing around like a couple of flies or something." He sat up as tall as he could manage and began searching for his pants, his gun, a quick exit. "What the hell's goin' on here?"

"Hold yer horses, Charley. There ain't nothin' goin' on other than the fact I'm hungry and I'm tired and you know how dangerous that can be." She wiped her hands on her apron, feeling the burn of the phenol, wishing she'd taken two seconds to pull on her rubber gloves before reaching into the soaking tub.

"Well, hell, let's eat somethin' then. You brought out that plate of Mama's chicken and biscuits, didn't ya?" He reached over to find a pack of smokes and tapped one out.

"Yeah," Joe said, regaining his confidence at the sound of Mayme's easy banter with the famous outlaw. "Why don't we have some supper first. No offense, Charley, but handling your infected penis is not the most appetizing thing in the world."

102

The cabin slowly erupted with unexpected laughter as Mayme and Charley both roared at Joe's surprising humor. Most folks wouldn't dare poke fun at Charley Floyd, let alone scoff at his privates.

"Shoot, Charley," Mayme said, "anybody ever tell you before that looking at your willie," she chuckled at her use of the new word, raised her eyebrows to Joe, "that your willie made them plum lose their appetite? Lawsy, Lawsy. I can't wait to tell Ruby that one."

"You hush, Mayme Holloway. And he's right. Let's have some of that fried chicken before you jab that stick in me again." Charley grabbed his pants, tossed a curious sideways glance to Joe. "A funny doctor. Well, that's not something you see everyday, but then again, neither is my willie."

6.

At the back of the church, O.C.'s mama stopped to talk to Mrs. Gellman, something about her making mulberry jam for the ladies guild sale. O.C. bowed his head respectfully to the two old women and strolled past them and out to the sunshine where small clusters of church folk gathered to chat before heading home for Sunday dinner. He smiled big for whoever might be looking and lifted his narrow-brimmed hat up to his head, tapping the right side gently as if he was saluting the town, then slowly made his way to a group of men, all regular customers. He liked to shoot the breeze with the boys after church while he waited for his mother.

"Well, Brother Jones, it's nice to see you in the Lord's house on such a nice day," O.C. said, slapping the younger man on the back, then grabbing hold of his shoulder, giving it a couple of good squeezes. "Guess that pretty new wife of yours figured out how to keep the fish safe."

Blinton Jones ducked his head and pulled away from O.C.'s grip. "Don't you worry, Brother Holloway," he said, "I know where the fish even bite in the middle of the day. I'll be out there soon as Lucy gets the dinner on. Day like this ya got to be outdoors. My daddy's goin'; you wanna come along?"

"No, no no," O.C. said. "Me and Mama's gonna have us some dinner and then I have some paperwork to take care. I have a Barber's Association meeting over in Tulsa next week," he explained. He was proud to be the

104

president of the Cherokee County Barber's Association, kept his appointment letter hanging on the wall of his shop for all to see.

"Mayme workin' agin?" Scotty Walker asked, knowing it didn't matter whether she was or wasn't. Everyone in town knew she didn't care for churches; she never did. It was only a rare and special occasion that Mayme Holloway accompanied her husband to Sunday service, usually a wedding and sometimes a funeral, though she tended to avoid those if she could.

"She is. She's helping some woman out in the country today. A new baby being born." O.C. smiled, almost benevolently at the mention of a baby coming into the world, though the very idea of a child passing through a lady's privates made him squeamish.

"Hey, O.C.," Scotty said, "You give any more thought to coming to one of our club meetings?"

O.C.'s right cheek flinched at the question. Scotty Walker's club was just the Klan in disguise. They might not wear the pointy hats and robes like they did a few years back, but they still pulled some dirty tricks on the negroes and any other folks they had a pick on. They didn't like anyone other than their own brand of white. The one thing he knew for sure was that folks in Scotty's club who had businesses charged black people more money for everything, just to make sure they didn't get nothing much in life. They had other tricks too, but O.C. didn't want to know what all they pulled.

"No, Scotty. I'm afraid ever bit of my time is tied up down at the shop or helping out with Mama. You know I'm all she has now that my Daddy's passed on. Something changes, I'll let y'all know."

O.C. looked back to see Mama coming down the steps, her right hand bracing the handrail with each heavy step. He hurried over and offered her his arm as she stepped out into the walkway for all to see how attentive he was to his mama, even though she got along perfectly fine without him. As he passed his friends, he tipped his hat farewell, nodding his head slightly, just as he'd seen Tyrone Power do so elegantly in a picture show, the chin dipping toward his left shoulder, his fingers barely lifting the hat from his head, before tapping it down with one jab of his index finger. He was happy to escort his mother on the short walk to her small home just around the corner where a fine meal would be waiting for him. Mama would fill a plate for him and when it was empty she would carry it into the kitchen. He would sit and read the paper while she washed the dishes, then they would drink coffee and he would tell her all the gossip he'd learned at the shop. Just him and Mama on Sunday afternoons. It was his favorite time of the week. He was glad to be there for her.

"When you gonna come and live with me and Mayme?" O.C. asked as they walked.

Mama swallowed a laugh, snorting in the process. "If there's one thing I know better'n my own name that's you don't need two women running one house."

O.C. didn't answer, just grinned vacantly as he watched their shadows leading the way, his long lean lines stretched far beyond the short round shape of his mother beside him. The shadows were almost dancing, he thought, as they floated along before him. He hummed a simple tune in his mind, one two three, two two three. He waved one arm out to the side gently, controlling the choreography and orchestration. It was almost a waltz.

"Glory," he said. "I do love the Lord's day, don't you, Mama?"

"It's the day the Lord hath made, let us rejoice and be glad."

"Amen to that," he said, guiding her up the path toward her front door, hoping there would be a pot of chicken and dumplings waiting for him. And maybe some apple pie. He loved apple pie almost as much as he loved his mama.

7.

By the time Mayme ground the old truck into second gear, the old cabin was swallowed in darkness. A low ceiling of clouds barred even the yellow light of a full May moon. She drove slowly, the headlights shining into a path of blackness, bald tires slipping over loose gravel and dirt on the narrow road that led away from Horseshoe Bend. Joe sat beside her, his right arm dangling out the window, his left arm resting on the alligator bag at his side.

"Thank you, Mayme," he said.

"For what?" she asked, risking a quick glance his way, knowing full well he was staring at her. She could feel the heat of his gaze flush her cheeks making her feel again like a young girl with a bad case of puppy love. Had she only imagined that moment on the lake, that unspoken flash of simple wanting so real it was palpable? She knew it was wrong to want someone like she wanted him, but it was hard not to sidle up close to a blazing fire and bask in its heat when her body literally ached from being out in the cold for so long.

"For letting me come along. It was one of the best days I've had in a long time, and I mean a very long time."

She forced a laugh and shook her head in feigned disbelief. "You need to get out more if trucking out to Horseshoe Bend to treat a case of the clap is your idea of a good time."

His attempt at a subtle laugh sounded like a throaty groan, more painful than funny. "You're doing it again," he said.

"What's that?" She was smiling, hungry for some joke at her expense, something to shift her wicked thoughts to harmless laughter, to something silly, or some patient. Her thoughts on this warm spring night were more dangerous then any outlaw out there.

"Never mind," he said, then turned away to peer into the darkness ahead. The lights on the old truck didn't reach very far and sometimes it seemed as if they were heading straight into the thick scrabble of brush and oak, but Mayme showed the same focus and skill behind the wheel as she did at the hospital. She was fearless.

"Naw, now you can't say something like that and just leave it hanging there like a dead fish. What am I doing?" Stupid was easy. No matter how much she knew, folks seemed to expect a pretty woman or any woman for that matter to be half ignorant.

Joe took a deep breath and exhaled loudly, sounding exasperated and amused too. "You're driving me home," he said. "That's what you're doing."

"That's not what you meant neither." Mayme breathed a heavy sigh in mocked exasperation, relieved and sad that the flirty chatter was fading with the day. "Men," she muttered and for a full five minutes, neither one of them spoke. The thrum of the wheels and yammering shocks bouncing on the rough road were the only noise. Each of them rambled about in their private thoughts and dreams, unspoken versions of the same story, the ending unwritten.

Mayme drove quietly and continued to shuffle the possibility that there had been a glimmer of romance out there on the water. Long ago she had learned to trust her intuition, that it rarely failed her. She could argue with her self all day, but in her heart, she knew. That moment had been real, and that was a problem she had no idea how to handle.

"I'm sorry," Joe finally said, breaking the silence, reaching over and touching her on the knee. "I don't want you thinking you were doing anything wrong when I said you were doing it again. You're not."

"That's alright," Mayme said. "I know I get carried away, forget my place and sometimes say too much."

"You see, that's exactly what I didn't want you to think. I have the utmost respect for you, who you are and what you do. What I meant was..." He breathed in a gulp of courage, then blew it out through pursed lips, slowly, measuring his words. "You're so interesting and brilliant and funny too. You're charming me, Mayme. That's all. You're not like anyone I've ever known before and it's... well..." he shook his head, and though she couldn't see him, the pause was there, cautious and heady. "Let's just leave it at that."

Mayme was grateful for the darkness and the need to keep her eyes forward, away from his gaze. "Well, thank you," was all she said, completely lost for any of that country girl wit he seemed to love so well. She swore she could feel the blood flowing through her veins, pumping through each chamber of the heart.

"You're quite welcome," he said, a phrase she'd heard him say countless times to patients when they thanked him kindly for stitching them up or doling out cough syrup. Every time he said it, "you're quite welcome," he sounded so sincere, his voice warm and reassuring, but now Mayme thought he was just falling back on the familiar haunches of his tried and true words, only now they weren't so reassuring; they were tired and sad. He fumbled in his jacket pocket and pulled out the flask. "I think there's a sip or two left; would you like a little?" He held it out to her, again letting his fingers brush up against her bare skin, this time on her forearm.

"Don't mind if I do," she said, taking the small bottle. She lifted it to her lips, never taking her eyes off the road. "Damn, that's good stuff," she said, smacking her lips big, daring to say what she really thought. "You bring that hooch and you can come with me every time I make a run to the hills."

"Promise?" he asked, taking a small sip himself. "I'm going to put in a very large order first thing tomorrow so that I'm prepared."

She laughed again, nervous and confused by the heaviness in her chest, the dryness of her mouth, the strange desire she had to stop the truck and just sit alone in the dark with this man beside her. "Promise."

For the rest of the drive back to town, they limited their talk to stories of patients, Mayme filling him in on back stories of the odd case or two that had shown up in his office or that might. Safe talk, like on the trail, Mayme thought. That's what would save her, safe talk.

"Hey, did you know Mabel Winslow really believes you cure a headache by spitting under a clod of dirt and walking backward ten feet?" he said. "I tried to tell her she'd have better luck with a couple of aspirin, but she wouldn't hear any of that."

"Well, that's better than wearing smashed worms on your forehead."

"What?" he cried. "Smashed worms?" He laughed so loudly Mayme nearly ran off the road. The truck swerved and bounced and they laughed even more at her recklessness.

"That's what Jasper Tatum does. He goes out and digs up a mess of worms, smashes 'em up, then rubs the whole gooey mess all over his head and temples. Swears by it."

"Does it work?"

"Next time you feel a pain in your head, come see me and we'll go out to the crik and find some worms and do some research."

There was always something more to say to each other and as long as they were talking, they were safe from the unspoken feelings Mayme was sure they shared.

When they finally pulled up alongside Joe's big house, Mayme was sorry she had such a heavy foot on the gas.

110

The ride back to town was over too soon. "Here you are," she said, "home again, safe and sound."

Joe nodded slowly. "Yes, home," he said. "I hope you'll call on me again." He reached one hand out to touch her forearm gently, warmly. "And, if you're ever walking past in the morning and want a cup of coffee, come tap on the kitchen door and I'll tell you about any dreams I had, at least the good ones. I'm always up early."

"How'd you know I walk past . . . never mind," she whispered, knowing already that he watched her, that he saw her doing things when she thought no one was looking. The thought of his eyes on her while she went about her day was a bit frightening and thrilling too. Again she felt a dryness in her mouth and a heaviness in her chest that ran down her legs. "Good night, Joe."

"Good night, Mayme. Get some rest."

"You too."

He was still standing on his brick walkway as she pulled away from the curb. "Sweet Jesus," she said to no one. "I can't be thinking like that, not about him."

O.C. was sitting at the kitchen table reading the newspaper when Mayme came through the back door.

"There you are," he said.

"Here I am," she answered. "Tired and powerful hungry, but here I am." She bent down and kissed his upturned face, a small peck on his thin lips. He still smelled sweet as honeysuckle, even at the end of the day. Such a flowery aroma on an empty stomach made her a little queasy.

"Mama fixed you a plate, it's in the ice box. I could warm it for you, and there's half a cherry pie there on the counter."

"Hmmm. I think I'll just have a little pie, but first I want to take a bath. I feel like a gritty mutt. Smell like one too." She lifted the collar of her dress and turned her nose down to her bare chest and sniffed.

"Well you don't look like a gritty mutt, but you do look worn out, maybe a little shaggy mutt." He eyed her more closely, tilted his head to one side. "Why don't you come by the shop tomorrow and let me give you a little trim, clean those ends up a bit." He reached up toward her face and brushed a stray hair off her face, already seeing her another way, his way.

Mayme backed away, brushing the offensive strands behind her ears. O.C. watched her too, she thought. But his eyes were looking for ways to make her prettier, to make her more like him, clean around the edges. "Maybe," she said, her fingers already loosening the buttons of her dress. "If there's time. I go on duty at four and I need to sterilize those sheets that Charley slept on before I go in."

"Sterilize?" His eyebrows arched. "Why that's not very nice. Charley's like a brother to . . ."

"Trust me, O.C." she interrupted, "you want me to sterilize those sheets. I won't trouble you with the details, but there's a reason I pulled 'em off the bed 'fore I left the house yesterday. I also need to make another house call out to your little friend. My hair style is the least of my worries."

He vexed her, that's what he did, and all with such politeness she couldn't even say what exactly he did that set her teeth on edge. In the words of her dead mama, O.C. vexed her. The only thing that she looked forward to doing tomorrow was getting out of bed just long enough to turn around and get back in and take a nap. A week of night duty was waiting for her and she had a feeling her days might be swallowed up with something other than sleep.

O.C. didn't say or do anything, just sat there with his newspaper, listening to her with deaf ears.

"I'll do what I can," she finally said, caving in to his pitiful face, all hangdog and stunned, like she'd slapped him with a slice of bacon.

"Well, if you can manage it, come on in, I'll do you up nice. I can make you look just like Marion Davies. I even

112

have a nice piece of ribbon I been saving just for you, I could tie it around your head like she had it in that movie we went to. Remember?" He nodded his head intently, willing her to agree, to remember, grinning like a fool. He didn't ask for any more details about Charley or what else she might need to do. He never did.

Mayme didn't answer, just offered a weak smile, a sad attempt to pacify his sweet need to try to make her more beautiful.

The small bathroom was just off the kitchen. As Mayme soaked in the hot tub of bubbles, she could hear O.C. whistling some old church song. She couldn't remember the words, but she'd heard it many times when she was a child, back when she had a mother and father and a normal life. They'd gone to the First Baptist Church every Sunday no matter what. After Peggs, she and Daddy spent Sunday mornings out at the river, fishing together, or she spent it wandering on her own while he worked through his own pain, usually ending up spending the night with Leora. Leora, her stepmother. She didn't know much about her, but she didn't like her. Not then and not now. She was just the woman her daddy left with.

O.C. switched whistling tunes to a jaunty number the band had played the night before. His shuffling feet in a perfect two-step rhythm skittered across the floor. Mayme could picture him, holding an imaginary partner in his arms, spinning around, dipping, grinning like a school girl. She closed her eyes and slipped below the surface of the water, drowning out the music, the dancing. She stayed there suspended in watery silence until her air starved lungs forced her up, gasping for air. He was still whistling.

Mayme rested her head back along the edge of the tub and let the day play on before her, like a vivid dream, or a motion picture that featured her and Joe in the starring roles. The rocking boat. The warm sun on her bare legs. Colorful tanagers watching overhead. Joe's fingers brushing her hand. The smell of him, strong and raw, not

113

the flowery sweetness of fancy aftershave. As her breasts rose and fell in the warm water, she let her fingers move down between her legs, and it wasn't O.C.'s startled grin she saw as she let her knees fall open wide. It was Joe, his dark hair curling and falling forward just above her open mouth. She wanted to taste him and smell the sweat of a man who knew what a body could do, how it could ache, and how it could split open with pleasure. She squeezed her thighs together tight around her eager hand and rolled to the right, her thumb pressing hard against herself as her own body shuddered in waves of painful pleasure. She'd never felt that way with O.C., with anyone, just by herself.

By the time Mayme stepped out of the warm water, she was lightheaded and weary, ready for a long night of dreamless sleep. She ran a comb through her wet hair before pulling on her nightgown, feeling ashamed of herself and her wild imagination, ashamed of her secret desires, her lonely pleasures. Dr. Stern just thought she was a good nurse, someone he could talk to about patients and some of the strange ways folks had. She spent too much time alone, star gazing, waiting on the sun and listening to crickets. Like a penitent child she shuffled into the kitchen to say goodnight to her faithful husband. He deserved better than her.

O.C. was back to sitting at the kitchen table, his worn black Bible open before him. He was reading from the book of Romans and had a piece of pie and a fork there ready and waiting for his wife. He probably wanted to share some special verse with her, the only way he could be sure that she'd get a little Bible learning.

"You can have my share, Sugar," she said, moving up behind him, placing her hands on his bony shoulders. "I'm just gonna hit the hay; I can barely hold my eyes open. I'll warm the sheets up for ya."

He patted her hand and turned his face toward her, knowing a good night kiss would be given. Another small peck on the lips. Neat. Clean. "Good night, Darlin'" he

114

said, "I'll be along shortly." He collected his kiss and reached for the slice of pie.

"Good night, O.C."

Mayme slept as still as a stone, as though her body somehow knew of the sleepless nights to come.

8.

The clothesline stretched along the far side of the backyard, away from the constant shade and bird droppings of the dogwood tree. By late morning, Mayme was pulling dry sheets off the line, letting them fall over her face with the first tug, then taking them up in her arms, careful to keep the edges out of the dirt. There was nothing like the smell of a clean sheet right off the line, all that fresh air clinging to every thread. She carried the bundle of crisp linens into the house, not bothering with a basket, then tossed them onto her bed.

She had slept soundly after all the excitement at the dance and then caring for Charley out at Horseshoe Bend. She faced the new week fully rested with a fervent vow to be a better wife. She had worked fiercely all morning, dusting, sweeping, washing sheets, even made a batch of hotcakes for O.C. before he left for the shop, promising him that she'd be in for that new hairdo by three o'clock. No later.

All morning she tried to imagine how her new style would look with her face, what exactly O.C. would do to her once he got her in that chair and under his control. It really was a small thing, she reasoned, really a lovely thing, her husband simply wanted to give her a haircut, to try to make her prettier. That's what he did best – clean folks up to a shinier version of themselves. She studied herself in the mirror that hung over the bureau, pulled the sides of her hair back and held them up to look like short hair and decided she didn't look much different then she did with it all braided and twisted up like she already did. She gave up on looking at herself and returned to the long list of chores she had made that morning before the sun was even up. Despite her plan to sleep late, she had woken early as if her body ached for the sunrise. As she carefully folded the sheets, her thoughts drifted to the small boat on the lake, the feel of Joe's hands around her own. She had to force her thoughts to return to only the tasks before her, laundry and housekeeping, the things a good wife does.

Once the clean linens were returned to their shelf in the small bathroom closet, Mayme stretched out on the bed for a catnap though she wasn't the least bit tired. Willing her body to rest in the middle of the day was a necessary skill she had mastered during long shifts in nursing school. More often than not, she would be exhausted beyond sleep, her body trapped in a state of strained wakefulness with only a six-hour break before another shift, no real time to let the weight of a long day ease away slowly. She discovered the trick to rest was to start with her toes and work her way up, relaxing one inch of her body at a time, mindfully, slowly, so that by the time she reached her neck, she was either asleep or nearly there.

The room was darkened and cool and the fresh scent of the outdoors lingered. Mayme closed her eyes and wiggled her toes, commanding the bottoms of her feet to relax and rest. She focused on the lower legs, telling herself they were too heavy to lift, to even move an inch. Just as she began to drift away, the telephone rang and shattered any hope for a little sleep. She jumped to her feet and hurried to the phone, not considering for a moment that she could ignore the annoying sound.

"Hello," she answered, her voice a breathy whisper, half hoping she'd make whoever it was think she'd been sleeping soundly and they had disrupted her time of rest. Especially if it was O.C. calling to see if she was coming for her haircut or his mama wanting to know if she could drop

117

off a little something for their supper. Either one of them would be better than somebody calling to ask for her help outside of town, some poor young girl having a baby and too scared to go to the hospital, or some fool with a bullet in him needing a little private care. She'd have to say no to them - there wasn't time for any extra work today. She already had Charley waiting. But it wasn't O.C., his mama or any stranger calling. Mrs. Daniels was on the other end, telling Mayme she was needed early; in fact, she was needed immediately.

"There's been some type of gun battle out on the highway outside of town, and Dr. Stern would like for you to assist him in surgery. How quick can you get here? Should I send Ernie?" It wouldn't be the first time the hospital director and chief nurse had sent the ambulance driver to pick someone up if they were needed quicker than their feet could carry them.

"No, I have O.C.'s truck; I'll be there in ten minutes. I just gotta throw my uniform on."

"We'll be ready for you."

Mayme hung up the phone. It wasn't the first time she'd been singled out to assist in the operating theater. Still, as she scrambled into her uniform and twisted her hair up into braids, a flutter of nervous anxiety flushed over her. Joe knew she was planning on running out to Horseshoe Bend before work. He wouldn't call her in for something simple; he'd just have Mrs. Daniels or one of the day nurses assist. And as much as she'd wanted to let O.C. try to turn her into Marion Davies, he would have to make do with his wife in twisted braids a while longer.

Dressed and ready in minutes, Mayme hurried out of the house and nearly ran head on into Mama Holloway as she waddled up the porch steps. Her face was expressionless as she handed a paper bag to Mayme. "I had a hunch you might need this," she said.

"Mama, I'm in a big hurry and have to get to . . ."

"Take it with you. It's just a couple of sandwiches."

"Why, thank you." Mayme took the bag and started toward the truck. She turned back to the old woman who stood staring at her, unmoving. "Really, thank you, Mama. I don't mean to be rude, but I got to go."

When Mayme drove down the long drive to park behind the hospital, Sheriff Bishop was outside the back door talking to a lawman she didn't recognize. Mayme guessed he was from another county, another sign that something big was happening. Her heart raced to keep up with her imagination, and she prayed desperately that it wasn't Charley Floyd waiting for her inside with another bullet in him. She mentally retraced her every step the day before and she was certain that no one had followed them, that their friend was safely hidden in the old cabin in the woods. Even so, the worry weighed on her like a heavy stone as the old truck rumbled to a stop.

"Morning, Sheriff," she said as she hurried past, keeping her eyes on the door, avoiding eye contact and any chance of delay.

"Morning, Mrs. Holloway." He tipped his big white hat to her and nodded his head.

Just inside the door, Mrs. Daniels was bent over a chart scribbling furiously when Mayme stepped in. She looked up, her face filled with concern. "Good, you're here. Get scrubbed and ready to go. We have a young deputy with a cranial gunshot wound. It doesn't look good."

Mayme flinched at the news. "Who is it?" she asked, already running down the list of local lawmen in her mind, who she knew, who their wives were, again praying it didn't involve Charley Floyd or one of his boys.

Mrs. Daniels continued talking as she followed Mayme up the stairs to the scrub room on the second floor. "It's a fellow by the name of Dwight Teague, from Muskogee. Dr. Stern thinks he has a good chance, but I don't know, Mayme, his mandible is shattered and there's still a bullet in there at the base of his skull. It won't be easy."

119

Mayme nodded; she understood full well what was in store for her that afternoon. She'd seen all manner of gunshot wounds but never had seen a man live after taking a bullet in the head. Hopefully, Joe would change that and work a miracle on this one. Saving a lawman was a crucial matter, maybe even more important, she hated to admit, then saving some poor farmer or merchant. She had no idea who pulled the trigger, at least not yet, but she knew as well as anybody that every officer west of Missouri would be on the hunt when one of their own was killed. It didn't take much to start a trail of endless blood when unleashed revenge wore a badge. There was already a massive hunt going on out there for Charley after he'd killed Erv Kelly; she'd hate to think what this place would be like if he'd added another dead officer to his long list of sins. The hills were full of people who loved him, but there would be no stopping the fury of Grover Bishop and every other lawman in the country, including that government bunch she'd been hearing about.

For the next four hours, Mayme stood at the side of Dr. Stern, anticipating his every move, passing him small instruments to pick away slivers of the deputy's shattered jawbone and broken teeth and finally the chunk of lead lodged just below the occiput. Not once did she look at the surgeon beside her and see the man with long curly hair and soft brown eyes rowing a small boat around a cove. Here, at the hospital, it was Dr. Stern and Nurse Holloway, a skilled surgical team, expertly tending to the wounded man on the table. Doctor Moody was there at the patient's head, delivering a steady flow of ether while Mrs. Daniels moved in and out of the room, removing contaminated sponges, chisels and gouges, replacing them with sterile instruments, always pausing long enough to monitor the situation.

"I wish you'd been with us in France," she said reverently as she finally watched the doctor stitch the torn tissue together, his fingers manipulating the fine curved surgeon's needle with expert precision, patiently weaving a man's face and head together with catgut sutures as best as possible. It was an art.

"My father was," he answered.

"Of course," she offered softly. "You inherited his skill, I think, and your mother's too." She peered in a bit closer.

"Thank you," he said, never turning his eyes away from the mutilated face before him. "Now if we can just keep him from vomiting from the ether," he said, talking to himself as much as his surgical team, "I think this officer will live to see another battle or at least another day."

Mrs. Daniels left the room with a tray of bloody sponges and the current status of the patient. She would keep his family and friends apprised of the situation, keep them hopeful, but also prepared for bad news should the surgeon's best efforts fail to spare their loved one's life.

Finally, it was Dr. Stern who stepped out to speak with Mrs. Teague, the wife, and Mrs. Teague, the mother. The young deputy would live, and hopefully there would be no lasting brain damage. "You need to prepare yourself for what you will see," he said. "Your husband will never look the same."

As gently as possible, Dr. Stern explained to a very young pretty woman, probably no more then nineteen or twenty years old, that while the bandages would hide the bullet's damage for days to come, the left side of the handsome face she had loved would forever be a sagging twist of scarred flesh, a constant reminder of his short and eager career as an Oklahoma lawman. Later, they could try some reconstruction surgery. There were new developments in medicine every day. After Dwight was stable, Dr. Stern assured her that he would arrange for her husband to go to one of the teaching hospitals where they do incredible things, moving muscle and bone to rebuild a damaged body part. But all of that would take time. Lots of time.

The two women clung to each other and wept tears of joy, tears of sadness, and tears of relief to know their prayers were answered. "I don't care what he looks like," the wife cried. "I just want him alive. I love him no matter what."

Joe took the young woman's thin hand and gave it a gentle squeeze. "You ought to go home now, get some rest. You can see him tomorrow."

"If it's all the same to you, I'll stay here," she said, turning to her mother-in-law for support. "You go on home, Mama."

"Actually, I think it would be best if you come back tomorrow," Joe said, his face and words filled with compassion, despite his own weariness. "Dwight's going to be out for several hours and he can't have any excitement whatsoever. Go home and get some rest. Nurse Daniels will call you if there's any change."

The younger Mrs. Teague watched him as he spoke and nodded her head, agreeing with anything the doctor said. The two women left, still clinging to each other as they shuffled out the double doors.

Mayme had removed her soiled gown and gloves and replaced them with a clean white apron that hung nearly to the floor. No one would believe that this narrow young woman had just minutes before pressed her fingertips into a man's shattered face, that with a steeled composure she had held the hemostat and opened a passageway for the surgeon to pick debris from the back of his throat, where the bullet had halted, narrowly avoiding a fatal intrusion into the cerebellum. She was just pinning on her nurse's cap when Joe came back into the small changing room.

"You're really something, Dr. Stern," she said. "I've seen some amazing things in my life, but I've never seen anything like what you just did in there."

"Why, thank you, Mrs. Holloway," he said. "I couldn't have done it without you, you know."

There was a moment of shared glory, pride in their work of saving a life, doing things most folks could never imagine. It always made Mayme a little giddy when a difficult surgery was successful.

"We have a little problem though," she whispered, leaning in close, but not too close should anyone walk in unexpectedly.

"Don't worry," he said, "I'll take care of it."

"How do you know what I'm talking about?"

"I know you didn't get out to visit my new friend and now you can't since you're on duty tonight, so I will. How's that?" He raised his eyebrows in mocking pleasure, his tired eyes brimming with mischief.

Mayme laughed at him, pausing to glance over her shoulder for an approaching Mrs. Daniels or Doc Moody. She moved in closer still, this time close enough to smell him, that same musky scent she'd imagined the night before during her bath. He had perspired heavily during the surgery. She knew that because she'd been there to wipe his forehead many times, always careful to dab the gauze pad just above his eyebrows.

"Aren't you too tired to do that? And do you even remember how to get there? Where to turn off the road? It's a bit tricky and you were blindfolded on the way out there."

"Of course I know how to get there." He lowered his chin and whispered, "I memorized every inch of the road coming back and besides, after that procedure, I'm too keyed up to be tired. The drive will do me good, give me a chance to unravel a bit. And I'd still like to help."

"Are you sure? It wouldn't hurt him too much to miss a day. It won't be a case of the clap that gets that one, believe me."

"No, it's better to stick with it. I'll go; I just wish you were going with me."

He looked right into her eyes when he spoke, as though he wanted her to read his thoughts, unspoken words.

Mayme flushed and suddenly worried that Joe somehow knew of her silly fantasies, how she'd imagined seeing his face hovering over her, his hair falling in her face, his arms surrounding her.

123

"Next time," she said.

As always, Mayme was hungry at the end of a long procedure and thought of the bag of sandwiches, the offering from Mama Holloway. She had left them in the truck, but they would still be good.

"Want a sandwich before you go?" she asked.

Joe looked at her, puzzled.

"O.C.'s mama brought me some sandwiches. I don't know what they are, but I'd be happy to share."

"Now that sounds like the best offer I've had all day."

Mayme was convinced that she had never before in her life enjoyed a better roast beef sandwich then the one she ate in the small break room with Joe that afternoon. She wondered how Mama did it, wondered if her mother-in-law would have offered up the bag of food if she knew Mayme would share it with a man, then wondered if somehow the old woman had a hunch about that too. In the end, there were still two sandwiches left for Joe to take with him, a meal for Charley. That was probably what Mama had a hunch about, not her own growling stomach, and certainly not Joe's.

Joe wasn't worried at the sight of a dark cabin. He could almost feel Charley watching him as he stepped up on the porch and pushed through the creaking door. Inside, the only sign that someone had recently been there was a faint layer of cigarette smoke lingering high in the dark room, apparitions drifting out the open door. The heavy smell of green soap and kerosene that had filled the room the night before was absent. Joe moved slowly through the dark room to set down the sack of groceries he'd brought along then turned his attention to lighting the lamps.

The box of matches was still where Mayme had left them, on top of her basket of clean linens and sterilized instruments in the corner. Charley had done as she'd told him and not touched a thing in that corner. "There ain't no hooch in there, so don't go pawing through everthin'," she'd

124

told him. "You'd germ it all up, then when you get treated, you'll make that pecker of yours more infected then it is now." Joe smiled at the thought of her chastising the infamous outlaw. He'd never known anyone like her before.

Just as he was spreading a clean white sheet over the rustic table, Charley leaned in through the door, looking more sheepish than dangerous, but there was something in his presence alone that could make even the toughest man feel small.

"Evenin', Doc," he said. "Looks like you come alone tonight."

Despite the inflated dose of confidence from the day before and that afternoon in surgery, a hitch of odd nervousness crept into Joe's throat at the sight of his patient, Charley Floyd, a machine gun hanging at his side, a handgun strapped to his chest, just a breath away. "Yes, sir, Mayme has to work at the hospital tonight, so I came alone."

"I'd figured y'all would make it out a might earlier. Why so late?" he asked, suspicious and wary.

Charley Floyd was no fool and Joe realized full well that Floyd would know something was going on for Mayme to send him out here on his own this late in the day. "It's partly my fault," he began, his voice sounding stretched thin and oddly nasal. "I asked for her to come into work early today, when she would have come out here, and assist me in emergency surgery. She's the best, you know, and it was a particularly difficult case, so I needed her there."

"Uh-huh," Charley grunted, never taking his eyes off of Joe or his right hand off the trigger of the biggest gun Joe had ever seen in all his life.

"A deputy was shot in the head," he explained, knowing how important it was for Charley to know it was a lawman that had been wounded, that it was severe. "But we saved his life; he'll live."

Every muscle in Charley Floyd seemed to tighten, his spine, his jaw, even his forehead turned to steel. "Who done it?" he asked.

"I don't know."

"Jesus, now these hills will be crawling with god damn cops. I gotta get the hell out of here." He looked left, then right, as though he would find something there to either help or hurt him, ready for either one.

"I think you're better off here," Joe said. "No one but Mayme and I know you're out here."

"Until someone slips and says something, or someone sees you heading out here with your little black bag and follows you to see who you're workin' on." Charley reached for his jacket and hat, again scanning every inch of the room, searching for anything he might need, not wanting to leave anything important behind.

"Sit down, Charley, please, think about this for a minute." Joe knew better than to move in closer or to extend a hand. No wild animal liked the prospect of being trapped, and sticking a hand out toward it might just cost you that hand. He stayed put but still tried to persuade Charley to wait it out a bit longer. "Come on, at least get one more treatment, have something to eat before taking off. I brought some food, sandwiches from Mrs. Holloway, O.C.'s mother, and even a little whiskey. Good whiskey."

Charley paused and studied the doctor, his eyes cutting up and down the tall man sharply. "Why are you so fired up anxious for me to stick around here? You don't hardly know me from Jesus. Maybe you got yer eyes set on that reward money after all. I hear it's a thousand dollars now." The tip of the gun lifted higher, the slight movement clearly threatening, though Charley did not aim it directly at the doctor.

Joe felt the color drain from his face, felt his knees weaken a little, but that weakness would never reveal itself. Not here. Not anywhere for that matter. Mayme could always fall back on her witty sarcasm to disarm the most agitated patient, but she wasn't here and he didn't have that charming wit. He was, however, a doctor and that was more than most folks could say. He knew that intimidated many of the men he cared for. He was the one that knew of their physical failures, their vulnerabilities. At the risk of sounding prissy and a bit uppity, the I'm a doctor card was the best he could think of, and he had to do something quick.

In his most sincere and professional voice, Joe tried to reason with the man holding the gun. "No, Charley, I do know you. You are my patient and that, I'm afraid, comes with a certain obligation. I don't care what you've done as far as the law goes; I'm only interested in treating your medical condition. And I'm certainly not interested in any reward money. I don't need it."

A shaft of dusty yellow light stretched through the open door and across Charley Floyd's handsome face. Joe could see a slight twitch in the weaker muscle of Charley's right eye and knew he was considering the situation wholly, the risk, his illness, the law, and the good whiskey and food that Joe had promised. When Charley half smiled, looking like the feral cat accepting the plate of fish bones and tossed his hat and coat back on the bed, Joe breathed a sigh of relief, impressed that he'd managed to hold his bladder.

"Okay, then," Joe said. "Why don't you have something to eat and I'll set up a work station. Oh, I also brought along a dose of morphine, but only one."

"That's alright; save that shot of hooch for next time. If you don't mind, I'd prefer to keep my wits about me. I'll take a pull on that shine though."

Joe nodded and smiled as he pulled the small green bottle of bourbon from the bag. "This is not shine, Charley. This is some of the best medicine there is, good Kentucky bourbon, available only by prescription. I keep a supply for, uh, special patients." He held it up as if he were a salesman, or a medicine man selling his magic potion to a crowd hungry for cures, knowing he was going against his own warning to avoid alcohol.

127

"Uh-huh, and yersef too, I imagine. And that little Mayme, too. I saw her cheeks glowing after you two had been out messing around. She'd had a healthy dose fer sure. O.C. just wants to slap it on his face, never touches a drop, but Mayme, hell, she can drink as much as any man I know."

As Joe passed the bottle of bourbon over, he noticed that Charley did not release his grip on the machine gun, not for a moment. A loaded weapon would be close at hand for the rest of the afternoon. Even as Joe inserted the urethral syringe into the man's infected penis, a machine gun would be resting at the side of Charley's bare hip.

Later, after the humiliating procedure was done, Charley moved from the table to sit on the edge of the bed while Joe cleaned up the aftermath.

"I hope I didn't scare you earlier," he said, his head dipping to point to the earlier talk. "But I ain't never going back to prison. I'd rather run like this for the rest of my life and die in some field then be locked in a cage." He shook his head at the thought, a forbidden image of a future behind bars flickering through his mind.

"No, well, yes, it was a bit nerve rattling, but I'm okay." He pulled the stained sheet from the table and shoved it into the old flour sack he'd brought along, just like Mayme had done the day before. "And I understand, at least I think I do. I've never been to jail, but I don't imagine I'd like it much."

Charley put a cigarette in his mouth and grinned as he struck a match, clearly amused at Joe's innocence or ignorance, Joe wasn't sure which and it didn't matter. He was just glad to see Pretty Boy smiling again.

"So you've been to jail before?" he asked, eager to know more about the life of an outlaw beyond the newspapers, radio stories and Detective magazine.

"Yep, I spent five long years at Jeff City, one of the worst bits of hell on this earth you're ever gonna find. I was on my way back one other time, but I got away from those fuckers."

Joe could see the pain of that time in Charley's face, the cringing at the idea of going back to hard labor and a life behind bars. He knew what agony looked like and, for a moment, it was there on the handsome young man's face.

"They treat you like an animal, hell, worse than that. Even a dog has a bit of freedom, can shit where it wants. It's unholy, that's what it is. When I think about the sounds of that place, the God-awful stink of that place, my skin turns cold."

"Is there somewhere you can go, I don't know, like Mexico or Canada, some place where you could live a normal life? Be with your family?"

"Maybe some day. Right now, I'm doing alright. I'm good at what I do, so I don't plan on getting caught no time soon. You know most the stuff they all blame on me I don't have nothin' to do with; I'm usually miles away from whatever they say I done. No, I'll be alright, but I might just lay low for a spell. I got me a little savings."

"Like I said before, if you ever end up in the east, I can arrange for you to have a place to stay back there."

Charley took a long drag on his smoke and studied the doctor again before speaking. "You're alright, Doc," he said. "You mind if I let a couple of my colleagues know where they can find a good bone man. Most of 'em already know 'bout Mayme, but in case they need a real doc, you know, something more serious."

"Mayme always knows where to find me," Joe said.

In just over an hour, Joe was ready to make his way back to town, the dirty sheets stuffed in the sack for cleaning at home; the instruments cleaned and sterilized for later use there at the cabin.

"Look," he said, "I don't imagine you're going to stick around long enough to go through the whole treatment, so I'm going to leave you with this medicine, the solutions already prepared for you. If you can't bring yourself to insert the syringe, just pour it liberally over your penis once a day. And take hot baths when you can, as hot as

129

you can stand it." He paused if for no other reason to give his next bit of advice some added effect. This was the most important thing for Charley Floyd to remember, important for the women who loved him. "And as long as you have any discharge and pain with urination, do not engage in any sexual activity. It's highly contagious."

"That I know, or I wouldn't be dripping fire, would I?" Charley was sitting on the edge of the bed, his pants still slouched down around his ankles. His flaccid penis, stained a deep purple from the dose of Protargol, rested limp along his inner thigh like a bruised thumb. He had refused to take the pants off during the procedure in case he had to make a quick exit. The last thing he wanted, he'd said, was to be captured buck-naked with a plunger hanging out of his dick. So he'd gone through the whole ordeal with his shoes and pants on, a gun at his side, and his hat and coat just a quick arm's reach away.

"I might be here tomorrow, but then again, I might not. Can't say for sure right now." Charley reached over and plucked another cigarette from a half-empty pack of Lucky Strikes and stuck it in his mouth. He struck a match and kept talking as he held the fire to the tip of his cigarette. "If you don't make the trip out here, I understand. Hell, I don't know why you or Mayme neither would want to go to so much trouble for the likes of me having the clap, but if you do, bring me a bit more of that there so-called medicine, a cup for the road so to speak, and a carton of smokes."

Joe nodded. "You really shouldn't be drinking alcohol, it causes the blood..." he looked over at the pathetic gunman, his beard rough and dark, half naked with a purple penis, and shook his head. "Never mind. I'll bring you some, or send it with Mayme if she comes instead of me." He dipped his head to the side, one corner of his mouth twitched. "Maybe we'll both come. I might be able to do something about that ankle."

"Much obliged." Charley pushed himself off the table and pulled his pants up, a burning cigarette clenched in his tight lips, his eyes squinting to avoid the curling smoke. That was the last thing Joe saw as he ducked out the door, Pretty Boy Floyd, grimacing, a circle of smoke surrounding his head like a distorted halo fading away.

As he drove down the narrow road away from Horseshoe Bend, contemplating the recent hours of his life, Joe felt as if he could almost fly the car home. Such overwhelming lightness filled him that he was certain that if he pressed firmly on the gas pedal, with only a tug on the wheel he could command the long hunk of metal to lift its wheels off the ground and soar above the tree tops. Nothing could compare to this day. Nothing. He had felt this way as a child when he and Adam Cohen had sailed around the point in a makeshift sailboat, a sheet rigged onto Adam's canoe, and again when he'd survived that first day of surgery, actually running a scalpel along someone's flesh, opening them up and, in his case, removing an inflamed appendix. Today, though, was even better then all of that.

In one day, just a matter of hours really, he had removed a bullet from the head of one man, the man who enforced the laws of the state, and then he'd turned right around and treated Pretty Boy Floyd, one of the most wanted men in the country. He had done what so few could do, what so few would ever dare even imagine. Not only could he repair the unspeakable physical damage that men did to one another, but he could cross that invisible line and travel in both worlds of lawmen and outlaws. He couldn't wait to see Mayme. She knew what this felt like even more than he did. He couldn't wait to talk to her, to hear her laugh. She really was more dangerous than any gun-wielding outlaw. His heart raced as he pressed harder on the accelerator, anxious to cross another invisible line.

131

9.

It was near daylight by the time Mayme finally left Officer Teague in the care of Judith Gosley, the day-shift nurse. Judith had two children and didn't like working nights, so she and Mayme always worked opposite one another. Though they only saw each other briefly each day, Mayme liked the way Judith talked to their patients, almost like a bossy mother, scolding the ones who didn't respond to treatment as though she could badger them into getting well. She had served in the Army with Mrs. Daniels, married her a soldier she'd met in the hospital back east, and somehow convinced him they should live in Oklahoma. She was older than Mayme by at least a dozen years, had treated every disease and injury imaginable, but she never hesitated to ask Mayme for advice with patient care.

Mayme had stayed at the hospital a little longer than normal, just to fill Judith in on the amazing job that Dr. Stern had done, how he had meticulously picked through the shattered tissue, removing bits of teeth and bone and finally the small bullet, how he'd carefully woven the man's jaw and face back together, working tirelessly for hours and hours, never wavering.

"If I didn't know any better, Mayme Holloway, I'd say you were a little sweet on the doctor," Judith had said when Mayme finally stopped gushing on about how great a surgeon he was.

132

She'd blushed but covered it right up with outright truth. "Shoot yes, I'm sweet on him, who wouldn't be? Just wait, you're gonna be swooning too, but let me warn you, I saw him first. He's all mine, ya hear?" They laughed at their easy competition since they both had husbands at home. Judith couldn't see the dull ache that lingered in Mayme's chest, an ache there simply was no cure for, no matter how long you spent working on it.

Now, as Mayme climbed into the old truck, she wished she'd let Mrs. Daniels send Ernie for her so that she could walk past Joe's house, maybe tap on his door, just to tell him that Officer Teague was doing fine, so long as she kept the morphine going. Maybe he had a dream to share. As she inched the squeaking truck down the drive, it occurred to her that she should find out what happened out at the cabin, but she would only stop if his light was on. She wouldn't even go inside, just make sure everything went okay with Charley. No one could fault her for that. Especially not O.C. should he ever know or ask why she was visiting the doctor before the sun was full up.

As she approached the big house, she could see the soft glow of a buttery light from the small window at the back of the house, the kitchen. There was also a small light coming from the front of the house. He was in there, probably getting ready to leave for the hospital. Mayme slowed down, made a right turn and parked on the opposite side of the street, as if she was headed out of town and not on her way home.

Joe was at the door waiting for her, watching her as she scurried across the street and up the brick path. She moved quickly, pulling her light jacket tight around herself, her eyes scanning the street for any early risers that might see her entering the doctor's home before breakfast.

"Are you leaving?" she asked, almost breathless at the sight of him standing there, waiting, the light circling him.

"No, come in." He stepped back and opened the door wider. "In fact, I've been watching out the window, hoping

133

I'd see you walk by, but it was getting late; I thought maybe I'd missed you."

"I have the truck." She nodded to where the old Ford was parked in the shadow of an ash tree.

"I saw the lights, but then you turned so I didn't think it was you until you stopped." He was smiling.

"Just being careful," she explained. Mayme didn't quite know herself if she meant that she was being careful of her reputation or for their secret patient, so she just left it at that. Careful.

Joe closed the door and fell in close behind Mayme. With his right hand, he took hold of her left elbow and guided her past the fancy parlor and brocade sofa where they'd sat just two days before, a place for greeting formal company. This time, he guided her back to the kitchen, the place for more intimate conversations where family and loved ones everywhere share meals, coffee, news, worries, and secrets.

It was a large kitchen, bigger then some of the homes Mayme had been in. Sage green cupboards with glass door fronts lined two walls revealing a display of the widow's old plates and glasses, everyday items left behind. An enamel sink sat below a large window with a view to the backyard of the home; a small dinette set tucked away in a breakfast nook looked out over a private side yard. Only one small window up high above a tall cupboard could be seen from the street. Outside, the day was beginning, the light growing stronger, as though it began in the earth, moving upward, spreading up and out.

"Lord, " Mayme said, "you could darn near fit my whole house in this kitchen. I never knew there were two sets of stairs in here." She pointed to the less formal stairwell that led up to the second floor .

"And that door leads to my office. It doesn't take me long to get home in the evening."

With an ease that surprised Mayme, he lifted up on the back of her jacket collar, allowing her arms to free themselves quickly, a motion that somehow seemed to shed an outer layer that held her down. She turned around to find herself facing Joe. He still held her coat by the shoulders, a loose frame of herself swaying free in his hands. Standing close to him was not unusual. They stood side by side for hours at a time when they worked on a patient, but this was entirely different. Face to face in the raw hours of the morning. It was a quiet moment that shattered all pretense and uncertainty.

Without shifting his gaze from Mayme's face for a moment, Joe draped her jacket over a chair back, removing every barrier that separated them. For a full minute they simply stared at each other in that quiet, each searching the other's face for a sign, a question, an answer. Neither said a word. They barely breathed.

Joe reached toward her, ran the back of his right fingers along the side of her face.

Mayme felt her lips part at the feel of his touch. Like falling in a dream, fearless and frightened to death in the same breath. She was wading through the creek on slippery stones wearing her finest dress, a test of balance and gravity while a school of minnows brushed through and around her legs, shining bolts of black lightning. It all seemed unexpected yet the very thing she had been waiting for all her life, fire and tenderness in one quick breath.

They would later argue about who reached for who first, but they would never argue about how good and right it seemed, coming together, her arms wrapped around his waist, his arms pulling her in tight, their lips meeting for that first kiss. The first real kiss of her life.

Their mouths opened and the muscles of Mayme's face stretched in unfamiliar ways, their tongues soft and warm, searching and tasting in a slow dance of want and need. As much as she knew about the human body, she had never known the depth of this new journey, the unfolding of some tucked away secret, forgotten with the disillusionment of married life.

135

"I shouldn't be doing this," she said, pulling away from him. "I'm married."

Joe held her upper arms loosely, but never let go. "Mayme Holloway, you don't really want to leave. At least I hope you don't want to go." He released her left arm, reached up and ran his long index finger again along the side of her face again, tracing her jaw line, then her mouth. "I can't stop thinking of you. I've wanted this moment for longer than you know."

"But I'm married," she repeated, not knowing if she spoke to Joe or to herself.

"I know that; I wish you weren't," he said calmly. And he kissed her again.

Mayme felt his hand move along her right breast, felt all will and resistance fade away as he undid the top button of her white dress. She tugged the back of his shirt free from his trousers as he slipped the uniform down around her shoulders and let it drop to the floor. Mayme unbuttoned the front of his shirt and clawed at the thin cotton undershirt as they embraced again, kissing his face, his mouth, his neck. As they kissed and caressed one another, Joe reached down and pulled Mayme's white slip up around her hips and tugged at it, pulling her closer still. She pushed him away, stepped back and pulled the slip over her head, held it in front of her for a moment then let it drop to the floor. She bit her lower lip, nervous, but not afraid, standing before a man who was not her husband wearing nothing but a brassiere and a skimpy pair of step-ins that held up her white stockings. She had never done anything so scandalous before in her life.

"All of it," Joe whispered, his gaze intent on every expression on Mayme's face, their eyes searching, questioning, knowing. "I want to know every inch of you."

Mayme did as he asked, her body moving beyond her will, beyond all rational thought. Her cheeks were flushed pink from passion and shyness. She reached behind her and unsnapped her brassiere, revealing her small round breasts. She took a deep breath, then gently took hold of

136

the edge of the step-ins and worked them down, maneuvering each white stocking carefully down her leg, until she stood entirely naked before him.

"Now you," she said, exhilarated and bewildered by her boldness. Even now, she and O.C. respected one another's privacy, rarely seeing the other unclothed. This was different. She and Joe both knew better than most folks what the human body looked like, inside and out, all different shapes and sizes, but the same basic parts, most of them always hidden under clothing. The unseen flesh was the medium of their work, and now it would be a secret they shared and enjoyed, the medium of their affection.

Mayme stood motionless, her hands trembling at her sides as she watched Joe pull his undershirt over his head, then drop his slacks and underpants to the floor. She did not move away when he stepped out of them and toward her, naked, a perfect male specimen. Her mind retreated to the safe routine of charting, mentally recording the details before her. Long and lean. His chest was covered in soft curling dark hairs that led in a diminishing line down to his navel and then another patch of the dark curls. He was circumcised. He was fully erect.

"You're beautiful," he said, cupping the back of her head in one hand, his kneading fingers sending small hair pins flying to the floor, causing her braids to collapse and fall into wild confusion. "Come with me. Upstairs," he whispered in her ear, his teeth tugging at her tender lobe gently, sending a chill from the top of her head to the backs of her knees.

It was only then as she climbed the stairs before him that Mayme was seized with a moment of modesty and reached one hand back around to cover her bare buttocks from his view.

"Don't hide yourself," Joe said, pulling her fingers away, stroking the side of her hip as she turned her back to the wall, pausing for another long kiss, this time with Joe's hand firmly on her breast and her fingers clenching his butt to pull him closer, his penis hard against her belly. They staggered on the stairs, all sense of balance lost to the frenzied moment.

"Come on," Joe said, moving ahead of her, taking her by the hand, leading the way. He took her into his bedroom where they stood beside the bed he had only made an hour before, never imagining the morning that lay before him. Mayme reached up and quickly yanked the rest of the pins from her hair, undid the childish braids and ran her fingers through the loose strands, letting the shaggy mess fall down around her face. She wanted every part of her to be free, even her crimped and wrinkled hair.

Joe sat on the edge of the bed watching her, waiting for her to sit beside him, his face a painful knot of pleasure. Mayme stood directly in front of him, close enough for his arms to reach around her hips, pulling her onto the bed beside him, their bodies immediately moving together as one, stretching out long. Joe took his time, first kissing each nipple while his fingers explored between her legs. His touch was tender and fleeting, teasing her senses, causing Mayme to gasp and long to feel more, to satisfy a growing need, her hips searching for his hand, willing it to continue. He touched her again, this time letting his fingers caress her with greater pressure, but knowing where to touch ever so gently so that her body arched and seized with a kind of pleasure she had never known with a man. Only her own fingers had ever known what just a touch in the right place could do. She reached over and held him in her hand, ran her fingers up and down the length of his firm penis as he touched her and kissed her neck and chest.

Joe's mouth moved downward from her nipples, kissing her ribs, then all around her navel. The room seemed to spin; a chorus of unfamiliar tunes and cricket songs seemed to pour in from some distant land. Mayme drew her fingers through his long hair and along his neck, closed her eyes and let the music in her head carry her away. When Joe scooted down toward the end of the bed

138

and parted her knees, pushing them back, one hand on each ankle, Mayme lifted her head and gasped at the sight of him, his dark curly head moving downward, kissing first her inner thighs, gentle nudges and light kisses that made her tremble all over. It was better than any fantasy she could have dreamed of.

"Oh my God, what are you . . . " she moaned as his kisses traveled, his tongue now the flickering tease. The distant chorus now rang loud and beautiful, unlike any song she'd ever heard, as though she stood at the river's edge and the music rose from the trees and ran through her, becoming her. "Sweet Jesus," she cried as her entire body shuddered and jerked in a wave of intensity, a bolt of electricity running from her toes to the top of her head. He took her hands into his own and the intensity only grew as he pressed the back of her hands against the mattress. Mayme was sure she would faint if he continued.

"Please, stop. Please," she pleaded.

Joe released her hands and moved over her, kissing her again just below the navel, then all along her stomach and up to her mouth. In one moment, the hollowness of a lifetime was finally filled, the easing of a deep pain that had been dulled on occasion but had never been fully sated. They moved as one, their bodies responding and melding one to the other, patiently, anxiously, until they both lay spent in each other's arms, their legs a tangle of pale limbs.

The room had filled with morning light, still soft enough for dreams, but only briefly. The rising sun glared in on the lovers as the soft shadows of the room dissolved to a sharp edge.

"We gotta get up," Mayme finally said. She was curled up alongside him, her head resting on his chest, his arm draped around her thin shoulders. "I gotta go home, try and make some kinda sense out of this. Figure out what I just did." She turned and buried her face into him, hiding from the harsh light of this new day and her awakening sense of reality and shame.

Joe sighed, shifted his weight to face her, forcing her to lift her eyes to meet his gaze. "Mayme, some things are not sensible, but that doesn't make them wrong. Please don't think you did anything wrong here." He shook his head and touched her cheek gently.

Mayme breathed a mournful laugh, as though she'd just discovered a trunk full of confederate dollars. Worthless treasure. "That's easy for you to say; you don't have a husband at home wondering where you are. I should have been home over an hour ago."

"I know," he said, pulling her closer, kissing the top of her head. "But I don't regret one minute of this. I'll never regret it." He leaned back, to see her fully, caressed the side of her face with one hand and whispered, "I think I love you."

Mayme stiffened. "Don't," she said, shaking her head.

"Don't what? Don't love you or don't say it?"

"Both of 'em are dangerous," she said, drinking in every line of his beautiful face, memorizing every speck of him, the light on his shoulders, the salty taste of his skin, the smell of him, a musky but clean scent, and the feel of his hands on her face, on her body.

"Dangerous?" He laughed at her. "You're hardly dangerous, my dear. You have no idea how delicious you are. I wish you could see yourself through my eyes."

Mayme stayed quiet and still, fearful that if she opened her mouth to speak, the wall of tears long stored up inside her would spill open and never end. She swallowed the pang of regret and hugged him tighter then she remembered ever hugging anyone.

"Oh God, Joe, I never felt like this before. Is that what love is? I don't even know. All I know is I have done what I swore I'd never do."

"Then it's definitely love. Mayme Holloway, you are the smartest woman I know, and the most loyal. Only something as illusive as love could make you confused."

140

He kissed her gently this time, their mouths coming together easily, as tender as the first kiss of young sweethearts.

"Definitely love," he repeated. "But if you do that thing with my tongue one more time, I'm never leaving this bed."

Mayme laughed. "What thing?"

"Where you kind of suck on it."

"Is that nice? I never did nothing like that before. I actually don't believe I've ever had another person's tongue in my mouth before."

"How is that possible?" Joe asked, genuinely perplexed by such a statement from someone like her, from a married woman.

"O.C. and I don't kiss like that." She shook her head in her own puzzlement.

"How do you kiss?"

"He keeps his mouth closed. I keep mine closed."

"Then I'm guessing no one ever," he shifted his gaze downward, "kissed you there before?" His fingers drifted to touch her lightly on the thigh, a gentle reminder.

"Heavens, no." Mayme covered her face with one hand, suddenly shamed at their recent performance. "I can't believe you did that. I'd heard of it, but ..." Her voice stalled, unable to express in words what played out in her mind, a wish that they could just stay there for a month and do it again and again and again.

He grinned, mischievous and pleased, pulled her hand away from her face to find her biting her lower lip again. "I'm glad I was first. And I can't wait to do it again." He lowered his face to kiss her nipple and began stroking her upper thigh, the tip of his finger just brushing against her, again teasing her senses.

"Oh, don't tempt me," she moaned pushing his hand away, knowing what those fingers could do to melt her resolve. "I gotta get myself home. It's late and I'm just praying O.C. is gone by the time I get there. I'm not sure I can face him just now. I need some time to, I don't know, I

141

just need a little time alone." She swung her legs off the bed, then stopped short of standing and gripped the side of the mattress. "I'm lightheaded."

Joe rose up to sit beside her, took her wrist in his hand to feel her pulse, his face a blank slate as he concentrated on her internal rhythm. "You're just exhausted," he finally said, now bending close to look into her eyes as though he could see straight through her. "You've probably been up for twenty-four hours straight and hardly eaten a bite, not to mention the exhilarating sexual experience you just enjoyed. Am I right?"

She nodded her head, smiling weakly at his seamless transition from secret lover to physician. Now if she said she stopped by the doctor's to discuss Charley and because she wasn't feeling well, she'd be telling the truth. Charley. She hadn't even asked about him.

"What about Charley?" she blurted out in alarm, her voice sounding more shrill then she'd intended.

"Who?"

"Charley. Did you go see him? Was he alright?"

Joe grinned, the thrill of the experience treating Pretty Boy Floyd showing on his face. "Charley is fine. When I told him about Deputy Teague, he got pretty excited, wanted to take off right then, but I talked him down, gave him a bologna sandwich and a flask of bourbon. That calmed him down enough for me to give a second treatment."

"No doubt he got excited. Shoot, if I know him, he'll be wanting to get as far away from here and as fast as he can." Mayme looked around for her clothes and remembered they were somewhere downstairs, in the kitchen. The thought of traipsing down the stairway into the bright kitchen with green cupboards bare-ass naked sent her stomach into a twist.

"I told him we'd go back out today, but in case he felt like he needed to move on, I left him the Protargol solution and told him to just pour it on. I don't think you'd ever get him to insert the syringe."

142

Mayme smiled at the very thought of it. "No, I don't imagine Charley Floyd would ever do that to himself." She searched around the bedroom for something to cover herself with. "Do you have, I don't know, a robe or a towel? Something." Though naked bodies were common to both of them, she was overcome with shyness and wished she could just crawl under the covers and hide until he was already seeing patients at the hospital. And if she could, she would just lie there and sleep the day away; she was so tired.

Joe moved unconsciously to his closet, comfortable to be without clothes in his own bedroom, even with Mayme sitting on his bed. He made no attempt to hide himself from her, even glanced at his body and smiled.

"Yes, as much as I hate it, you need to cover up or we're not leaving this room." He pulled on a robe and headed for the door. "I'll be right back with your clothes. And mine."

Mayme sat naked on the bed, more terrified than she'd ever been in her life. She was, she realized, more afraid of herself than anyone.

Joe appeared with his clothes and her uniform and undergarments draped over one arm and her shoes in the other hand. "Here you go," he said, dropping the clothes onto the bed beside her.

Mayme looked away as she put her brassiere on first, then stepped into her stockings. They dressed silently. By the time she pulled her dress over her head, Joe was standing before her, buttoning his shirt, fully clothed.

"My hair," she said, touching the loose strands. "I think I'll just leave it. If O.C. is still home, I'll say I had a headache, had to get those pins out. I was supposed to get it cut yesterday. He wants to make me look like Marion Davies."

Joe tilted his head, surprised at what she said. "Why would anyone want to cut that hair? And why would you want to look like Marion Davies? She'd be better off looking like you."

143

Mayme scoffed at his flattery, but his manner belied any sense of mockery. He was sincere and again she knew to speak would be to open a watershed of tears. She simply hugged him, her ear pressed against his chest, listening to the music of his tender heart. He was right. This must be love.

10.

O.C. was long gone. The house was quiet and still, a silence waiting to be shattered by her presence. Away from Joe, back in the home she shared with O.C., a crushing weight fell over her. Mayme went to the pantry and pulled a bottle from the top shelf, poured a bit of the clear liquid into a coffee cup and drank it down in one gulp, letting it burn her from the inside out. She was hungry, but the thought of swallowing any bite of food made her stomach roll into knots. She made her way to the bathroom and began filling the tub with hot water.

It was there, alone, submerged in water, emotionally and physically spent, that Mayme gave in to the threat of tears. She didn't know what was worse, her betrayal of O.C., or knowing that she wanted Joe more than anything she'd ever wanted in her life. The future played out before her, the lies she would tell, the pain she would cause, and the love. The love they would make, the love they would share. She felt robbed and cheated of a life she could have had if she'd only been patient, not married the first man to ask her. If she was by herself, she could have Joe forever.

Mayme looked down at her naked body. Faint bruises were forming where Joe had touched her, around her breasts and down on her thighs, tender places. He had left his mark on her and while the bruised flesh would fade, she knew the ache in her chest was there for a lifetime, no matter what happened in the future. She had crossed some line that could never be uncrossed.

145

Mayme slipped into the cool sheets, her skin still warm from the hot bath, and stretched out, careful to stay on her side of the empty bed. The scent of lavender was strong in the room, the sweet smell haunting her sleep. She dreamt, oddly, that she was in bed dreaming and awoke in a large room of soft yellow curtains, drifting with the breeze through the open windows. The room was filled with flowers and leaves swirling all about her. She reached over to wake O.C., then realized it was Joe in the bed. They kissed and laughed at the cyclone of daisies and roses until there was a pounding at the door. They tried to break through the flowers to find their clothes. Someone needed their help, but the flowers were now violent, barring their way to the door. They scurried about the room, battling the petals, Joe pulling Mayme through a wind tunnel that nearly sent her flying, both of them shielding their eyes pushing toward a patch of blue light. Before she could escape the tornado of wild flowers, Mayme awoke, first in the dream and then in her bed, a double awakening that left her confused and uncertain about where the dream began, where it ended, how the pieces came together in some kind of beautiful storm. For the first time in her life, she knew the weight of a guilty conscience.

An illusion of night permeated the modest room, all light blocked from the windows to accommodate Mayme's upside down life of dark days. Mayme lay still, barely breathing in the struggling darkness, imagining herself invisible, nothing more than a slight ripple in the unmade bed. The dream puzzled her, so disturbing and terrifying, but so beautiful too.

It wasn't a hard one for her to make sense of. Shoot, she thought, any fool could reason it was that sweet smelling O.C. raising all kinds of hell, a flowery hell at that, half crazed his woman was in another man's bed, but, Lord, the way Joe had held onto her hand, his grip so firm, their need to help others pushing them forward through the harrowing wind, and that shining blue patch that was bluer than any sky she'd ever seen. Though her body

146

needed more sleep, Mayme pushed herself out of bed. Even a silly dream could be dangerous. Wanting things you can't have is always dangerous.

After a splash of cold water in the face and a hasty dash to Conley's market for all the essentials and some extras besides, Mayme set to work. She whirled about the kitchen like a house afire cooking one of the finest meals she'd ever made. With fierce energy, she cut up a fresh chicken, happy to have something to slam the heavy cleaver through, the sound of the small bones cracking, the flesh parting at her will. She dumped the pieces into a large mixing bowl, doused them good with flour, salt and pepper, then used her bare fingers to evenly spread the powdery mix to cover each piece thoroughly, reaching down and pulling the breasts up from the bottom, then the thighs and the drumsticks. The plump flesh rolled thick and heavy in her hands, the pieces tumbling until the clammy skin turned smooth and dusty, like they'd been dusted in talc after a nice shower.

As she worked, her mind drifted back to the morning with Joe, the things they did, the sense of falling, then shattering. She worked harder, desperate to push those images into the deepest corner of her heart where she could hide them away from O.C. and the rest of the world. She wanted to say it was a mistake, that it would never happen again. She wanted to make amends for her transgression, to feel free of the guilt that would haunt her forever. But she knew better, even now as she dropped each leg, each thigh, each breast, one by one into the black iron skillet Mama Holloway had given her as a wedding present. She would do it again. The hot oil sizzled and splattered, hot drops burning her neck and forearms.

While the chicken cooked, slowly turning a crispy golden brown, she made fresh biscuits, boiled a pot full of potatoes for mashing, and cut up some tart green apples for baking. She would sprinkle thin slices with a generous amount of sugar and cinnamon, dot the whole mess with butter and bake it until it turned into a soft gooey mess. It

147

wouldn't be quite a pie, but it'd be warm and sweet all the same, and rolling out pie dough was more than she could tackle in one afternoon. Though she would not be there to see O.C. eat a single bite, she knew how much he would like that, coming home to a house that smelled like his mama's house, a fine blend of grease and cinnamon apples lingering in the air, a big dinner waiting for him in the kitchen.

Every time Mayme's thoughts strayed back to Joe, his face twisted in thrilling agony, his hands on her, in her, his tongue, warm and soft, she pushed herself to work harder. She chopped, pounded, fried and scrubbed as though she could atone for her desires by sweating in the kitchen. She made more than plenty, enough for O.C. to stuff himself silly, enough for her to take to work, and some for Charley, too. If she hurried, she could make it out to Horseshoe Bend and back and still be to work on time. She didn't have to be in till six tonight and it was not even three yet. Plenty of time.

Mayme covered O.C.'s supper with a clean kitchen towel and left him a note, telling him she was terrible sorry she missed him that morning, but she'd had to take care of some business on her way home and it couldn't be helped. He would never ask for any details. Not that morning or any other.

With a fresh basket of clean linens and a hearty helping of hot chicken and potatoes for her and Charley in the seat beside her, Mayme began to ease the old truck out from the driveway. She looked back and startled at the sight of Crazy Cora and her little boy Henry standing still directly in her path. She stopped to wait for them, but they stood there, not moving an inch.

"Cora Hon, you like to scared me half to death," she called out the truck window. "What y'all doin' standing in the drive like that? That's how you get yourself run over, girl." She waved her hand as if she was shooing away a fly.

Cora just stood there, grinning foolishly the way she always did. Even when they were kids, Cora stumbled

148

through every day with a dazed smile plastered across her round face. Some folks made fun of her back then, but over the years that meanness had turned softer, to a kind of tender pity. Some man, probably more'n one in Mayme's opinion, had taken advantage of her simple mind and made her pregnant. Of course, no one ever stepped up to the plate to claim Henry as his own flesh and blood, and Cora never told nobody who it might have been. She either didn't know his name or followed his orders to never tell. No one knew.

So, all these years later, Cora and Henry lived in the same old shack she'd lived in all her life. After her momma died, some folks in town talked about moving her out of there, finding her a home where someone could watch out for her, but nothing ever happened, and before you knew it, Cora was having Henry, and it just seemed better to leave her where she was at the end of a dirt road on the edge of town. She did odd jobs for what little bit of money she could get, but mostly she just went around asking neighbors for whatever she needed. Mayme had heard more than one old biddy in town refer to it as begging, like those poor hungry boys heading out west, but that put a whole different twist on what the true situation was. Cora didn't beg; she simply asked her friends for what she needed.

Cora and Henry walked up to the truck window, the young mother grinning like she'd just found two dollars and little Henry looking like a slight breeze might knock him over. "Hi there, Henry," Mayme said, reaching her left arm out to touch his dirty head of hair. It felt thick and sticky, and she didn't want to think about what might be crawling around in there. "How y'all doin', Miss Cora? You getting along okay?"

Cora leaned in through the window and breathed in deep, her eyes falling to the basket of supplies, the covered dinner plate right on top. She grunted low before speaking. "Hi, Mayme," she said, her lips smacking, her breath rancid.

"Hi, Cora," she repeated.

"Can I have that? Me and Henry's hungry." She reached across in front of Mayme, pointing to the covered dish of hot chicken and potatoes, Charley's and her supper.

Her eyes were narrow slits in her round happy face. She had not bathed for several days at least, and her ripe odor caused even Mayme to wince, and Mayme had smelled some horrible smells in her days. It wasn't that the poor girl liked being dirty or that she was lazy. She just wouldn't think to do something like take a bath or brush her teeth, or for that matter, tell Henry to take a bath or brush his teeth either. She only needed to be told what to do and then she would do it. When Cora got this nasty, Mayme knew that no one was taking her in and feeding her and no one was givin' her any jobs neither. Not if she smelled worse than gangrene and gut rot.

"Tell you what, Miss Cora. I will give you all this food if you promise me to go straight home from here and take a good hot bath and get nice and clean. And you make Henry take a bath, too. Y'all wash your hair and brush your teeth, too. I want you both smellin' like sunshine before you go to bed tonight. You do that and then you come back tomorrow this time and I'll have some work for you to do. How's that sound?"

Cora grinned bigger and jiggled all over in happy agreement, a happy gurgling sound rolling from her open mouth. Mayme handed her the plate of food.

"Go on now," she said, waving the dirty mother and son on down the street.

By the time the hungry pair reached the road, they each had a piece of fried chicken in their hands, Cora walking in an awkward balancing act as she ate and carried a plate, Henry holding the plate pressed against him, making a worse mess than he already was. There wouldn't be a scrap of food left on the plate by the time they reached home, their bellies too empty to wait a minute longer to shove it into their mouths. Mayme felt good knowing the strange little duo would sleep tonight with full bellies and clean bodies. She watched them drift away, like two dry leaves chased by the wind.

Mayme turned off the truck and hurried back into the house for another plate of food to deliver to her patient hiding out at Horseshoe Bend. She considered just taking the dish she'd made up for O.C. He'd never know she'd spent the whole afternoon over a hot stove, she reasoned, but the smell of her efforts lingered heavy in the air. He might find out or at least suspect and then he would be hurt that she gave it to someone other than him, and she didn't want to hurt him, especially not now.

Mayme pulled three cans of Campbell's noodle soup off the shelf and settled on taking four of the half dozen biscuits she'd left for O.C. to go with the soup. He'd be tickled just to have fried chicken and baked apples, none the wiser that there had been a full dozen biscuits.

The cabin was empty, just like before. Mayme heated the soup and lit the lamps, certain Charley would show up sooner or later, but he never did. He was gone. She took her bowl of soup and a biscuit and went and sat on the front porch to have her supper.

The late afternoon sun was warm, too warm for sipping on hot soup. And though she didn't really have much of an appetite, Mayme forced a couple of bites down, more broth than noodles. It was going to be a long night and she knew she needed some fuel in her to keep her from keeling over. The biscuit was easier to get down and seemed to settle some of the queasiness that had plagued her since her spell that morning. She wasn't sick; she was just overcome with guilt or excitement or maybe even love like Joe said. She didn't really know. All she knew was that she felt like she was standing on the edge of a cliff and diving off with her arms spread open wide seemed like the only thing she wanted to do. She could almost feel the rush of air in her face, all cool and lovely, the falling sensation like a new drug she longed for. She struggled to

151

balance herself, trembling from deep inside, trapped on a dangerous ledge and no matter what, she didn't want to be saved.

The sound of tires crunching on gravel woke her to the moment, her reaction to company more curious than frightened. Expecting to see Charley or maybe even Wilma and Matthew, the sight of soft powder blue made her heart leap, her stomach tighten. Joe.

"What are you doing here?" he asked as he slid out of the pretty car.

"Me?" Mayme sat the soup bowl down on the porch and rose to her feet. "The question is what are you doing here?" She couldn't help but turn happy at the sight of him standing tall, almost radiant in the perfect slant of afternoon light.

"I was sure you'd be too tired to make the trip so I thought I'd come and then you wouldn't have to." He moved slowly toward her, his hands in his pockets, smiling sweetly. The Cheshire cat, she thought. He wasn't wearing a jacket and he had his shirtsleeves rolled up half way to his elbows.

"How was I supposed to know about that?" She brushed the front of her dress, removing any stray crumbs that might have landed there and wiped the corner of her mouth with her fingertips.

"I guess I didn't think that part through."

He stopped directly in front of her, his gaze never leaving her face, but he didn't touch her or reach for her. He just looked at her. Mayme thought his eyes were like soft dark pools she wanted to dive deep into, a nicer fantasy then diving off some cliff. He looked better than she'd ever seen him, but she wasn't sure what was different now from the hundreds of times she'd stood this close to him. Of course, only a few hours ago, they'd been closer, skin against skin, naked and joined together, their bodies as one. Mayme couldn't help but blush at the memory.

152

"Where's Charley?" he asked, finally looking over her shoulder toward the open cabin door, his expression now the one she knew best, the doctor asking about his patient. "Did you already give him the Protargol?"

"He's gone," she said. "I never saw him."

"Gone?"

"Yep. I stuck around, thinking maybe he was just out for a spell, wandering the woods, but I ain't seen no sign of him. I think he's moved on; that's just how it goes."

His chin moved only slightly, but Mayme saw it. She knew what he was thinking. She was thinking it too.

"You want some soup and biscuits?" she asked. "I made some biscuits this afternoon," she explained. "They're probably not as good as Mama Holloway's, but they're not bad."

"I'd love some."

Joe followed her into the cabin. Anyone watching the two of them would have thought they were simply moving inside to visit. It was only after the door had closed behind them, in the near darkness of the woodsy hideaway that Joe reached for her, pulled her close and pressed his mouth against hers.

"I can't stop thinking about you, about this morning," he said.

"I know," she answered, her face buried in his chest. "I have the same problem. I'm ashamed of myself but I think maybe I'm more alive or something, more excited, scared and confused than I've ever been, but more alive."

He kissed her again, this time more tender, then took her hands and led her over to the small bed.

"Oh no," she said. "Charley still might come back. And besides, those sheets."

"Aren't those clean sheets?" Joe nodded toward the basket of linens Mayme had brought then reached up and lightly lifted a loose strand of her fine hair and let it fall.

"Yes, but Charley."

With the back of his fingers he touched her right breast, up and down, then in small circles, never shifting

153

his gaze away from her face. "I don't think he's coming back," he said and sat down, pulling her down beside him.

"We don't have any way of knowing that," she said, taking a deep breath of resolve. "It's too risky. Really."

Joe sighed, dropped his roving hand to hold her fingers. "You're right. As always."

"And besides," she said, looking at her watch, "I go on duty in just about an hour. I got to get going myself."

"Are you sure you've had enough rest?" he asked, his concern genuine. "You couldn't have slept for more than a couple of hours if you're out here eating soup and you made biscuits too." He dipped his face close to her, smiled slightly as he examined her eyes, using his thumb to gently pull down on the lower lid.

"You don't know the half of it," she said, moved by his concern for her, humored by his feigned examination. She was usually the one offering up worry for other folks' well being. It didn't come her way too often and she liked the way it felt, all warm and soft inside her.

"Well, at least we can have some dinner together," he said. "Have a little more soup. Eat with me." He nudged her with his shoulder, two friends being chummy, simply enjoying a chance afternoon in the woods.

"I think I left my bowl out on the porch."

"I'll get it. Just sit. Let me wait on you."

Mayme moved to the table and watched Joe spoon the canned soup into their bowls as if it was the finest meal in the land. He carried the last biscuit to the table as if he carried a tray of precious jewels. They sat and ate the simple meal and talked about Mrs. Daniels' latest plan to buy a bigger building, patients, movies they'd seen, their favorite things to eat, anything and everything. Mayme told him about her dream of flowers, the patch of blue, and the grand meal she had cooked and given away to Cora Lillard.

"I know her," he said. "She came to my office one day and asked if I had some cookies for her. I guess Mrs. Hardy used to bake cookies for her and the little boy."

154

"That's right," Mayme said. "I remember that. So did you give her some cookies?"

"No. I didn't have any, but I gave her some money. She looked hungry." His face tightened to the worried concern Mayme had often seen at the hospital. "I told her to go buy her and the boy a nice dinner at the diner then have the cookies after."

"That was a nice thing you did," Mayme said.

"How does she survive? She's mildly retarded and has a child alone. Of course, I wonder how half the people in this country are getting by these days."

"It's bad everywhere," Mayme said. "Let's just hope FDR wins the election."

"Here, here," Joe said, lifting his biscuit as though it was a glass of champagne.

They sat and talked, moving effortlessly from lovers to colleagues to friends, the threads of their relationship magically weaving and tightening into a seamless gown of the finest silk made for Mayme alone. It clung to her hips and draped around her shoulders like a second layer of skin while Joe held the long train in his hands, careful and loving as though he held the greatest treasure on earth.

"As much as I'd love to stay and talk to you for another three hours, I gotta go," Mayme said. "Mrs. Daniels will have my hide if I'm late again."

It was only then, at the moment of parting, that they fell together in a tight embrace. Mayme now had her own reason for hurrying out of the hospital where she would hide in the darkness as she let herself in through Joe's kitchen door, away from the view of the neighbors. She would simply mention to O.C. she was working a little extra and he'd never ask how, where or why. He would never question her absence in the morning. His practice of turning a deaf ear and blind eye to her activities was now a welcomed neglect.

"Will you come by on your way home in the morning?" Joe asked.

"I'll be there," she promised.

11.

All summer long, Mayme and Joe worked together like nothing more than a chicken sandwich had ever passed between them. They worked side by side in the operating theater, Mayme slapping forceps and scalpels into Joe's palm with solid precision, every ounce of attention directed to the body lying limp on the narrow table. Out of surgery, they would pass each other in the hallway or out on the patient ward with only a friendly nod or casual conversation about wound care or pain medication. But there was rarely a morning that Mayme didn't find herself praying for the sun to hide itself just a few minutes more, longing for the extra span of darkness that lingered in winter. Those were the moments she lived for, there in the shadows of Joe's bedroom on those luxurious days when there was time to spare, or even just sitting at his kitchen table, talking over a quick cup of black coffee, sharing dreams and wishes while life commanded their presence elsewhere. Fortunately for Mayme, O.C. was usually gone to his shop by the time she got home, and she was always gone before he returned. As she'd predicted, he never bothered to ask where she'd been or where she might be going either. He just whistled silly tunes and visited his mama, whether she was off at the hospital or loving another man. For a while, it seemed like those summer days might stretch on forever.

It was the killing of Susie Sharp up on Braggs Mountain that snapped every man, woman and child over the age of eight into a tailspin. Not a soul that sat in O.C.'s chair didn't have some morsel of gossip about who done it and where they might be hiding out.

Ernie Bell had been driving ambulance for Baptist Hospital that night, said he'd never seen such a horrible mess. Poor Mrs. Sharp was dead on the scene, slumped over in her seat, her daughter shot up in the back seat, but still breathing. Even Susie's five-year-old grandson had a bullet in his scrawny leg. Larry Owings couldn't wait to tell everyone how his own boy had been on a Boy Scout outing, driving down that steep grade off the north side of the hill there when they stopped to investigate a wrecked car. There they were just peeking into the empty wreck when the killers come crashing out of the brush and stole the scoutmaster's car and left them all stranded on the side of the road. Ernie Bell couldn't understand why they never saw those Boy Scouts when he went up that same road after the Sharps. O.C. offered his explanation that the poor kids were probably hiding in the brush scared out of their wits. Even Peggy Miller, a quiet woman who never missed a meeting of the First Christian Church women's Bible study, had a bit of gossip to share while she waited on her grandson to get his hair trimmed up for the new school year. She told O.C. that her good friend, Eunice, had sold the criminals hamburgers just before the killing. "Can you imagine?" she asked, "actually feeding the very men who killed your neighbor?" Sitting at the Normal Club Barbershop was more informative then reading the newspaper, and every paper in the country was carrying a story about the heinous slaughter of innocent citizens. Even the governor said he was disgusted by such a terrible act. O.C. was sure he had more of the details than any reporter or lawman out there.

When Grover Bishop walked in one evening, just before closing time, O.C. got so excited he could have danced a jig. Now he would get some real scoop, some honest-to-goodness truth about the investigation that he could pass on the next day, maybe even what the officers had found at the roadblocks they'd set up all around the county. He wanted to know if it really was Luther Joliff that did it, like some folks claimed, and hoped to shout nobody was claiming Charley had anything to do with this mess. He knew his old friend would never do something like that, no sir. Charley robbed banks, but he didn't shoot defenseless women. Sitting back in that chair had a way of loosening up folks' jaws. Even Grover Bishop's.

"Afternoon, O.C."

"Why afternoon, Sheriff."

"Deputy Sheriff, O.C. Deputy Sheriff."

"All in due time, all in due time." He motioned for the tall lawman to take a seat. "Hop on up here, let's see if we can't clean you up a bit."

Bishop tossed his big white hat onto an empty seat against the wall before taking his place in the barber's chair. He pressed his neck to the left and then the right before laying his head back against the headrest. The motion made a loud pop and crack as the muscles released their tense grip.

"Lord, that sounds like bones breakin' in there." O.C. released the lever to lower the seat back to a reclining position and studied his client's stubbled face while he cranked the seat higher with a foot press. Dark circles seemed to shadow the piercing eyes. "You look a might weary, Grover. Guess you been working a little extra these days."

"That would be an understatement, O.C. I shouldn't even be in here, but I just wanted a minute to myself to think. And I'd like a clean shave. You might give a little trim to the back."

O.C. recognized the subtle clue to leave him be for a spell, so he let him just sit quiet, didn't even whistle or hum while he snapped the white apron around the man's thick neck. He brushed a heavy lather of shaving cream around the broad face, then opened his favorite pearl-handled straightedge razor. It was then, between strokes, as the blade ran up along the underside of his neck, that Bishop began to talk a little.

"You know I'm gonna get those boys that done that killing. Them that shot Susie Sharp and her daughter. And anyone who helps any of them out is gonna pay the price too."

"I've no doubt you will, sir." O.C. spoke softly, as if he was only half interested in anything his client had to say.

"O.C., you know I hear things now and again, things that cause me to wonder."

"Hmmm mmmm."

"Most folks don't talk much 'round here, especially them that live outside of town, but occasionally someone trips up and I catch wind of some little thing that makes me curious."

"Uh huh, I imagine that would happen." O.C. swirled the dirty blade in a basin, then lightly placed two fingers on the man's chin to tilt his head to the right, a move that kept Bishop quiet until the barber turned again to clean his blade.

"I heard th'other day that Mayme sometimes gets called on by folks, some who are, shall we say, less than honorable to help 'em out if they're sick or wounded, folks that don't want to go to the hospital."

O.C.'s mind flashed back to that morning last May when Charley showed up at their back door, a bullet in his ankle and Lord knows what else wrong with him. Charley had said something about Mayme having a good reputation. Now he was curious too. Reputation? With who?

"Oh, she delivers a baby now and again, young girls out in the sticks who can't afford to see the doctor, but she mostly stays busy at the hospital these days."

A small tremble began at the base of his spine, but he caught the nervous rumble and held it clenched in his belly. He didn't have to look to know there were two fiery eyes fixated on him, studying his every response. He could feel the officer's gaze burn right through him like fire.

160

"Well, she might hear of something now and again, around the hospital, you know, people sometimes tell their doctors," he paused to swallow, his Adam's apple rolling up and down under O.C.'s fingertips, "or their nurses things in passing about somethin' they seen. Somethin' private she might pass on to you."

"She ain't mentioned nothin' special," he said, deftly rolling the lawman's head to one side, positioning his arm to block the man's view. He was grateful that he didn't know anything at all about what Mayme might know or hear.

"Well, she can't be too careful 'bout who she aids. You hear about that doctor and nurse that helped out Dillinger? Back east somewheres." He didn't give O.C. an opportunity to answer, just took a quick breath and kept on with his story. "They got two years for taking care of Mr. Dillinger's injuries. Claimed he forced them, but they went to prison anyway."

O.C. took a hot towel from his sterilizer and wiped the remnants of lather from Grover's face, leaving the warm cloth draped there to steam open his pores and to hide the broad, clean-shaven face completely for a moment. Again, with the big lawman resting before him, vulnerable and blinded, his block-shaped head stretched back, offering the jugular vein for the taking, the gentle barber was seized with a glimmer of unimaginable power, unimaginable rage. Luther Joliff, Ford Bradshaw, Jim Benge, and Charley Floyd would give anything to be in his polished shoes right now, their ruthless hunter lying before him like a sacrificial lamb. O.C. squeezed his eyes closed to force away the evil thoughts, hating himself for letting them into his head. Mayme, he thought. Grover Bishop has heard something about Mayme. It finally occurred to him that he had no idea what she was up to, where she was half the time, but maybe he should find out.

Tonight, after he closed up shop, he would go to the hospital and visit her, tell her he needed to talk to her in private, maybe even see if she could take a short break for dinner. He could stop and get a couple of sandwiches to go from Dewey's Diner. He hadn't done that in, Lord, forever, it seemed.

O.C. had made it a habit to avoid the hospital since he'd made a terrible fool of himself there. Once upon a time, Mayme had arranged for him to go to the hospital and shave those patients that were in there for a longer spell, maybe give them a haircut, make them feel better by looking better, or some nonsense like that. No sooner had he opened his traveling barbering case than old Melvin Casey tossed his cookies into a little bowl not five feet from him. The smell alone made him almost faint. He packed up and ran, nearly tripping over his feet as he dashed down the stairs and out the front door. Mayme'd told him how they all laughed at the sight of him, all white faced and pale, running like a scared rabbit.

How on earth did barbers in the old days do blood letting? And why on earth did he sometimes get those ugly thoughts in his head? The sight of blood always made his stomach roll over, so why did he conjure up those images all by himself? It was a God-awful mystery, but surely the good Lord had some purpose in it for him.

About the time O.C. made it up the hill with his sack of sandwiches, he could hear the sirens wailing, coming his way. He cringed and dashed to the far side of the road, his stomach knotted in fear, when a Muskogee County Sheriff's car raced up the street at breakneck speed. He watched the car slide down the drive right up to the back entry where two doors opened wide for carrying ambulance patients in. Mayme came running down the small ramp with a gurney as the driver was pulling his wounded partner from his vehicle. O.C. lifted one hand to wave to her, but she didn't see him. Her eyes were fixed on the two other sheriff cars that sped in after the first one.

O.C. never moved any closer to the action, realizing it was probably not the best time to invite his wife to join him for dinner to tell her about Bishop. Whatever was going

162

on, it was big news, and it was playing out right in front of him. Two Muskogee deputies carried the wounded man into the hospital, Mayme already bending over him, checking out some wound in his belly area, then motioning to someone inside the door, turning to see what was coming out of the second car. He could hear her holler to the officers, "Hang on, a gurney's comin'." Ernie Bell came flying out after the first man had passed through and helped the officers bring in a second man. O.C. couldn't be positive from where he stood, but he was pretty sure they was both lawmen that was shot or they wouldn't be so fired up to get them in to the hospital. Lord, he thought, have mercy on them that done this 'cause them officers sure won't. No sir.

The two tuna melts that Dewey had made special for him would be cold by the time he got home, but they would still be tasty. And unless Mayme packed them for her supper, he was pretty sure there was five or six persimmon cookies left in the jar on the counter at home. Mama had made him a big batch for Sunday dinner, and he'd tried to make 'em last all week, limiting himself to three or four after supper. He was nearly home when he caught sight of the young doctor flying up the hill in his fancy car. He'll be working all night tonight, O.C. thought. But that's the price you pay to be a doctor.

Shifting the bag of sandwiches from one hand to the other, O.C. picked up his pace, already thinking of all the news he would have to share with his customers. He may not have had a chance to talk to his wife, but he had a bird's eye view of what was going to be front page news. Lord, he was hungry enough to eat a horse and chase the rider. Was there milk in the ice box to go with them cookies? Mayme wouldn't have been to the market, and he was pretty sure he drank the last of it last night.

One thing he knew for sure now, and he would make sure he let old Grover Bishop know it too - Mayme really was spending her time at the hospital. Poor scrawny thing really ran herself ragged. She never even had time to use

163

that hair waver he bought her, just wrapped it all up in braids all the time. He'd have to ask her about that young doctor there. O.C. couldn't remember the fellow's name, though he knew Mayme talked about him all the time. But O.C. didn't cut his hair and didn't know much about him really. It occurred to him that the man must go all the way down to Louie's Shop over on Vinita for his barbering. Course, he didn't go often enough, by the looks of him. Even from fifty yards away, O.C. could see the man needed more than a trim, the way his brown curls hung over his collar. Did nobody at that hospital own a mirror?

12.

It was just a small wound in the upper quadrant of the chest, not much bigger than a fifty-cent piece, but once they rolled the patient over a bit, the real damage was clear. The hole where the bullet left his body looked like he'd been hit with something the size of a softball, not the small soft-shell 30-30 of a Winchester rifle but something meaner. His chances were slim to none and everyone, even the wounded man, knew that, his sweat-dripping face twisted in a knot of pain, but that didn't mean you don't try your damndest to save his life.

"Good Lord," Mayme said to Joe, cutting the remnants of a blood-soaked shirt off his arms, "it's Webb Reece." She raised her voice to a cheerful tone and gripped his wrist. "Hey there, Webb Honey, you hold on and we'll get you feelin' better here quick like."

"Get him upstairs, and get Dr. Moody up there, too," Joe ordered, already headed up the stairs to the scrub room. "Mayme," Joe said, his voice urging her to follow him.

"Wait, there's another one," she said, and turned back outside to help another deputy drag a second bleeding man from the back of another shot-up patrol car. Joe turned and followed her, knowing they would have to decide who made it to the table first and who would have to wait.

Upstairs, Mayme and Joe quickly slipped on muslin skullcaps and sterile gowns and took their place side by side at the porcelain scrub sink. They each stomped on the heavy foot pedals under the sink and held their arms and hands under the stream of hot water that began to gush from a long gooseneck faucet, scrubbed their hands with disinfectant, fierce and rough, more frantic than usual. There was not a second to spare.

"I know him, too," Joe offered, finally picking up on the thread of conversation that began under the portico outside. He worked the brush across his nails, then his knuckles.

"I know his whole family," Mayme answered, never shifting her gaze from her own scrubbing task. She ran the hard bristled brush across the back of her hands and up her forearms, remembering the night he'd been there with his wife, Lily, when their baby was born, not so very long ago. A boy, they'd had a boy, but she couldn't remember the baby's name for the life of her.

"He spent a lot of time here visiting Dwight Teague."

"They've been friends as long as I can remember." Mayme dropped the scrub brush and held her hands and arms under the hot water, letting the last bits of soap rinse away. "Dwight'd probably been out there with him if he hadn't been hurt."

He was a big baby, she remembered that, and he had a thick head of dark hair. It was a funny name. Webb had been so happy, had sat and snuggled the new baby up to his cheek, kissing the top of his tiny head.

Mayme was just tying her mask up when Doc Moody took his place at the long wash basin. "I'll do anesthesia," he said to Joe, as if he still had a say in the assignment of duties. There was no doubt this was Joe's surgery to perform, but it was still Moody's house as far as he was concerned. The only one he deferred to was Mrs. Daniels. Joe nodded in agreement but didn't exchange any sly knowing glance with Mayme as they might have on another day. He was deep in concentration, considering options, risks, knowing all chances were worth taking.

"There's another one right after this one," Joe added.

166

"Two of 'em?" Doc asked, obviously not completely aware of the entire crisis.

"Yes sir," Mayme said. "The other one is hurt bad, too, shoulder and mouth, but this is the more urgent. Gunshot to the chest."

"We need to get a bigger hospital," the older man said. Mayme tied his mask for him while he finished scrubbing, hurrying him along with a quick tap on the shoulder. "Douglas is over in Tulsa today, but I'll have Edna call him back."

"Not a bad idea," Joe answered. "Looks like we might even see if someone from Baptist can help out."

Normally, three doctors were more than enough for the nine-bed hospital, but this was not a normal time. Two officers with bullets in them more than likely meant there would be more gunshot wounds in the days to follow, and unless the shooters were quick to get out of the territory, there was a good chance any survivors would end up there.

Mrs. Daniels made sure the patient was prepped and ready in a prone position on the operating table, facing downward, arms above the head, his face turned to one side. His body was draped in sterile sheets, a thick layer of large gauze covering the open wound that had been doused with betadine and saline. Though a heavy dose of morphine ran through his torn body, he was not yet unconscious when Mayme pushed through the double doors to the small operating theater. It had been only minutes since he'd been carried through the back door, but they were ready to go, fully aware of every crucial minute that passed.

"Hey there, Webb," Mayme said as she came up alongside the wounded man, taking her place beside the tray of sterile instruments. Everything was in proper order; they were just waiting for the doctors who were only moments behind her.

Weak with pain and sedation, and no doubt fearful of the unknown just a breath away, Webb Reece was all raw emotion. Tears slid silently down over the side of his nose and pooled on the forearm stretched out near his face. Mayme reached over and held his head in her gloved hands and looked into his bleary eyes. "Too-ra-loo-ral," she sang, sweetly and low, the Irish lullaby she remembered from her own childhood, her mother's voice soothing her fears of the dark.

Joe moved up beside her just as she finished crooning her lullaby, the last note merely a soft whisper of breath. She moved back to her position, left Webb to drift off to sleep, and prayed he would wake, that he would live to hold that baby and love his wife for years to come.

"Hi, Webb," Dr. Stern said, "we're gonna get that bullet out of you now."

Webb blinked slowly, and Joe nodded urgently to Doc Moody to begin the ether drip as Mayme slapped a probe into his hands, predicting his need to first take a look at the mess he had to deal with.

"Take care of my family," Webb whispered to Joe, his voice dry as dust.

Just as Moody placed the mask over the man's face and Joe pulled the gauze back from the wound, Webb released a loud gurgling sound, as if his lungs drained of fluid and air in one gush. Mayme looked to his face where his eyes had rolled up to the right and fixed there as if he had caught a glimpse of something so grand he dared not blink for fear of losing sight of it. He was dead.

"He's gone," Mayme said, turning her face away for only a breath, a half second to gain her composure, to realize once again her prayers were not answered, at least not to her liking.

Joe reached over and placed his fingers on the man's throat, then quickly moved to the foot of the bed and placed his hands along the base of his sternum and pressed down hard, his hands working to resuscitate the man, to force air into his lungs. "Breathe," he whispered, but the body refused to obey.

"He's gone," Doc Moody said.

168

Joe continued to work, unwilling to accept what the older doctor and Mayme already knew. Nothing worked. Finally, with two fingers, he closed Webb's eyes, then took two steps backward away from the table but did not yet turn away.

Mayme looked to where Nurse Daniels was standing in the hallway, watching through the small window above the double doors. She slowly shook her head to let the older nurse know to move on. Webb would be removed and Deputy Freddy Edmondson brought in to take his place under the bright light.

Jonas. Webb had named his boy Jonas.

By midnight, one officer was dead and one was in critical condition. There was not a badge within five hundred miles that wasn't out looking for the sorry bastards that did this to two of their own. Other men, farmers and mill workers, eager to play a part in the manhunt, armed with service-issue revolvers and hunting rifles, would sign up to serve as temporary deputies. These were their boys and no cash reward mattered as much as the satisfaction of punishing those that hurt their own.

"Nice work, son," Doc Moody said, placing a warm hand on Joe's back before heading down the stairs to go home, heavy footed and weary.

Mayme smiled at her old friend, knowing this day had been rougher on him than usual. He was getting too old for such long hours on his feet, even if it was just managing the flow of ether. "Good night, Doc," she said.

It was just the two of them now in the scrub room. "Guess the Lord has His ways, giving you another face shot so soon," Mayme said. She had pulled off her soiled apron and was busy placing the contaminated scalpels and probes into the large sterilizer just outside the operating room door. Many of the utensils had been cleaned in the smaller device during the surgery, ready to be used a second time during the long procedure.

"This one was actually far less challenging than Dwight's, poor man. He should heal up nicely." The face that flashed through both their minds had healed in a ghoulish manner, his features twisted into a strained permanent half grin, but he could eat solid food, and his wife really didn't seem to care that her husband had a face that would frighten small children.

Joe moved to the basin and let the water run freely, scooping up handfuls to splash on his face. He dragged his wet fingers through his hair, tucking the loose strands behind his ears. "I need a haircut," he muttered to himself.

"Hmmmm, maybe so," Mayme said, her attention on other matters, her mood somber. She glanced over at him standing there in the doorway and forced a smile and a bit of humor. "You need more than one cut - you need a whole crop of that sheared." She turned the dial on the sterilizer and gathered up the soiled drape from the utensil cart, tossing it in the laundry bag filled with bloody sheets and napkins. Housekeeping would be busy tomorrow.

The hospital was quiet. All the patients on the main ward were sleeping for a change. There was an extra nurse on duty sitting at the small desk reviewing charts. Mayme realized Mrs. Daniels must have called in extra help from the Muskogee registry during the surgery because Mayme didn't know the woman. Judith Goley, the nurse Mayme expected to see manning the desk, sat with Freddy Edmondson in a separate room alone, making sure he stayed calm as the ether left his body and a steady supply of morphine took over. He would need to remain sedated for several days while his wounds began to heal.

"You need a ride home?" Joe asked as they made their way down the stairway.

"No, I got the truck. Besides, I'm on until three. I came in early so I could work a twelve and be done by three. Judith was going to cover the next twelve. I wanted to . . ." Her voice trailed off, both of them knowing what she had planned.

"Let's sit and have a cup of coffee," he suggested.

"Sure." One of the things they knew they could count on after a night like this was that a pot of coffee would be waiting for them in the kitchen when they were done with their duties. It might need to be heated up on the stove, but it would be perked. Mrs. Daniels was good about those little things.

They sat on the front porch and let the cool night air wash over them, neither of them speaking for at least five minutes. Mayme sipped on a cup of lukewarm coffee, and Joe sipped on a bit of brandy from the flask he kept in a small cupboard in the doctor's workroom.

"Did you hear what Webb said?" he asked, breaking the silence.

"To take care of his family?"

"Yeah. I keep thinking about that. What on earth could I ever do for his family?" He tilted his head back to drain the flask and wiped his mouth with the back of his hand.

"You were the one there to hear it, but it was really for everyone. He was just thinking of Lily and Jonas, his little boy, not who he was asking." She reached over and patted his knee but kept her gaze fixed on a divided moon, half dark, half light. Jonas wouldn't have a daddy; no one could fix that. Even if Lily got another husband, he wouldn't be his daddy, and it would never be the same as the one who made him.

"Still, I was the one to hear it. I want to do something for the family. Should I give them some money? Do you think that would be okay?"

Mayme felt a warm burn deep in her belly. She loved this man sitting beside her. Most surgeons wouldn't have even remembered a dying man's words, let alone take them to heart.

"That would probably be welcome. Nobody has two cents extra these days."

"I do."

She turned to look at him but knew he'd be staring at the stars, seeing something beyond her view.

171

"It was very touching," Joe said.

"What's that?"

"The way you sang to him."

"He looked so scared, just seemed like the thing to do."

"Well, it was a moment I'll never forget."

Mayme felt her cheeks warm and an unexpected lump in her throat. It wasn't that he liked what she did, but he saw it, and it meant something. It was him feeling something about what she did that affected her so.

"I gotta get back inside," she said and scooted forward in her seat.

"And I need to get a little sleep."

As Mayme turned to go inside, Joe tugged at her hand. He didn't need to utter a word; she followed him willingly into the deep shadows on the side of the house. There, hidden from the eyes of a sleeping town, away from the glow of light that shined through the windows of the hospital, they held each other close.

Joe lifted her chin with two fingers and kissed her mouth, a gentle kiss, soft and sweet, then wrapped her in his long arms and held her tight. Losing a patient was always difficult, but the death of Webb Reece hit both Mayme and Joe in a soft spot, a place they didn't let many see. He kissed her lightly on the lips, the forehead, each cheek, then on the lips a final time.

"Well, ain't that somethin'?" a voice said from the shadows behind Mayme's old truck. "Night time sho brings out the secret sides a folks."

The lovers parted, but Joe never let go of Mayme, pulling her by the waist to move her back behind him before speaking. "Who's there?" he asked. "Show yourself, please."

From the black wall of shrubs and vines that stretched along the driveway emerged two men. They moved slowly and kept their distance, but Mayme was sure, by the sound of the voice, a nasal drawl filled with hungry spite, that they were from out in the hill country

172

somewhere. She also recognized their shuffling stance, hunched over and menacing, like scared dogs that would tear your throat out in a heartbeat. The shorter one carried a long rifle, cradled in his arms like a baby. Though the bigger man didn't seem to have a weapon, Mayme had no doubt that at least one revolver was tucked down in his pants or strapped to his chest, on the ready in case he needed to shoot anyone that he deemed worthy of shooting.

"Evenin', Miss Mayme."

The voice was familiar, and he was no stranger if he knew her by name.

"That you, Luther?" she asked, recognizing the self-proclaimed mayor of Cookson.

"The one and only." He stepped closer and his friend followed along.

"Hey, Skeeter," Mayme said, now recognizing the shorter fellow, too. "How's Junie and the baby?" It hadn't been so many months ago that she'd made her way to their small cabin deep in the woods near Cookson to help his wife deliver her little girl.

"They alright," he muttered, his jaw working a mouth full of chaw.

Joe tightened his hold on Mayme's arm as she moved to the side of him, out from under his shelter but still in his grasp.

"Looks like we interrupted a couple of love birds sneakin' around in the night," Luther said, his voice thick with moonshine and a heavy dose of malice. Mayme could feel the slimy toothless grin that she couldn't yet see.

"Do you need something, sir?" Joe asked, his voice cracking slightly, but only Mayme would know that. "Is someone needing a doctor?" As his voice grew stronger, he stood taller and his grip on Mayme loosened, allowing them to stand side by side, together.

"Matter of fact, I was hoping to get Miss Mayme to pay some kin folk a mine a little visit this evenin', but seein's how y'all are thicker'n molasses, yer comb getting' red and all, mebbe the two of yous ought just come together."

Mayme avoided looking over to see Joe's face. She could feel an anxious current flow between them, a dizzy jolt of dread igniting the moment the intruder's words pierced the night, the witness to their indiscretion. The initial wave of shock now exploded into absolute fright at what they might be dragged into. This was not the time to be sneaking off to care for some old rambler with a bullet in him, not with every lawman west of Ft. Smith combing through these hills. And, Mayme knew, whoever needed help more than likely caught that bullet from Webb or Freddy and may have even been the one that got one or both of them in the process.

"Luther, you know I always help when I can, but I'm on duty for a couple more hours still. We been short handed 'round here. It's been a hectic night and I can't just pick up . . ."

"Didn't look to me like you was workin' too hard," he interrupted. "I think you need to go inside and tell 'em you got to get off a little early, and bring that big ol' sack you had witcha last time."

Someone was hurt bad, someone that mattered an awful lot to him. Luther liked to give orders from his sagging porch front; he wouldn't have made the trip to town in the middle of the night himself if it wasn't important. He would have sent one of his kids or some other hungry fool on this errand.

"I can go," Joe said, inching forward. "Leave Mrs. Holloway here, and I'll go."

"No," she snapped, startled at the desperate edge in her voice. "I can go with you; just give me a minute." She gave his hand a squeeze and pulled away.

"Mayme, I can take care of whatever it is," Joe whispered. "I'll be fine. Really."

He reached over and grasped her forearm as if he could convince her with a simple touch. He stood as confident and fearless in his resolve to attend to the unknown injured as if he'd been doing such things his whole life. Mayme swelled with confusion and anxiety at the situation and his odd behavior. He didn't need to protect her; she was in just as much danger here as anywhere, especially now. O.C. was bound to find out now and that was just as frightening as traipsing off to some hovel in the woods to dig a bullet out of some fool. What was she thinking sneaking around in the shadows like they did? Especially right here out in the open? Of course they would have to be caught eventually. She was surprised they hadn't been caught before, all those reckless mornings, slipping into Joe's house through a side door, her white dress gleaming in the moonlight, or her familiar truck sitting on the road nearby. Of course she would be caught. Stitching up a bullet hole wasn't no more risky than what she'd been doing right here in town in front of God and everybody else for the past few months. Of course she would be caught. Of course.

A light breeze tickled the back of her neck and sent a shiver of goose bumps down her arm as she caught a whiff of the men, their unwashed stench smelling worse then even the putrid odor of a nasty wound or loose bowels and vomit she'd spent years building up a tolerance to. She whispered to Joe, "I think with everthin goin' on, it's best if there's both of us out there. Just give me a minute."

"Don't forget that happy juice y'all keep in there," Luther said. "Grab us plenty of that."

"I'll help you get what we need," Joe said.

"No," Luther said, "I think you'd best stay right here and left Miss Mayme do what all she needs to do." He looked at the long-nosed Ford that gleamed in the darkness. "That your automobile there, Doc?"

"Yes."

"Why, ain't that fine lookin'?" He turned to the fellow with the shotgun. "Skeeter," he said, "I believe I'll ride out with the good doctor here, get me a chance to ride in that fancy thang. You follow us in the truck."

175

Skeeter just nodded and spit into the dirt, a glop of brown sputum landing with a splat somewhere near Joe's feet; but Joe didn't flinch or object to Luther's decision to ride in his car. He liked the idea of having his own ride back from wherever they were headed.

In no more than five minutes, Mayme appeared with her famous knitting bag, stuffed to the brim with a half dozen vials of stolen morphine, a syringe case, bandages, gloves, surgical kit and peroxide. "I grabbed what I could," she whispered to Joe. "Told Judith I had an emergency at home, something about O.C.'s mama. Hope she doesn't ask Mama about it."

"How's our patient?"

"Seems to be doing well, sound asleep. Everything is quiet on the floor, so they'll be fine. Good thing Mrs. Daniels got that extra nurse from the registry or I'd really be up the creek. No way I could leave if she wasn't there."

The road wasn't much more than a narrow strip of gravel winding through a tunnel of scrub oak and hickory out to a small clearing on the banks of the Illinois River. Joe drove, desperately trying to keep his car on the crunching scrap of road, his headlights bouncing off the thick vines and foliage scraping up his pretty car. Mayme knew where the dirt road ended, how it widened to a hulled-out square of three small wood-framed cabins and one larger house made of field stone, hand built by Luther and his daddy long before she was born. The small enclave was only about a half mile in from the town of Cookson, named after Luther's granddaddy, who once upon a time had run a post office out of his front door when the area was still Indian Territory. Now, with all the laws and privileges of Oklahoma statehood, there was an actual little town resting on the bank of the crystal clear Illinois, under a bluff two hundred feet high. Luther's clan hadn't ventured far from the area, but the store and post office were now run by the Ballew family while Luther ran a different sort of operation back in the brush.

Even the small cabins were bigger than the old fishing shack out at Horseshoe Bend. They had to be to hold everybody in the family and maybe a cousin or two extra. There was always a couple of skinny kids hanging off the porch watching their mamas smoke cigarettes while they shelled peas or scratched around in some patch of a vegetable garden. It seemed they were always doing something to do with food, yet every single one of them always looked half starved to death.

Mayme'd been out to Luther's place more than a few times in the past couple of years. He lived in the big house and was a bit like the mayor in that neck of the woods. One thing she knew for certain was she didn't want Luther Cookson on the other side of the fence from her. He might be smiling that goofy grin all the while he was patting you on the back, his blue eyes gleaming right into yours while he told you how you made his heart sing, then he'd piss down your leg and knife you in the back when you reached over to wipe it off. Then again, if he liked you, he'd kill or darn near kill anyone that made you miserable. Luther was dangerous in a sweet kinda way.

The boy in the bed was hurt bad. Luther's old wife, Sarah, was busy wiping an endless stream of sweat off his face, kneeling beside his bed, cooing to him like a baby, praying to Jesus.

"Ease his pain, Lord, ease it up right now. In your sweet name, Lord Jesus."

The dirty sheets he lay on were soaked in blood despite the old woman's efforts to bandage up the hole in his side with what looked like it might have been a flour sack or dress at one time. An odd spread of small flowers could be seen in the soak of dark red.

"How's he doin'?" Luther asked the minute they walked in, keeping a distance from the bed, his weight shifting from one foot to the other, his grimy hat held in front of him like a shield.

"Not so good, not so good," Sarah sighed, her withered face drawn in sorrow, pushing herself up to her feet as she

177

spoke. An old apron worn over her faded dress was smeared and splattered with blood and vomit and specks of flour from her afternoon biscuit making. "He hurts real bad."

Joe went right to the injured man, his bold approach enough to send Sarah skittering off to stand with her husband, wiping her blood stained fingers in the dirty apron. While Joe began his assessment, Mayme pulled her knitting sack open and went right to work preparing a syringe of morphine. She could at least ease his pain and allow Joe to take a good look at the wound, figure out what they should do for the man.

Within seconds of the needle going into his vein, the strained look of agony relaxed and his eyes closed, his thin body exhausted from the struggle of the past few hours and weakened from the loss of blood. Mayme quickly removed the dirty makeshift bandages and cleansed the area with the clean gauze and peroxide she'd carried in her bag.

"Who is this?" she asked, looking to Sarah for an answer. "I don't recognize him from around here."

"My cousin, Leroy," Sarah answered nervously. "He's stayin' with us for a spell. We grow'd up together over in Vian." Her chin quivered slightly as she spoke, but she didn't look away.

From the top of the stairs a child coughed. Three skinny kids, a girl and two boys, a trio of dirty ragged nightshirts, sat hunched like nervous crows, their eyes fixed on the bleeding man on the table, their uncle, the one who had just yesterday whittled the boys a sling shot and a little doll for the girl.

"You kids get to bed!" Sarah ordered. "Rhat now, I tell you. Don't make me get my switch." She started toward them, her right hand reaching out toward a willow branch hanging on the wall.

With that, the three of them scampered away, pushing each other ahead, tripping on the stairs and over their own dirty feet. Mayme had no doubt they'd be back before long or at least find another way to spy on the gruesome activity going on in their kitchen. She wondered briefly if they'd had any supper with their momma so busy tending to her cousin.

"How'd this happen?" Joe asked, rolling up his sleeves before pulling on the gloves Mayme had known he'd need no matter what the situation was.

As soon as he spoke, Mayme raised her eyebrows and shot him a look of warning, shaking her head slightly. The one thing she'd learned over the years was to do what she could, but leave the questions for other folks. That wasn't her job, not Joe's either.

"Jes a lil huntin' accident," Luther muttered.

"Can you bring that light closer over here?" he asked Mayme. "I need as much light as possible, so you're going to have to hold it, lean it in."

Joe grimaced and looked around the room, finally taking in the area he had to work with, a lesson he'd learned from Mayme out at Horseshoe Bend. He wiped the oozing blood and examined the wound, pulling the body toward him to see if there was an exit wound. There wasn't. The bullet was lodged in there somewhere.

"Abdominal trauma," he said, reciting his findings aloud, his clinical practice. "Gunshot wound to the upper abdomen." He looked to Mayme, briefly, then to the worried family members. "He really needs to be in the hospital for treatment. He needs proper surgery to get that bullet out and repair whatever internal damage was caused by the perforation."

The puzzled look on Sarah's face made it clear that she didn't quite understand. "His insides are shot up, they need to be fixed," he explained in more simple language, "and he needs to be in the hospital, where it's clean. The germs in this room alone could kill him with this open wound."

"No hospital," Luther said sternly. "You fix him here or not at all." He reached for a half full jar of clear liquid sitting on the kitchen table and took a big swallow from it,

179

letting a bit dribble down his chin, not bothering to wipe it away. His still was famous in these parts. The liquid sloshed over the edge when he slammed it down on the table.

Mayme and Joe exchanged a familiar look of anxious worry, nothing more than a flash of eyes, a slight nod of the chin, but there was no mistaking that not at all was not an option they could choose. They could not simply say no to these folks and head back to town.

"We'll do what we can," Mayme answered.

"You fix him up and I'll ferget what I saw over there in the bushes 'hind the hospital."

Mayme ignored his threat. There was work to be done and the sooner they tended to it, the sooner they could be headed home.

"Luther," she said, "I need you to boil me up a big pot of water and light the baking oven. Can you do that? Or let Sarah do it and you hold the lamp in close."

She looked from one to the other, not sure which one would fare better watching her and Joe dig around in their cousin's belly. It wasn't easy to see someone's guts opened up, let alone someone you care about. "Someone has to hold this light."

"I'll do the water," Luther said, "Sarah'll do jes fine with the lamp there."

While Luther Cookson filled a soup pot with water, Sarah held the lamp over the patient while Mayme cut the remnants of Leroy's filthy clothes off him. She couldn't help but notice how Sarah turned her eyes away from the sight of her cousin laying there naked, his limp penis stained with his splattered blood. She then pulled the soiled sheet out from under him and motioned for Joe to hold him up so that she could spread a clean one in its place.

The first order of business was to douse the wound thoroughly with peroxide hoping to create the most sterile field possible in the dirty room. A couple of clean sheets and peroxide was all she had to work with, but she'd done more in worse conditions with less.

"When you get that water going, I need a couple of small pans full over here," she said, knowing she'd need a makeshift wash basin for instruments to kill a few germs and keep the scalpels and forceps clean during their procedure. "If you got any salt, pour some in there." Mayme looked around the room, carefully considering what was available. "And bring me that ironing board." She looked at Joe and explained. "Instrument table." And though he didn't say anything, she could tell by a twitch of his left eyebrow and the tilt of his jaw that he was impressed with her improvisation skills. From her knitting sack, she removed an array of surgical tools, fresh from the sterilizer, and a small bottle of chloroform. Her gut had told her they'd be needing more than a suture kit if Luther himself had come for them. Ether would have been better, but the chloroform was handy. It would do in a pinch.

Joe leaned in for a closer examination of the wound, considering the best approach for dealing with the injury in such primitive surrounds. He nudged Sarah's arm, urging her to remove the flicker of shadow from her head. She followed his unspoken command as though she'd been assisting in surgery all her life.

"It would sure be better if this was the middle of the day," he said to himself as much as anyone else. "This lighting is not good, not good at all."

After dosing their patient with a bit of chloroform, Mayme took her place next to Joe. She slapped the scalpel firmly into his outstretched palm. He made a clean incision to extend the opening in the flesh, then wiped away the seeping blood while Mayme clamped off a bleeder. Using a long probe, he pulled back the torn flesh to see the extent of damage inside.

"Missed the spleen at least," he muttered, still talking to himself. "Looks like it's lodged in the stomach."

The room smelled bad, like an old rag had been left in the corner to rot. The stench of Leroy's lacerated stomach

181

only made the matter worse. Joe and Mayme didn't seem to notice, but Luther sure did. "Good God, what's that stink? Did Leroy shat himself?"

"Not exactly," Joe said, never lifting his face to see Luther covering his nose with a dirty handkerchief. "It seems the bullet entered his stomach. None of us smell too good on the inside."

Joe didn't elaborate on the source of that smell, the leaking bile, a green ooze that would work to kill much of the bacteria that lived in the belly. The pain and trauma had induced vomiting that emptied most of Leroy's belly, but there was still the remnants of his morning meal, half chewed meat of some kind and lumps of corn kernels that had not had time to work their way into the intestine.

"Well, I'll be waiting outside," Luther said as he refilled the pot of water for the cool pan Mayme'd asked for.

"Don't wander far," Mayme said, her voice thick with the sound of the hill folk, taking on the speech patterns of those she spoke to, as if she spoke a host of languages. "If'n we need somethin', you gonna have to fetch it. You keep to the front porch where's you can hear me if I holler. Ye hear?"

Luther was never needed. The wounds were messy, but Joe and Mayme were able to do a fairly decent job of removing from Leroy's stomach a lump of lead that had more than likely come from a .45, probably from a good distance or the damage would have been far worse than it was. There wasn't a doubt in Mayme's mind that old Leroy had been in the same battle as Webb Reece and Freddy Edmondson, just on the other side of the shooting. Luckily, he was new in these parts so no one would be looking for him in particular. It was the likes of Troy Love, Ford Bradshaw and Jim Benge the law was after. They were well known in these parts for their meanness, though not as famous as Charley to the rest of the world. This fellow stretched out on the bed was just Leroy Nobody, some old relation to Luther and Sarah.

182

They cleaned him up as best they could under such dire conditions, rinsing the wound with saline, cleaning instruments in salt water, and finally stitching up the torn tissue with catgut sutures. The sun was creeping up by the time Mayme taped a large gauze bandage over Leroy's abdomen and chest. It was still dark out, but more purple then black. Leroy moaned in pain when she pressed the tape into his ribs, so she gave him another injection.

"I wish you'd let us take him down the hill," she said to Sarah. "He's gonna hurt like hell when he wakes up. And the risk of infection is too high in here. He needs to be in the hospital where it's clean and someone can watch over him."

Luther had returned to the make-shift operating room at some point during the night and seemed to be sleeping in his chair, his dirty boots resting on a small stool in front of him. "Tha's why y'all gonna leave me some of that happy juice here. Sarah can stick a needle in his butt just as good as you can. And she can watch him too."

"Luther," Mayme said, "I'll leave you a little hooch if that's what you want, but let us take Leroy back with us. Please. He'll die if we leave him here."

"You take him to that hospital, he's good as dead. You know that, Mayme Holloway. And you wouldn't do so well neither." He leaned over and spit in an old iron pot next to his chair.

He was right. Back in Tahlequah, there was a dead deputy and one in serious condition. Anyone showing up with a gunshot wound would be suspect, especially one that had to be treated out in the middle of nowhere. There would be questions, lots of questions, for Leroy, for her, for Joe. Luther was right. There was no way this man could go to the hospital.

"What if I took him to my house?" Joe offered. "I could set him up in that downstairs bedroom. At least he'd be close."

"Joe, you can't do that," Mayme said. "If you got caught, you'd go to jail or worse."

"What's the difference between treating this patient in the woods or in the office. We'd go to jail for this, too." He swung his arm in an expansive gesture, a wide sweep of the room.

Mayme stood speechless, exhausted. If she'd come out here alone, she'd just leave Leroy and hope for the best. She would never have considered taking him to the hospital before. Why, she wondered, was she worried about this man? Why should they jeopardize their own lives and careers over some hillbilly with a gun? She was changing.

"But he'd be by himself when we're at the hospital. What if there was a problem and we weren't there?"

Joe considered the situation. "Like Luther said, Sarah can stick a needle in his butt as well as you can. I propose that Sarah come too. You can show her what to do when we're not there."

"It's dangerous," she said, looking from Joe to Sarah, whose eyes grew wide with fright or excitement, Mayme wasn't sure which. "But I think we could make it work. What do you say, Sarah? Want to be a nurse for a couple of days?"

Sarah first looked to Luther for approval. Poor thing, Mayme thought, she's just as tired as me and Joe, but she'd work harder if she stayed here tending to Luther and however many kids was sleeping somewhere. She hadn't seen any children since Sarah had shooed them off to bed, but she knew there was a grip of them lurking about the place spying on the family drama. She could feel their curious eyes on her.

Luther spit again. "Hell," he muttered, "it's just Leroy, Sister, but tell you the truth, I don't want the law finding his bleeding soul in my house." He dropped his feet to the floor and stood. "I'll get Skeeter to hep ya carry him out to yer car." He shuffled out the front door without ever looking at his wife.

Joe had grimaced a little at the mention of his car. "I'll stretch a blanket out over the back seat," Mayme said quietly, "in case he starts bleeding again."

Luther and Skeeter walked into the house just as Mayme was packing up her knitting sack. "Mayme, I'd like to remind you that you was gonna leave me a little something."

Mayme considered arguing with him. He wouldn't have the faintest idea how to load up a syringe and give an injection. Morphine wasn't the easiest thing for her to get her hands on, not with Mrs. Daniels keeping that log in the drug room. But, she decided, she didn't want to push her luck with this one. He had the goods to hurt her in more ways than she wanted to think of, not the least of which was witnessing her and Joe in a compromising position. She pulled out the remaining vials of morphine, three of them, and left two next to the nearly empty bottle of shine, saving one for any emergency on the ride home. "That's not easy to come by," she said.

The ride back to town was easier by the light of day, even pretty, as the car wrapped around the cliffs above the flowing Illinois, a ribbon of dark green water that cut through limestone rock. Just beyond the dramatic ledge of bluffs, the fancy car inched along the gravel road through a dense growth of hickory, the driver trying to make the ride as smooth as possible for the groaning man in the backseat. Sarah held his head in her lap and cooed gently for him to hush, to sleep, offered more simple prayers to Jesus for his healing.

Once they hit the main road, Joe was able to pick up speed. The sun was rising higher, which meant the town was awake and moving about. Just getting Leroy into the house unseen was the next challenge for them. At the sight of a fast-moving car approaching, Mayme motioned for Sarah to duck down. The sight of the patrol car heading in the very direction from which they'd come caused Mayme's heart to leap into her throat and the fine hair on her arms stood on end. The driver of the car was none other than Grover Bishop, and even though the cars were moving, she was sure he'd seen her sitting next to Joe.

"Lawsy," she said, "that could 'a gone south in a hurry."

Joe looked to her, his eyes narrowed in concern. "You don't think they're looking for him, do you?"

"Naw, he's a nobody." She glanced back to Sarah, still scrunched in the corner. "Sorry, Sarah. But you know what I mean, so far as the law goes, they ain't lookin' for the likes of Leroy here. They's lookin for Charley Floyd or Ford Bradshaw, bigger notches on their belts."

"They sometimes come up to the house lookin' for folks," Sarah said, her voice weak with exhaustion and worry.

"Let's not fret about that now," Mayme assured her. "Let's just take care of Leroy for now."

Her words consoled Sarah, but her own thoughts raced in panic. Just half an hour longer and she and Joe would have been there when the sheriff arrived, if that's where he was headed. She never meant for Joe to get involved in this kind of mess; he couldn't risk it. Of course, she reminded herself, they'd been forced out there. They never would have been there if Luther hadn't caught them with their lips locked together. They had to be more careful about that, too. And now, Lord Almighty, they had Leroy here bleeding in the back seat.

Joe pulled the car right up to the back door, driving right over a patch of zinnias that were struggling in their final days, summer at an end.

"We need a gurney," Mayme said.

"I have a stretcher," Joe offered, searching his mind for where he'd stored the thing. "It was one of my father's, a war souvenir. Just wait here, I'll go get it."

Joe returned with a military field stretcher, a worn dark green canvas stretched between two poles.

"That'll do her," Mayme said. "Sarah, you take one end and I'll take one end, and we'll let Joe here lift him

186

outta the car." She pressed her lips together in a line of worry, then sucked in a long breath through clenched teeth as she considered their plight. "Sho' wish we had one more person. Getting him from that backseat to this litter ain't gonna be easy."

From the side of the old house, there was the sound of footsteps and an all too familiar voice sounding more then a little sheepish. "I can help."

"O.C.," Mayme gasped, "what in tarnation are you doing skulkin' around in Dr. Stern's bushes?" She was frantic with thoughts of him being there on other mornings, hiding in the shadows, watching her sneak into her lover's house where she would sometimes linger for hours, long after she should have been home from even the longest hospital duty shift.

"I was worried when you didn't come home, so I was gonna go up to the hospital and check on you. I was bringing you some dinner yesterday when they brought those boys in and knew it was bad. Anyways, you had the truck so I was walking and saw you in the car there. What's going on here?"

Joe stepped around the car, his lean face a knot of worry. "Let's do this inside," he whispered, urging them to stop talking and get moving. "O.C., you take one end there with Sarah. Mayme and I will lift him out."

"Seems like I should be the one to help you, Doc," O.C. offered. "Mayme's such a bitty little thing."

Mayme rolled her eyes and opened her mouth as if to speak, but it wasn't necessary. Joe handled it.

"Don't worry; we're used to lifting patients, and I need you holding that litter up when we get him on there." He looked at the barber's clean round face, a blank slate of fear suddenly visible.

"He's bleedin'," O.C. said, his mouth stretched in a grim line of disgust and terror. He ducked his head and peered up at the three anxious faces from beneath the brim of his grey hat, the right side tilted downward ever so slightly, a careful placement before the mirror.

187

"Yessir, he is. So we need to get him inside. Quickly."
Joe's brown eyes roamed the empty street before opening
the car door.

"Is he gonna die?"

"That's what we're trying to prevent. Can you take
one end there? Help Sarah." Joe motioned with a nod of
his head to where Sarah stood holding two poles in her
rough hands, the other end resting on the ground.

O.C. nodded and picked up the poles, looking like he
might faint.

"O.C." Mayme said, "you're gonna have to hold him up
now. You hearin' me?" She knew how he hated blood and
sick people, and she hated having to put her trust in him
for this, but there was no other way. "O.C., get a grip," she
growled, a tone he'd only heard her use a time or two
before. "This is serious."

O.C. stood straighter, his grip visibly stronger, but he
looked away from the car, away from the injured man, his
gaze directed off to the odd-shaped crepe myrtle tree out
back. The branches on the east side had been trimmed off
by Mrs. Hardy in an attempt to give her tomatoes more
sunlight. The tree now grew lopsided, a wealth of pink
blossoms on one side, a flat line on the other.

With extreme care, Joe entered the side of the car
where Leroy's head rested. Beads of sweat covered his
white face, and the gauze bandage was soaked in blood,
but it didn't appear to be severe. He reached under Leroy's
shoulder blades while Mayme grabbed him by the legs
from the other side of the car.

"Let's first scoot him down so that his butt is on the
edge of the seat," she suggested.

Joe slowly and as gently as possible lifted the top half
of the man while Mayme guided the lower half down as
gently as they could. Leroy groaned loudly.

"O.C., move that stretcher right next to me," she
ordered. "Right here."

"I think we should change sides now," Joe said. "Let me lift him out. And you'll fit in here with him better then me."

Mayme nodded and they moved around, switching sides without speaking. In less than a minute they had Leroy on the old Army stretcher and carried in through the back door.

"In here," Joe said, leading the way to a small bedroom downstairs, beneath the kitchen stairs.

Mayme followed O.C. and Sarah through the narrow doorway, her stomach flipping and rolling like a small boat in a tornado when she spied the familiar bed of squeaky springs. More than one early dawn she and Joe had not made it up the stairs and found themselves stretched out on the old single bed, a remnant from Odette Jackson, Mrs. Hardy's live-in maid, a thin mattress on top of a bed of rusted coils. Odette still came and cleaned for the new doctor on Tuesdays, but he didn't want her living there, so the bed went mostly unused. She'd been there recently; the room was neat as a pin, the bed made up nicer then she and Joe ever would have bothered.

Leroy moaned even louder as they lifted him off the stretcher, no doubt feeling the pull on his incision, the burn of the hole in his stomach returning. He needed another injection soon or the pain would be unbearable.

"Help him, Lord," Sarah muttered, her face drawn in a line of sorrow.

"Sarah, just sit with him here for a minute," Joe said softly, pulling a straight back chair close to the bed. "Mrs. Holloway and I will just gather some supplies and then get him a bit more comfortable." He looked to Mayme, his eyes narrowed in concern. "He needs an infusion; I have a couple of bottles of Ringer's and a pole, but I'll need to get more from the hospital. And some more morphine."

Mayme nodded but didn't speak as she watched O.C. bend down and pick up a white hairpin from the floor. One of hers, she knew, and not from this morning. She needed him to be gone, away from the house, away from

Joe, just gone. It was wrong, him being there. She couldn't work with his presence filling up the room.

"O.C., shouldn't you be getting on to work," she said. "And what are you doin' here anyway."

"I was going to see you," he said again. He moved away from Sarah's earshot and took Mayme by the forearm, and pulled her close to him in unusual forcefulness. "I need to talk to you," he whispered. "It's important."

"Well, can't it wait?" She pulled her arm free and began making her way behind Joe, only to find O.C. dogging her every footstep. "I'll be home in a few minutes. Call me on the telephone." This was so unlike him, she thought, pushing himself onto any scene like this. What does he know? If he knew about her and Joe, surely he wouldn't be in the man's house, grinning like a first-class idiot.

"I can't talk about it on the telephone. That Angalene Baker might be listening in." He spoke in a hoarse whisper that seemed louder than his normal voice. "Grover Bishop come to the shop yesterday."

The sound of Grover Bishop's name stopped her in her tracks. "Just give me a minute, Dr. Stern," she said. "I'll be right there." She led O.C. out the back door, stopping him on the porch. "What'd Bishop want?"

O.C. pulled his hat off his head and wiped his forehead with a white handkerchief he pulled from his inside coat pocket. "He kept ratchin' on about that nurse and doctor that went to jail for treatin' John Dillinger, said you should think about that. I think he might be talkin' bout the time you helped Charley. He might be tryin' to get Charley by gettin' you."

Mayme never ceased to be amazed at O.C.'s endless innocence, or ignorance, she wasn't sure which sometimes. He had just helped to carry a man who'd been gut shot into the doctor's house, not the hospital, but a small bedroom off a kitchen, and he was thinking the sheriff was interested in her treating Charley Floyd for a case of the clap more than three months ago. It didn't even make sense to come up with that notion, but his blinders were on tighter than a fat man's britches. She couldn't begin to guess what he'd think or do if he knew the half of her adventures, not the least of which was carrying on with Joe, doing things he'd never imagined.

"Don't you worry about Charley none," she said. "Bishop's just running circles trying to catch those boys that shot Susie Sharp. And you and I both know Charley didn't have nothin' to do with that. They say it's Troy Love, and I ain't seen hide nor hair of that piece of work, so just go on to the shop and quit worryin' 'bout this stuff. I'll see you tonight." She stretched up onto her tiptoes and kissed his clean-smelling cheek and nudged him on.

O.C. nodded once and put his hat back on, ready to face his day of making folks look good. "You best get some rest, darlin'; you look a little peaked around the edges there."

Mayme closed the door behind her and let her eyes close for one second. She looked peaked? Lord Almighty, she'd tended to three men with bullets in them in the last fourteen hours, been on her feet most of that time, watched one of them die. A freight train of work and worry pounded through her veins; her head felt like it could split open and her empty belly howled for food. Feeling faint and almost too tired to breathe, she didn't know if she should laugh or cry or just fall down where she stood and sleep for a month of Sundays. She took a deep breath and followed Joe into his office.

It was handy having a well-stocked medical office attached to the house. Joe had a surplus of bandages, antiseptic soap and surgical instruments for the minor injuries he tended there and carried with him out to the children's home.

"Let's get some fluid in him," Joe said, "and really clean that wound and put a fresh bandage on him for now, but he needs a drainage tube."

191

Mayme nodded and carried peroxide, Ringer's solution, a handful of gauze and surgical tape while Joe collected an infusion kit and a tall metal pole to hold the bottle of clear liquid that would keep the man hydrated. He opened his mouth wide and let out a loud lion-roaring yawn. "I need to go to the hospital," he said, "check on the deputy and get that tube."

"You need to sleep," Mayme answered. "You can't see patients today. And you need to eat something."

"I'm okay," he said. "That's why they nearly kill you in medical school. I can go for a week on a couple hours sleep."

She smiled a faint smile of encouragement. "I don't go in until six tonight. Want me to stay here with Sarah? I could sleep upstairs and be here if she needed anything. You could at least catch some sleep without being disturbed." She smiled at him, knowing he would refuse to sleep. "Just a couple of hours at least."

"What about O.C.?"

"He'll be at the shop all day. I need to talk to him, but I can call him and say I'm staying here today. After what he saw this morning, he won't think nothing of it. In fact, he won't want to know anymore than he does already."

"Why was he here?" For the first time, it seemed as if he realized the troubling implication of Mayme's husband showing up on his doorstep in the wee hours of the morning. Any other morning such an appearance could have been disastrous. Today it had only been unfortunate.

Mayme told him about Grover Bishop's visit to O.C.'s shop.

"He knows something," she explained, the story taking on more significance with the telling. She nodded her head fiercely as she spoke, as though she was talking to herself more than anyone else, agreeing with her runaway imagination. "We can't be too careful right now, Joe. First, old Luther spying on us last night, then O.C. popping in out of the blue like that. Let's just pray no one saw us haulin' Leroy into the house. Or me coming and going here before sun up every day. What were we thinking?" she asked herself as much as Joe.

Joe didn't react to Mayme's avalanche of panic and dread. His calm demeanor remained as passive as though they'd just come in from nothing more than a morning stroll or tending to a regular patient in his office.

"Don't panic," he warned her. "I learned long ago that the first step to failing is to panic, and I have no intention of failing now, or ever. Stay calm and it will be fine. Trust me."

Mayme nodded, but the weight of worry still felt like it might suffocate her.

"If you could stick around here for a while, that would probably be a good idea," Joe said with a yawn as he pushed through the white painted door that led back to his kitchen.

Mayme couldn't help but feel an initial twinge of exasperation at Joe's calm. She was a bundle of nerves, nearly delirious with exhaustion, and there he was just as cool as a cucumber. As she watched him, noticing the slight slump of his shoulders, the dark circles under his eyes, his shirt stained and dirty, she was reminded how tired he must be after so many hours in surgery, so much commotion and excitement. He was just doing what he had to do to get through the day. Mayme didn't want to add her problems to the rest of the burden he carried, but she wanted him to understand how dangerous things were getting. Even though he wasn't the one caught in a marriage that felt like sticky syrup running down her back, her being married would cause him trouble if they were found out. And even though they weren't the ones who robbed a bank or shot a deputy, they would both be punished for caring for those that did.

Much of the trouble they were in was her own doing, and she needed to be the one to bear the responsibility if things went south on them. This man, she thought, put everything at risk for her. If Charley Floyd hadn't been pissing fire, she would never have knocked on his door looking for Protargol, and he'd be treating pinworms at the children's home right now, not hiding a cop killer in his bedroom. Lawsy, she had a way of messing up good peoples' lives without even trying.

Mayme nudged Joe with her shoulder and offered her own plan for the morning. "Why don't I tend to Leroy and you go take a hot bath. You know I'm not half bad with a needle and thread if he ripped a stitch or two along the way. And when I'm done with Leroy, I could rustle us up some eggs; I don't know about you, but I'm half starved to death, and I know Sarah is, too."

"Mayme Holloway," he said wearily, "you're not half bad with everything you do and yes, I'm as you say, half starved to death too."

Before moving another inch, he leaned over and kissed her on the mouth, a friendly kiss, mouths closed, both of their arms occupied with bundles of medical supplies.

"This was where it all started," he whispered, looking around the room where they had first come together not so many months before. He laid his armload of goods on the table, then pulled her toward him, taking the bottle of Ringer's and bandages from her hands. He wrapped an arm around her waist and pulled her close, resting his cheek on the top of her head. "This is all the rest I need, right here."

Mayme could hear his heart beating through his stained shirt, a steady rhythm of comfort. She had come to love the smell of his sweat and the taste of his skin more then she thought possible. She wanted to stay here, to be hidden away for a few hours where no one could find her. Sleeping in Joe's bed, even alone, seemed less frightening then going home to her own house where she would be alone with her shame and fears, where she could be found.

"Go on," she finally said, pulling away from his embrace, looking over her shoulder to assure herself that no one was spying on them again. "Go take a bath; leave this." She pointed to the gauze and antiseptic splayed out on the table. "I'll take care of Leroy and fix us all a bite to eat. While I'm at it, I'll give Miss Sarah there some lessons on taking care of Leroy and fix her up with a nice comfy chair so she can doze a little too."

"I'm glad you're staying here today," he said. "After breakfast, you go upstairs and get some rest. I don't want you staying down here taking care of Leroy all day. I want you to sleep."

"You know I will."

It was nice to have someone worrying after her well-being, telling her to sleep and rest. She hoped that at some point in the day Joe would join her for a short nap. The thought of lying curled up next to him, even for a few stolen moments, satisfied another kind of hunger, one she couldn't quite get her fill of, no matter the risk. Only later, when she was alone, would she allow herself to sink into the certainty of a windstorm of trouble that was blowing her way. She didn't need Mama Holloway for this forecast; it rumbled deep in her gut and bristled the fine hairs on her forearms. She was scared.

13.

It was a slow day at the Normal Club Barber Shop. O.C. hung out his "Closed for Lunch" sign and headed next door to Maudie Owens' Café for a ham and cheese sandwich, a tall glass of sweet tea and hopefully a slice of cherry pie, if it was fresh baked. He was just locking the door behind him, humming a happy tune of his own making, when he heard the angry growl of tires skidding around the corner. He edged closer to the side of the road to see the Sheriff's car screeching to a stop in front of Reed Culver Funeral Home.

"What in tarnation?" he muttered as he scrutinized the gruesome sight before him. Were his eyes playing tricks on him again?

The trunk of Bishop's car was open and what appeared to be a human leg and a bloody arm dangled out the back end. O.C. shuffled closer for a full view that made his head swoon and his knees grow weak for the second time that day.

Bishop moved fiercely and violently, bursting from the driver's seat like a lion escaping an iron cage. His body jerked and swung with each angry step. Without a moment's hesitation, he yanked the dangling arm and leg of a lifeless man and tossed him effortlessly onto the grassy front of the funeral home. The lump of flesh and bones landed with a loud crack as the brittle bones snapped for a final insult to the body. In one more swift arc of his bulking back, he hoisted out another victim, tossing him

196

alongside his partner. Outlaws Troy Love and Kyle Carlisle were nearly shredded with bullets from Bishop and his deputies, and they were not done yet. They intended to hunt down every man believed responsible for the death of Susie Sharp.

O.C. was still standing on the curb when Jeff Reed and Newt Culver ran out to remove the gruesome sight from the lawn of their establishment. A small crowd had gathered to witness the crude delivery of corpses. Mrs. Brewer stood with her hand over her mouth, pressing her daughter's innocent face into her thigh.

O.C. turned around and returned to the safety of his barbershop. Only then, faced with the aftermath of a manhunt, did it occur to him that the fellow he helped Mayme and that doctor man haul into the doc's house that morning just might be one of them Bishop was looking for. The man sure looked like he'd been shot in the belly. Sweet Lord in Heaven, he prayed, what had his wife got herself mixed up with now? The only thing he could do was ask her and ask her now. She would probably be home sleeping, but this was one time he would interrupt her slumber. If what he just witnessed was the fate of them that Grover had in his sights, she was in more trouble then she realized.

Again, O.C. locked the door behind him, but this time he turned right and headed home instead of to Maudie's. A half block from his little house, his heart skipped three beats and his feet nearly stumbled at the sight of the patrol car out front and Grover Bishop standing on his doorstep, pounding on the door.

"Well, hey there, Sheriff, is there somethin' I can do for you?" His voice sounded shrill and high in the still afternoon air.

"Where's Mayme?" he asked as O.C. joined him on the narrow porch. The big man's square face was drawn tighter than the gun belt around his waist.

"Why, she's inside sleeping. She's been working the night shift lately." He bent down and picked up two stray bobby pins, the white ones Mayme used to hold her cap in place, just like the one he'd picked up at the doc's place that very morning. "She's probly dead to the world and can't hear you knocking."

"I need to talk to her."

"Well, can it wait? Calling on her at the noon hour's like rousting me outta bed at midnight. It ain't pleasant." He gave his best Sunday school smile despite the feeling that he'd just swallowed a big gulp of sour milk. There was a dark-colored streak down the front of the deputy's shirt, no doubt a parting gift from the dead men he'd just dumped on Reed's lawn. O.C. thought again of the thud of the lifeless body hitting the earth, the hairy leg flopping out of the trunk of the car. He needed to sit down.

"No. It can't wait. Get her up, O.C."

O.C. didn't offer any further objections. He did as he was told and led Bishop through the front door of their small home.

"Have a seat there," he said, pointing to the comfortable chair his mama loved so well. "I'll just go get her. Gimme a minute."

Even in the darkened room, it was easy to see their unmade bed was empty. Mayme hadn't come home. His mind raced to the wounded man at the doctor's house, and he knew Grover must know something about that old boy. That's how she was, looking out for everybody but her own self. If Bishop found out she'd patched up one of them killers, it would mean a world of hurt for all of them. He closed his eyes and prayed to God that he wouldn't do or say anything to lead the lawman to his wife.

Grover sat impatiently on the edge of the seat, his tall hat clenched by the brim in one hand, his other pressing against his upper thigh as if he had to hold himself down in his seat.

"Well, sir. She apparently got called out on another medical emergency. I seem to recall her saying one of those gals out near Hollow Oak was 'bout ready to hatch one any minute. I don't recall which gal it was, so I don't

198

rightly know where she might be." He scratched his head and shook it back and forth, offering his best look of bewilderment. "You know I don't always listen like I should to everthing she says."

Bishop shoved his hat on his head as he rose to his feet. "Tell Mrs. Holloway I need to talk to her. Today." And without another word or glance, he was out the door and gone.

O.C. bounced on his toes as he peeked out the window, making sure the officer drove away. He then raced out the front door, not even thinking to grab a couple of cookies or a biscuit until he was a block and a half away. He'd have to grab something quick at Maudie's after all. What on earth was Mayme up to, he worried, his legs moving back to the shop as fast as they could. Where was she now? He would call the hospital to see if anyone there knew anything. Or maybe Wilma would know. It was only when he passed through the front door of Maudie's that the jingle of the bells that hung on the doorknob startled him to realize where she was. Why, he thought, she is still at that doctor's house, tending to that young man. She must have needed to sit with him a spell. He smiled at his ability to solve the mystery on his own. Not many men could figure their wives out like he could. Of course, he realized, Mayme wasn't tough to figure. She was just a good old girl who loved nursing folks more than anything. Now if he could just get her to do something with her hair and go to Sunday service with him, their married life would be just about perfect.

"Afternoon, Maudie," he said, flashing a toothy smile to the plump woman behind the counter. "I need a quick sandwich to go. Can you bring it to me next door?" He looked down the counter and took a happy gulp of air. "And a piece of that pie there might be nice."

"Why sho, O.C., anything for you, darlin'. I'll bring it myself." Maudie wiped her pudgy fingers on her stained apron before lifting the clear plastic cover from a half-eaten cherry pie, its lattice top a perfect golden brown.

199

O.C. tipped his hat and scooted toward the door. It was nearly 1:30, and there would be somebody wanting a cut or shave any minute now. His whole lunch hour had been used up by that Grover Bishop.

He couldn't help but release a sigh of relief when he looked out over the street and saw that the bodies were gone from the lawn of the funeral home. The town was once again peaceful and orderly, even shady on the south side of the road. His stomach was roaring mad, but lunch was on its way. Mayme was working too hard, always doing good things for good folks who got themselves into a patch of trouble, and even if they was like Charley, they still had good hearts. Why, life ain't quite so bad as everbody says, he thought. It's all a matter of how you want to look at it. He read the papers and listened to the radio like every other man, but while they moped around about the dust and being hungry, even jumped off buildings, he and Mayme rolled up their sleeves and worked to make the world better, whether it was cutting hair or giving shots. Kinda' like Charley too, he figured. The banks robbed the people, and Charley and them other boys just worked to even things out. Yessir, he reasoned, it all comes out in the wash, one way or another.

He reached down in his pocket for his door key and pulled out the white hairpins he'd gathered that day from the doctor's house and on the porch. He needed to call Mayme and tell her about Bishop, but in a cautious sort of way, in case that Angalene was fishing for some gossip. He let the door close behind him, turned on the lights and dropped the pins on the shelf behind his chair before picking up the telephone.

"Hi, Angalene," he said. "This is O.C., down the barbershop. Can you connect me with that new doctor, Dr. Stern?"

"I'll try, O.C., but I couldn't get another call through there to his house earlier. You might try the hospital." She paused and coughed a short giggle. "I hope he's planning on coming to see you; I saw him the other day, and he's starting to look like a girl with those pretty ringlets."

"Well, maybe I'll offer him a free shave. How 'bout that?"

"Sounds good, O.C. Let me connect you."

His thoughts drifted while Angalene connected the wires. He should have asked Maudie to bring him an iced tea to wash that sandwich down with. The phone rang shrilly in the distance. No one answered.

14.

The light slipped through a narrow gap in the closed curtains. The softness of twilight was disorienting. She had not intended to sleep so long, but her body and mind were equally exhausted by the time she'd crawled into the big bed, laid her head on Joe's chest and closed her eyes. They did not make love. They had simply held each other close, skin to skin. Her handy bag rested on the mahogany highboy and her dirty uniform was draped over the footboard. Joe's blood-stained shirt and trousers lay in a crumpled heap on the floor. She was still naked. Wishing she had a clean dress to put on and a few more hours sleep, Mayme resigned herself to get up and get going.

Downstairs, Sarah sat quietly next to her cousin, her mouth open and eyes closed. Mayme could tell she wasn't sleeping by the rhythmic nodding of her head as though she were keeping time to a quiet melody that played on endlessly in her mind. The door to Joe's office was open and Mayme could hear him in there shuffling through papers, his chair squeaking at every shifting of his weight.

"How's Leroy?" she whispered, interrupting the woman's moment of silent contemplation. It occurred to Mayme that Sarah probably didn't get too many days where she got to just sit and dream in the middle of the afternoon. She wondered what the poor woman dreamed of? What must she think sitting here in this fancy house, so big and empty, all for just one man?

"Oh, Miss Mayme, you're up." She straightened her spine and forced her weary eyes open wide.

"Yes, I guess I slept the day away." She stepped close to the bed, placing her hand gently on Sarah's thin shoulder, keeping her from rising out of the chair, believing this woman had earned every minute of rest she'd ever get for the remainder of her days on this earth.

"Has Leroy been in much pain?" Mayme asked. "I was sure he'd need another dose of morphine and you'd come get me to help even though I knew all along you could handle it." She leaned over, lifted the limp wrist, felt the weak pulse, a little slow, but steady. That was a good sign.

"Dr. Stern give it to him." She seemed embarrassed to mention his name, embarrassed to think what she might know about Mayme and him, both of them going upstairs together, and her eyes shifted away. "He showed me how to do it too."

"Good, good. Well, I'm going to go talk to the doctor a minute and then I'll be going. You'll be okay here?" She touched her shoulder again, gently, reassuring.

Sarah nodded. "Yes'm. Thank you, Mayme, for all you done for Leroy."

"Oh, don't thank me. It was Dr. Stern saved him."

"His people moved out to California so me and him is all that's left of our clan here. Pickin' oranges, I believe."

Mayme offered a nod of her head in understanding but had no words. It was an old story anymore. Folks were moving out of Oklahoma faster than she could keep up with. She left the worn out woman with a weak smile and turned away.

Joe sat at his desk, bleary eyed, but certainly looking better then he had that morning. He'd probably slept some, but not much, before leaving her in the bed alone, dead to the world. Mayme couldn't remember the last time she'd slept so soundly.

"Hey there," she said.

"Why look who's up and about." His face seemed to glow in the soft light of a late afternoon. "I was just going up to wake you."

"I can't believe I slept so long. I need to get home and clean up; I go on duty in just about an hour."

"Do you really need to go home first?"

"Of course. I can't hardly show up wearing this dirty uniform. Mrs. Daniels would have my hide."

"What will you tell O.C.? I mean about where you've been all day."

"He won't be home before me so he won't ever know I haven't been there and, trust me, he won't ask. I told you, let me worry about O.C. You got enough to worry about with Leroy and Sarah camped out in the side room."

Joe leaned back in his chair and extended a hand to her. "Come here." He patted his knee. "Just for a minute."

She inched toward him, biting her lower lip, her heart pushing her to him and her head yanking her back. "I really have to go."

"I know. I just want to touch you one more time before this day's over." He stretched his arm out toward her, his fingers beckoning, and as if an invisible cord was tied around her waist she responded.

Mayme rested her head on Joe's shoulder. "You were something out there at Luther's place, you know that?"

"Me? You were the one with the portable operating room in a bag. I still don't know how you knew what we'd need. Luther never told us what we were in for." He stroked her fine hair, combing it with his long fingers.

"Instinct, I guess." Mayme closed her eyes and let herself sink into him, enjoying again the beat of his heart, the weight of his chin on the top of her head. She had a vague memory of sitting on her mother's lap like this, her mother's fingers lightly stroking her hair, telling her a story about a little girl and boy lost in the woods and a witch who lived in a house made of candy.

"I think that's what it must have been like for my father and my grandfather," Joe whispered.

"How's that?"   His heartbeat was strong and reassuring, a steadiness at the center of chaos.

"My grandfather was a Yankee surgeon during the Civil War and you already know my father was an Army doc with Mrs. Daniels. They served together in France."

"That's right."   She listened to him talk, but her thoughts were pulled elsewhere, returning to the dread she'd left behind earlier, the trouble that was making her ears itch and her skin burn.   It was still there waiting for her.

"I grew up hearing stories of men getting a leg amputated in a ditch or digging out bullets with nothing more than a shot of whiskey for anesthetic.   Somehow the body survives."

"Somehow," she answered, her thoughts still resting in the rhythm of his heart.

"You know Leroy's doing pretty good," he continued. "I spent most of the afternoon here.   I went to the hospital and checked on patients, picked up some more morphine by the way, then told Mrs. Daniels that I felt a bit feverish and didn't want to infect anyone so I was going home.   I probably wasn't there for more then an hour, but it was quiet.   Doug Roberts was in today, so he can cover for me."

With just nine beds and a handful of nurses, three doctors had always seemed enough, but with Doc Moody slowing down, there was talk about adding at least one more.   Dr. Stern's extra efforts had forestalled the decision and earned him a day or two off for some unidentified illness.   No one would question it.

"I see you got a drainage tube in him."

"Yes, I grabbed one at the hospital.   Sarah was a pretty good assistant.   I even showed her how to fill a syringe and give an injection."

As much as she wished she could stay curled up there forever, Mayme slid off Joe's lap and smoothed her skirt.   "Well, here's a little secret.   I showed her that this morning even though I know full well she's probably given more than one or two of 'em in her day. I just wanted to make sure she did it right."

Joe stared at her curiously, waiting for some kind of explanation. Mayme kissed him on his chin and didn't offer anything more. He didn't need to know everything, at least not right away. It wouldn't take a smart man like him very long to figure out the country folk around here, even the less than friendly ones.

"Did you get a chance to check on Freddy? The deputy?" she asked.

"Oh, he's doing fine. No complications whatsoever. I don't know if he'll be doing any more police work, but he'll recover in good time."

"Good."

"You know, it's still a bit thrilling, caring for both sides, so to speak. It's the true Hippocratic oath, caring for each man, every man, regardless of the color of his uniform."

"You playing like you're back in the Civil War with your granddaddy?"

He laughed low, rose to his feet and squeezed her tight around the middle. "I guess I am."

"Now I got to go." She pulled away from his grasp, lifted up on her toes to kiss his puzzled face, then quickly scooted out of the room without so much as a glance back.

With long, almost skipping, strides, Mayme hurried toward the front door. There was no harm leaving a doctor's house by the front door at the end of the day. Anybody could look at what a mess she was and know she'd been hard at work. And if her luck held out she'd be washed, changed and gone before O.C. made it home.

The front door opened just as she was fixing to turn the knob. The unexpected motion startled her, but the sight of Grover Bishop standing on Joe's front porch nearly knocked her to her knees.

"Hey, Sheriff," she said, "you got an appointment with Dr. Stern? He has a side door 'round there that goes straight to his office. He's still in there." She pointed to the back of the house and closed the door behind her, hoping to keep the lawman from just strolling through Joe's house unannounced. Her heart pounded in her throat as she studied the blood stains around the hem of her dress, a spread of fallen roses, smashed and torn. "I didn't want to scare his patients so I'm sneaking out through the front." The best thing she knew to do was keep moving, get the man away from the house where a wanted man was laying there recovering from surgery. At least if he went into the office, he would run into Joe before he ran into Sarah and Leroy.

"No, I don't have an appointment with the doctor," he growled. His head shook in irritation, his feathers rumpled at the end of a hard day. "Though I do believe I might oughtta talk with him about a thing or two. But right now I want to talk to you, Mayme Holloway." He stomped after her, following her down the porch, his dark eyes fixed hard as stones on the back of her head.

"Can it wait, Sheriff? I've got to be on duty in about an hour and I need to get home first. Clean up a bit." She stopped at the walk and turned toward him, feigning interest and cooperation. A practiced smile flashed across her face, but her left eye twitched involuntarily. She looked homeward then turned her gaze back to Bishop, silently pleading for him to let her go without answering the dangerous questions he intended to ask.

"No, it can't wait, but why don't we start with where you've been this whole long day, what you're doing coming out of the good doctor's house looking like you been run over by a truck. You got blood all over yo dress there, in case you hadn't noticed."

The forced smile faded. "Like you, Sheriff, my work often leaves me with a little blood on my hands. All in a day's work, Sheri . . . excuse me, it's Deputy Sheriff; I forgot." She started walking away, moving toward the road home, her pointy chin jutting out like an angry beacon.

But even as she took that first bold step, she knew he would never let her simply walk away.

"Get in the car, Mayme." Like a mad bear, his glare froze her in her tracks. "Now," he ordered. "I'll drive you home and we'll talk on the way." He spit into the dirt and stood his ground, never moving a muscle toward her, simply controlled her with his command.

Refusing Bishop was never an option for the unarmed, and the deadly stare she met when she turned around unraveled her from the inside out. Like a penitent child, Mayme quietly made her way to the dirty police car. The passenger door had a hole the size of a dollar where some bullet had missed its mark and buried itself into the side of a seat cushion. Bishop held the door open for her while she slipped in quietly. He grinned as the blood drained from her face as she picked up the nurse's cap from the seat beside her, the one he had removed from Luther's house just that morning. He slammed the door hard, then strutted around the tail end of the car like a cocky rooster.

"Looks like you left somethin' out at Cookson," he said. "That weren't all you left out there, Mayme, so don't go saying it ain't yer hat. We both know it is."

"I never said it wasn't," she answered, her spindly fingers working their way around the edge of the white cap. Her mind worked furiously, recalling the look of the cabin when they'd carried Leroy out to the car. What had Bishop seen? What did he really know? Her future and Joe's depended on her recall and her imagination. There had been a pile of bloody sheets and rags, the clothes they'd cut off Leroy, and probably a morphine vial. One thing she knew he didn't see out there was Sarah. All he knew was that someone had been cared for and that there had been a lot of blood.

"Sarah had a terrible incident, Sheriff. Didn't Luther tell you about it?"

208

"He didn't say nothin' 'bout Sarah. And you and I both know it wasn't Sarah done lost all that blood. If it was, he'd a told me to keep me from locking him up."

It wasn't as if she didn't think about this moment, when she'd be caught in some precarious situation, in the company of someone she shouldn't be with or her handiwork suspected. Like her daddy told her years ago, people know what you tell 'em, so tell 'em what you want 'em to know and nothin' else. Mayme's mind raced. She'd always kept the worst medical story she knew tucked away if for no other reason than it refused to leave her memory. She never talked about it either, but now might be the time to use such a tragedy. Course she'd have to tell Sarah what she'd said and Luther too, but they'd either adjust or not. None of that mattered so long as she kept all of 'em, including herself, out of jail.

"I'm not so sure Luther feels like talking 'bout what he saw. I know he wouldn't want me to be telling folks." She turned her head away from him, as if the image that haunted her was too much to bear. Long shadows stretched across the lawns of the big houses along Kiowa. The air was lighter now, the brutal summer at an end. A few leaves had begun to fall, a promise of cooler days. Everyone prayed for rain.

"You best not be yanking my chain, Mayme Holloway. I could arrest you right now with what I know. And now that I see you comin' outta that doctor's house, I could probably arrest him too. So if you got a story to tell, you best get to talking now. I got a dead deputy and one near dead, and my patience is run out with you."

He parked the car in front of her little house, but made no move to get out. His grey eyes were still fixed on her, waiting to hear her story, holding her captive in the passenger seat. Mayme would later swear there was heat comin' from those beady eyes.

"I'm sorry to say that Miss Sarah done lost another baby," she said, her voice serious and professional, but oozing with concern, just like she talked when she had to tell someone bad news about some loved one. "This time was different though. It was just awful, Sheriff. We had to do what's called deconstructive surgery."

"We?"

Mayme had weighed this carefully in her mind as she doled out her sorrowful fabricated tragedy. She didn't say we by mistake. As much as she hated to drag Joe into it, there was no way to avoid it. Not now. Bishop had just seen her coming out of his house looking like she'd been run over by a milk truck, blood stains splattered down her dress, her dirty hair hanging limp as an old dishrag. Shoot, Sarah and Leroy were just inside. For this story to play out and keep Bishop off their heels, she might even have to go so far as to stick Sarah in that little bed and stick a needle in her vein. There was, she decided, no keeping Joe out of this.

"Yes, sir. I had to call on Dr. Stern to help me. That's why I was at his house. We took Sarah to his office for some extra care. He has a little sick room there where Sarah's staying."

"Why didn't you take her to the hospital? And what was so God awful that she had to hide her away? And what the hell is decomposing surgery?"

"Deconstructive surgery, sir." Mayme paused for effect. "Are you sure you want to know about this? It's a terrible thing to know."

"Mayme, I hauled two dead men in the trunk of my car today, one of 'em with half his head blowed off, the other with his guts open. And that was what I done before lunch, so I don't think you can tell me anything that could be more upsetting than anything I done seen in my life."

And so she began her story, a tragic tall tale to save her and Joe and Leroy and Sarah and Luther too.

"Dr. Stern was still at the hospital late last night, caring for Deputy Edmondson, and of course I was still there too. Anyway, Luther showed up and asked if I'd come and help Sarah. He said she'd been in labor most the day, but he didn't dare come near this place with all

210

those police cars around. You know he's scared a y'all. Everbody around here knew there was a shootout, and he feared you'd think he was involved. And apparently he was right since you was up there nosing around his place."

"So you're tellin' me all that blood and mess and those morphine vials is just from old Sarah delivering a dead baby?" His words almost exploded from his mouth; a spray of spit splattered across the dashboard and landed on Mayme's nose. She wiped the wet mess from her face, then wiped her hand on her dirty dress.

With narrowed eyes and clinched teeth, she growled her reply. "It was more'n a dead baby, sir. Though, yes, a lifeless baby was the end result. You men," she started, but finished the sentence with a disgusted shake of her head. She went on, her face turned away from him, avoiding his eyes. "Dr. Stern come along with me, thought she might need a cesarean. By the time we arrived out to the Cookson place, Sarah was in considerable distress. To tell you the truth, I'm surprised she made it through this ordeal a'tall. The baby, God love her, was a breech birth."

Mayme sniffed as she inhaled deeply, released the air slowly, as though the memory was too painful to reveal quickly. She went on. "A foot had presented by the time we arrived. Thank the good Lord I had those vials of morphine. And yes, there was a lot of blood already, but what happened next, well, it's just awful." She turned toward Bishop who sat frozen, his face an irritated question mark. "Are you sure you want me to go on? Maybe you've heard enough to know all you need to know."

"I'll be the judge of how much I need to know, and right now I need to know every last detail, Mayme Holloway."

"Alright. Don't say I didn't warn you. This is not an easy picture to carry around in your head. And I know you seen some horrible stuff, but this is . . . this is . . . well, it's just God awful."

"Get on with it, Mayme, and quit yer jabbering."

"The baby was dead," she said bluntly. "By the time we got the body pulled through the birth canal, Sarah's contractions stopped. Her body just shut down after all that struggle." She took another breath. "Let me make this clear. The baby's head was stuck in the birth canal, but the torso and limbs were out. There were no more contractions and nothing we did would release the head. If we'd been there sooner, we could have delivered the baby by cesarean, but it was already a vaginal delivery by the time we arrived."

"That's it? Babies die all the time, Mayme. You know that more'n I do so, why are you making a fuss over this one?"

"I didn't finish yet," she narrowed her eyes and glared at him. "I told you we tried everything and could not get the head out. The baby was blue. Sarah was, thank God, unconscious, partly from the morphine and partly from the loss of blood and exhaustion. Ultimately, we had to perform the deconstructive process. The head was delivered by cesarean; the body was delivered vaginally."

Mayme watched the sheriff's face closely, waiting for the realization of what she said to land home.

"Are you telling me you cut that baby's head off?"

Just the reaction she expected and hoped for. He would never want to talk to Sarah or any of 'em now. It was too gruesome, even for the man who walked around town with a big gun and a big hat for his big old head.

"There was no other way," Mayme whispered, her eyes lowered and head shaking, no, no. "It was either that or Sarah would die too. We later discovered the baby was hydrocephalic." She pronounced the medical term slowly, as if that would help the sheriff to understand, but she gave him the diagnosis in laymen's terms anyway, a subtle hint that she might know a thing or two more than he did. "The head was oversized due to fluid on the brain. He wouldn't have lived no matter what."

"Good Lord."

"That, Sheriff Bishop, is why my dress is bloody and why we put Miss Sarah in a private room in Doctor Stern's house. She is not only physically impaired, but in a very delicate way emotionally. We had to tell her."

"Why in tarnation didn't Luther tell me all this? He wouldn't say one word about nothin' when I asked him about your hat and that little bottle."

"To tell you the truth, he don't know too much. He knows the baby didn't make it, but he'd been drinking some of his own mash, and we didn't want any trouble, so we just told him to come see her this afternoon. I wondered why he never showed up but figured he was sleeping it off somewheres."

Her whole twisted, gruesome, bald-faced lie worked like nobody's business. She could see it in the sheriff's slackening jaw, the usual cement block melting at the edges. He was so consumed by the thought of a doctor and nurse actually cutting off a newborn baby's head, imagining the unimaginable, that even he forgot all about his suspicions of Mayme treating men he hoped to capture or kill. His mind was elsewhere, at least for a second or two, long enough for her to escape from any more of his questions.

"Now, Sheriff, if you don't mind, I'd like to take a quick bath before heading in to work the night shift. I still got to care for your deputy and God knows who else Ernie carried in today. I wish there was time to take a nap, but like you, sometimes I don't get no sleep." Her lips pressed together hard as she glared at him, daring him to keep her a second more.

"Okay, go on," he growled, shooing her away as if he was swatting at a fly, "but you best not be yanking my chain, Mayme Holloway, or so help me God, I'll make sure you pay the heavier price."

"I got no secrets," she lied.

"Yeah, and I got a million dollars."

He was still sitting there in front of the house when Mayme slammed her front door behind her. If she hurried, she actually could have a quick wash and be gone before O.C. got home. She didn't know if she had another round of creative horseshit left in her to deal with his cockamamie worries. And Lord knows if she told O.C. that same story she'd be wiping up his puke and picking him up off the floor.

Scrubbed and clean, her damp hair pinned up under he cap, Mayme was ready for whatever the night delivered. She scribbled off a note to O.C, telling him she was taking the truck and that he should go to his mama's for supper. She read it over, then added a bit, telling him that after the crazy morning they'd had, she had gone home and slept the entire day and he shouldn't worry about her. She left the note on the table and scooted out the back door just as O.C. came through the front.

Mayme was not there to see her husband read the note, to witness the way he sat rigid in his kitchen chair, flattening the scrap of paper against the table with the palm of his hand, again and again. She would never know how he reached into his pocket and gently pulled out the hairpins he'd picked up that day, two from the floor at the doctor's house and two from the front porch. Something was not right. Not right at all. Maybe he should talk to Mama about it, he pondered. He picked up the hair pins, one at a time, and rolled them gently between his thumb and index finger. Not right a'tall.

15.

"How's he doing?" Mayme asked.

"He's looking better this evening," the pretty young nurse said. She was a temporary from over in Muskogee. Mayme had seen her before but couldn't recall when or where or what her name was. Her brain was still weary from her conversation with Grover Bishop. "He's not so gray looking this evening. This morning, well, closer to noon, I guess, he was . . ."

Mayme cut her off mid-sentence, eager to get on with her own duties, her own assessment. "I'm Mayme Holloway, head night nurse," she said and picked up the chart from foot of his bed. She stood quietly, looking over his vitals and meds from the past few hours. She finally looked up and over to the younger nurse again and smiled. "My apologies, but I'm afraid I don't recall your name, and I know we worked together before."

"Peggy. Peggy Fletcher. Well, it's really Margaret, but I like to go by Peggy." She edged away from the bed to make room for Mayme to get closer to their patient. "He was awake earlier, but I just gave him a dose of morphine not fifteen minutes ago, so he'll probably sleep another hour or two."

"Best thing for him, right now," Mayme offered. She lifted his wrist and took his pulse. "I suppose your shift is over now?"

"Yes, I'm just leaving. Mrs. Daniels asked if I could come back tomorrow, so I'm going to stay in town over night. I have some people here that I stay with. My aunt and uncle. The Jamesons?"

Suddenly Mayme remembered the nurse clearly. She had only met her in passing, but Joe had gone on and on about her after one afternoon on the floor with her, claimed she was his first genuine case of diarrhea of the mouth he'd ever seen. She smiled at the younger woman, her mind drifting to the evening with Joe, the exasperated look on his face, the way he'd tugged at his dark curls as though he wanted to pull his hair out at the thought of the endless chatter.

"Oh, sure," she finally answered, "Willard Jameson. He teaches over at the college, right?"

"That's right. He's a mathematics professor, the smart one in the family. Of course, my dad, his older brother, tells him he's not a real doctor." She giggled awkwardly, her fingers fluttering at her sides. "By the way, I hardly saw Dr. Stern in here at all today. Do you know if he'll be around much tomorrow?"

"I really don't know," Mayme murmured. "If there's an emergency, his office is just a block away. Wasn't Dr. Moody in today?"

"Oh yes, Dr. Moody was here, but I just...well, I liked working with Dr. Stern so much last time I was here and was hoping to have another chance. He's so interesting."

Mayme picked up the chart to record her notes, refusing any further eye contact with Peggy. She did not want to encourage any more small talk, knowing that any bit of her small talk might stretch into tomorrow if she'd let it. She also clearly recognized the school girl crush that Pretty Peggy had on her Joe. Her Joe. That was a problem she wasn't ready to deal with just yet. How could he be her Joe when she was married to O.C.? Was she Joe's girl or O.C.'s girl?

As always, when the complications and consequences of her behavior crept into her consciousness, she forced her mind onto someone else's problems. Right now, it was Deputy Edmondson. He seemed to be recovering as well

216

as anyone could hope. A few hours ago, her attention was on the fellow that very well might have put one of those bullets in him. But now, he was the one stretched out in front of her, so now he was the one she cared about.

"You know, Mrs. Daniels said there might be a place for me here permanent, it's been so busy and all. I think I'd like that, so I'm keeping my fingers crossed."

Mayme glanced at her briefly but didn't comment further, her attention fully on the sleeping man's chart.

"Well, good night," Peggy finally said.

"Good night." Mayme didn't look up, just kept flipping the pages of the chart, the tip of her pen poised like she was ready to scribble something urgently.

Finally, left alone with her cluster of sick people, Mayme prayed for a quiet night, and for once, the Lord seemed to hear her. There were no emergencies and only four patients total. Deputy Edmondson was the most serious case, but mostly he slept, and the other three didn't need much of her attention through the night. She checked their vitals periodically and delivered medication, but most of the night she spent worrying about what was going on two blocks down the road where Joe and Sarah cared for Leroy or out on the road where Grover Bishop seemed to be chasing every whisper of an outlaw; but deep in her belly, gnawing away at her last nerve, was a worry about O.C. She couldn't for the life of her figure out why she was worried about O.C. He would believe anything she told him without question. But still, it was there, the unavoidable haunting intuition that she knew better then to ignore.

For the next two weeks, Mayme and Joe worked both ends of the middle, keeping both the deputy and the outlaw alive. Morphine eased their pain, and slowly their wounds began to heal; soon it seemed as if they were both headed for healthier days. Grover Bishop and his boys stayed busy combing the hills in search of any clues or information that might lead to finding any more of those heathens who were responsible for the death of a lawman, and O.C. stayed busy making folks pretty and eating his mama's fried chicken and biscuits. He was quieter than his normal self, but Mayme chalked it up to him worrying over her long hours.

It occurred to her that perhaps O.C. showing up that morning was simply a fortuitous event. She did not have to be so secretive about her coming and going from Dr. Stern's house at all hours of the day, at leasat not with him. He knew there was someone there that needed her attention, and it wasn't just Joe. And he knew better then to interfere or ask too many questions. After all, he'd helped to carry Leroy into the doctor's house so he was involved, too. During that time of Leroy healing, there were days when she didn't bother to go home at all. She took to keeping a clean uniform ready at Joe's house so that she could sleep in his bed, bathe in his tub, and share the slippery sunrise naked in his arms if the opportunity presented itself. Her worries about her husband and his suspicions simply faded away for a spell. Those private times alone with Joe were better then any shine she'd ever tasted, and they didn't leave her with a pounding head the next morning.

It was still dark when one early morning Mayme slipped through Joe's back door, her thoughts nearly drunk with the morning she'd imagined all night, her and Joe upstairs alone during that in-between time, her day ending as his began, daylight hovering just beyond the horizon. It was as though the sun waited patiently for the lovers to have a moment or two in the shadows. All those delicious plans faded at the sight of Joe and Sarah sitting together, sharing a cup of coffee at the kitchen table. He usually didn't come downstairs until after she'd arrived. Sarah had never said so much as a word about what went on upstairs and made it a point to stay out of sight until someone came into Leroy's room. They'd saved Leroy's life and that was all she seemed to care about.

"What's going on? Is Leroy alright?" Mayme asked.

218

"He's fine," Joe answered. "In fact, he's so fine, he's going home today."

Mayme poured herself a cup of coffee and joined them. "You want me to take him out there?" she asked. "I can go get the truck."

Joe smiled at her, but shook his head. "No, I don't think that truck ride would do him any good. It'd be better if I drove him in my car where he can stretch out on the back seat."

"Well, I'll go with you," Mayme said. "Keep you from getting lost out there in the woods." She shared a knowing smile with Sarah. The dense woods between the highway and Sarah's place were deceiving. Even though they'd been out there once before, the vines and hickory were thick as mud and never looked the same as the day before as fast as they grew and multiplied. There was a reason so many wanted men took refuge in those hills.

"I'd like that," Joe said, "if you're not too tired."

"My kids are gonna be surprised to see me back," Sarah said. "Lord knows they been running wild with me and Luther both gone."

"Who's been watching out for 'em?" Mayme asked. "I shoulda thought about that."

"Oh, we's all related some ways or t'other out there. We share the raisin' of our kids, and Dinah and Jinx, the oldest, do a good job a keepin' the little ones in line most the time. But they still like their mama to be there." She took a sip from her coffee and smiled, as if she saw something in that cup that pleased her. "You know, I can't thank y'all enough for all ya done, but someday I'll figure somethin' out."

"Don't worry about that," Joe said. "I wish we could have had him over at Holland Hospital so you wouldn't have had to stay away so long."

"I think we did just fine right here," Sarah said.

During Leroy's recovery, Mayme had come to realize that this simple woman was smarter than most folks she went to school with. She didn't say much, but her care for

Leroy was impressive. Mayme knew that if life had offered her some better choices, Sarah would have made a fine nurse. She had steady hands and a strong stomach. She never flinched at the less than pleasant chores that go along with caring for a man who's been gut shot. She held the bedpan, cleaned his wounds, and now could even bathe him without shame.

It didn't take long to get Leroy in the car for the trip home. He could walk some with a little help from Joe and Sarah. Once they got him settled into the backseat, Mayme covered him with a blanket and placed a pillow under his head. "Sarah," she said, "you ride up front with Dr. Stern and me so's Leroy can have the whole seat here."

The sun was just coming up as the four of them drove past the little house on Chickasaw Street. A faint light glowed inside, and Mayme knew O.C. was in there, probably sitting at their little kitchen table sipping on a cup of coffee, polishing his shoes with a flannel cloth, wishing his wife would come home and cook him a plate of eggs and bacon. She stared at the patch of yellow light, and for the first time, from God knows where, she felt real shame, deep shame, or maybe it was just nostalgia for what never was but might have been. Whatever it was, it hurt. She swallowed, hoping the terrible lump in her chest would ease, but it was like she'd swallowed a mouth full of gravel. It would take more than a gulp of air and a swallow to ease that pain. It was too deep and raw, too unexpected. This must be what it feels like to be shot, she thought; but no, that wasn't it. There wasn't enough morphine on God's earth to take this ache away. She knew as sure as she'd known anything before that she would live with it forever and eventually die feeling like she'd swallowed a stone.

Mayme didn't have much to say for the rest of the drive. The road was an empty stretch most of the way at this hour other than an occasional delivery truck headed for town. As they crossed the flowing Illinois, Mayme breathed a sigh of relief that they hadn't seen any lawmen who might recognize the doctor's car, and even worse, see her and Sarah riding with him. The only thing to see now was the shimmer of the water and the sunlight setting the limestone cliffs aglow. Mayme would never grow tired of that view and would never cross that bridge without feeling certain of a good day ahead. When a flock of geese soared overhead, even her new-found guilty conscious seemed to settle a bit, dropping from her throat to a knot in her belly.

Jinx, the oldest, and all the other kids were there to meet them. All of the little ones, Sarah's and the rest of the neighboring brood, gathered around the car, their necks craning to see Leroy in the backseat, their dirty hands pressed against the windows.

"Y'all get back 'fore I take a switch to ya!" Sarah ordered. She was shooing the curious bunch away as she jumped from the front seat, swatting at the air and scowling at the ones Mayme knew she missed so dearly. "Jinx," she said, knowing she didn't need to tell her grown daughter what to do. The girl began herding the children away, her arms spread wide.

Mayme smiled at the sight of her new friend, Sarah, who seemed to have turned into a feistier woman from the one who had held the light over her cousin just two weeks before. "You tell 'em, Sarah," Mayme added. "And don't y'all be jumping on your Uncle Leroy, you hear me?"

The children stood back in a cluster and watched silently as Sarah and Joe helped Leroy hobble into the house. Mayme took over for Joe and helped Sarah get him into a bedroom where he would have some privacy and maybe some quiet too. The house and the kids did not seem to have suffered too badly in Sarah's absence, just as she'd predicted. Jinx had learned from an early age how to do those things women did out there: cook, sweep, wash clothes, pluck a chicken, and take care of little ones. No doubt, Mayme knew, she'd have her own brood before too long. She was only fourteen, but that was about the time many of them took up with some boy and found their way to an altar, usually with a daddy and a shotgun close behind. She wished they could all have a better look at life

221

on the other side of the river, but that was just wishing, and that never did anyone much good.

"We best get back quick," Mayme said to no one in particular, just saying out loud what flew through her mind. "Sarah, I'm leaving you with some supplies here, but if you need something more, you send someone to see me or Joe and we'll see what we can do."

"Thank y'all," Sarah muttered, "thank ye."

"You know where to reach me," Joe said to her.

The days and nights they had shared were over but not the friendship and trust that had formed. It might be a trust bound together by secrets, but it was bound tight. Sarah stood at the door and watched the dusty car disappear around a sharp bend.

Though she would have liked to rest her head back and close her eyes for a short nap, Mayme sat up straight, watched the trees and twisting road slip past, and directed Joe back to the highway. For most of the drive, they were quiet, each caught up in their own thoughts and dreams. The sight of Tahlequah pulled them out of the quiet lull, a solid reminder of their destination.

"How was Edmondson last night?" Joe asked.

"He's coming along," she answered. "Your favorite nurse was on duty when I got there. She asked about you."

He grinned and shook his head as if he could shake the image of Peggy Fletcher from his head, or at least the sound of her voice. "Oh, dear, she's back on today too isn't she?"

"Yes, she is, yes, she is. In fact, she tells me she just might be a permanent fixture in our little hospital soon." Mayme couldn't help but grin at Joe's irritation. It somehow made her feel special, to feel truly wanted in every role she played.

"I'm sure she's a fine nurse, but God, that woman hardly stops talking long enough to take a breath, let alone to hear anything I say."

"Exactly. We got to be careful with her around, especially if we get any more Leroys showing up at your door."

"Let's hope that doesn't happen any time too soon," he said. "I'm exhausted from the endless worry alone." He looked over at her sitting in the seat beside him, then reached over and touched her knee. "You're the one who must be exhausted."

"I won't argue with you there," she said and rested her head back on the seat. "In fact, if you'll drop me at the house, I'll be forever grateful. I don't think I could walk four steps for a drink of water on a hot day."

"You're not worried about someone seeing me let you off?" He looked at her with concern, as though she might not be thinking clearly on her own, needing him to remind her of their unusual predicament, their ongoing professional and personal subterfuge.

"Too tired to care," she said and closed her eyes. She didn't open them again until the car slowed to turn down Muskogee Avenue. It was there that she sat up straight, looking like the nurse who had gone on a house call to assist the doctor and nothing more. The house sat lonely in the morning sunlight.

"What are we doing, Joe?" she asked aloud, though the question had been rumbling inside her for days.

"Well, I'm going to work, and you're going to bed."

"No. What are we doing? All this sneaking around like fools." Her gaze was intense, eager for some clarity in her sudden attack of conscience that morning. "What on earth do we hope to come from this?"

Joe didn't answer right away, letting the question hang there in the car like a wasp circling for a place to land and sink its stinger. He took a deep breath and gently brushed the back of her hand. "Mayme, we do what we have to do sometimes, even when it seems impossible, or even foolish. As far as providing care to the likes of Leroy, well, that's something I will never back down on. Everyone deserves to have medical care, and that was one of the first things I loved about you, the way you did that."

Mayme felt a bit of softening in her jaw, reminded of the true nature of this man she'd come to love. Her lower lip pushed forward a bit and she lowered her gaze to watch his hands take hers into his own.

"And as far as you and I go," he whispered, "I wish I knew where it was going. If I could have my way, I'd pack you up and take you far away from here and start a new life. You'd get a divorce and we'd get married. But I don't always get my way, and I could never ask that of you right now, at least not in this little town. So, for now, I just live for every chance we get to be together, even if it's just standing together at some patient's bedside. And, if it wouldn't cause a scandal of colossal proportions, right now, I'd wrap you in my arms and just hold you for a while."

She smiled weakly and squeezed his hand. "You're right," she said, "it would be a scandal of colossal proportions." Her smile grew. "I'm just tired, and my mind is running off in eighteen different directions." She turned back to look at the house and picked up her bag.

"Get some rest," Joe said as she slipped out the door. "I'll see you at the hospital later."

"I'll be there," she answered. "Lord knows, I'll be there." She climbed the porch steps, stopped before opening the door for a look back at him. She waved him on; all she wanted was a bath and a bed where she could sleep for at least a week without interruption or dreams. She would settle for six hours and a pot of coffee.

16.

O.C. was sitting at the kitchen table reading the evening Democrat-Star when Mayme stumbled out of the bedroom, still bleary eyed and thick headed from too little sleep. The sight of her husband sitting and reading the newspaper renewed the earlier stirrings of unfamiliar guilt. It seemed as if she'd been living her life with blinders on, refusing to see her life in the light of day, just running in the dark. She saw some of the terrible things other husbands did, and she knew she was lucky. She was married to a perfectly nice man, gentle and kind, handsome and sweet smelling. And what did she do? Fall in love with another man, the doctor she worked with. Even worse, she was intimate with him every chance she got. And even worse still, she liked it. It was downright bawdy and unseemly. Now, for whatever reason, a buttery light in the window that morning wreaked some kind of havoc on a conscience she didn't even know she had. Somehow, she had to make this right, one way or another, but she couldn't go on playing the games she'd been playing or she'd be in an early grave from the worry alone.

"You're home early," she said sweetly, rubbing her eyes.

O.C. looked up, then laid the paper down. "I've still got one more customer but not till after dark," he said sheepishly.

"After dark? Who needs a haircut after dark?" Normally, she might have teased him about some pretty

225

woman needing his personal attention, but a joke like that would only be more salt in her own wounds.

The words poured out of his mouth in a hoarse whisper as if someone might hear him if he spoke normally. "Charley give me a call this afternoon, didn't say his name, but I knew it was him. He said he's in the area and wanted to stop by this evening after supper, so I brought my clippers home on the chance he needs a little cleaning up and can't risk sitting in the shop." He smiled and nodded his head, clearly impressed with himself for thinking ahead.

"How about that? Tell him I said hi," she said and wondered if she should add any words of warning about the endless search for anyone who'd ever even thought of robbing a bank, but Charley knew more than she did about what was going on out there. "I can't stick around and wait for him; I got to get cleaned up and gone. My shift starts in an hour." She paused at the bathroom door. "Your mama been by? I smell something good." She closed her eyes and breathed in deep.

"Yes'm; she dropped off a pot of chicken and potato soup. She said she thought you might be in the mood for some soup. Not me, mind you, you."

"Hmmm, soup does sound good."

"And you thought Mama didn't like you. She even asked when you were gonna be home, said she had a little somethin' for you."

Mayme rolled her eyes in amusement before stepping into the bathroom, then called out through the closed door, "It's probably a recipe book so she can stop worrying that her baby boy would starve to death without her cooking."

Dressed in a clean white uniform, her hair neatly braided and pinned up off her neck, Mayme joined O.C. in the kitchen. "Did you eat?" she asked, taking a bowl from the cupboard. "Want me to scoop you up some of this?"

"I had a little earlier, just a taste though. I figure I'll wait and have some with Charley. No doubt he'll be hungry when he gets here."

"No doubt," Mayme said and took her seat at the table. She wished Charley was just another guy down the street and not wanted by every badge in the country. When he came to town, O.C. was a different man, excited and happy, really happy, not just pretend happy. Those days back in Ft. Smith when they'd shared plenty of meals and dances with Charley and Ruby were some of the best times she'd ever known. She had been so sure that her life with O.C. would be like that forever, but nothing is forever, she reminded herself. Her heart ached for her friend Ruby, knowing how she agonized every night about her husband, her son's daddy.

As Mayme sipped a spoonful of chicken broth, pondering the trials of loving a man like Charley Floyd, she couldn't help but notice her own husband fingering something in his hands, tapping out a silent tune on the table top, all rhythm, no humming or whistling the tune. Unusual for O.C.

"What you got there?" she asked.

"Oh, just some hairpins I picked up," he said. He made a clicking noise through one side of his mouth, then went on with the tap-tap-tapping.

"Off the front porch, I imagine. First thing I do when I get home is get those things out of my hair. I can't go to bed with 'em poking me in the head."

The tapping ended. O.C. smiled weakly at his wife and slipped the hair pins into his shirt pocket where he'd been carrying them for weeks, a reminder that all was not as it seemed. He recalled again how he'd picked them up off the floor of that little bedroom in the doctor's house, a day when her hair had been pinned up while they carried that wounded man out the door. He kept the hairpins to help him ponder what to think or do after hearing Mrs. Cooper, the doctor's neighbor, ask if Mayme was working in the doctor's office now since she was over there so often. He also had the note of lies she had written to him tucked safely in his wallet. He had not yet had the nerve or time to confront her with his questions, afraid to make her angry, afraid to learn something he didn't want to know.

"Do they ever just slip out of your hair, it being so fine and all?" he asked. "You know, like when you're working hard and losing track of things?"

"Oh, no, these little guys stay in tight. If they were loose, that could be a problem in surgery. Can you imagine one of my hairpins dropping into someone's open belly? Gettin' sewed up with that floating around in there? Lawsy, what a mess that would be. Lord knows what kind of infection would set in; probably kill the poor fellow." She laughed at the idea of death by bobby pin, then remembered who she was talking to. "Sorry, honey, I know you don't like to think of things like that."

His joy had seeped into a strange melancholy as she spoke, not his usual squeamishness. "No, I don't like to think about what you do," he said sadly.

"O.C., don't get like that. Hey, Charley's coming to town. You and him's gonna have some fun, even if you don't leave the house here." She reached over and patted her husband's hand. "You can put the radio on, catch up on how Ruby and Dempsey are doing, talk about all the crazy things you did when you was boys and tell me all about it in the morning. I'll make a point of getting home early, long before you leave."

O.C. nodded, happy to see his old friend soon, eager to ask him what he thought about O.C.'s suspicions. Charley and Mayme had a certain kind of friendship, each one knowing things about the other that they didn't share with O.C.

"You taking the truck tonight?" he asked.

"If you don't mind," she answered. "I'm still beat from workin' all last night and this morning, so I'd like to get home as early as possible and spend some time with you before you leave." She dropped her spoon into the bowl and leaned in closer to O.C. "Hey, I plum forgot to tell you; we carried Leroy back out to Cookson this morning before

228

the crack of dawn. Thank God. That's one less burden on my plate."

O.C. perked up at that bit of news, happy to be reminded that much of Mayme's extra activities were not made known to him because he told her long ago that he didn't want to know. He'd made that crystal clear from the beginning when she'd come home from nursing school all excited about seeing the insides of somebody. The thought of it made him sicker than a dog. Mama always said he let his imagination run to Georgia and back, and she was always right. Mayme'd probably taken care of plenty of folks in that doctor's house and that woman never did give two licks about how her hair looked. She might have just yanked those pins out to yank 'em out and left them where they landed. Shoot, he should have known better then to think there was any hanky panky going on between her and that doctor. Besides, Mayme wasn't even interested in that kind of stuff anymore. No sir.

They'd had their high time in the early days of their married life, but he couldn't think of the last time they'd had relations. He looked at her hunched over a big yellow bowl, sipping her chicken soup, no bigger then a half-pint snippet, and tried to conjure up the way her cheeks would flush when he touched her down there or the sounds she would make when he entered her. He knew there was a gasp or sigh or some kind of whimper, but he couldn't rightly recall what it was exactly. No, he realized, Mayme was no adulteress.

"Well," O.C. finally said, "you take the truck and get home as soon as you can." He thought of his expected visitor and added, "and you never know, Charley might still be here, needing to see you 'bout something. You never know."

Mayme was surprised to see Joe's car parked at the hospital. He was usually still seeing patients at his office or just closing up there. When she walked in the door, the air was electric, charged with the hair-raising anxiety of

229

crisis. She could taste it before she even talked to anybody or read a chart. Something bad was happening upstairs.

In less than a minute, Mayme was at Joe's side, nudging Peggy Fletcher to get out of her way. Deputy Edmondson had been moved to a Gatch bed in a private room where his upper body was elevated and his knees flexed. A bag of ice had been placed over his pericardium and the windows were open wide. Mayme took the man's thin wrist and felt his weak, thready pulse. His skin was hot to the touch, his breathing thick with the sound of bubbling and wheezing. It was pneumonia.

"What happened?" Mayme asked. "He was doing so well." She spoke to herself more than anybody, knowing full well that after any surgery, things can suddenly go south without warning.

"His lungs congested a bit yesterday, I'm sure you noticed, and his fever spiked this morning," Peggy said, as if the question had been directed to her. "We got him going on some codeine syrup and tincture of digitalis."

Joe turned his gaze to Mayme's, and no words were necessary. It was serious, very serious.

"Nurse Fletcher," he said, clearly irritated at her presence alone, "perhaps you should have Mrs. Daniels get his family together in the parlor downstairs to talk with me."

"You don't think . . . " she started, but Joe didn't let her finish.

"Please do it now, I'll meet with them in a few minutes. And let Mrs. Daniels know that I suggest you stay to cover the other patients. Mrs. Holloway will need to be dedicated to Mr. Edmondson tonight. He'll need constant care."

Peggy scurried out of the ward, looking happy to do the doctor's bidding, even when the errand was one of dire circumstances.

"Did you want to try cupping him?" Mayme asked, noting the protocol already ongoing.

"To tell you the truth, I don't really believe cupping cures pneumonia, at least not in this case," he answered,

230

studying the deputy's face for a moment, the healing surgical wounds along his jaw and the upper right shoulder. "Still, we don't have many options at this point."

"I'll get the cups," Mayme said.

"I should have been here earlier," Joe said.

"I was here all last night," Mayme said. "He was a little congested, and he complained of pain, but there was no sign of this coming on."

"Clearly, the morphine helped him sleep through most of his discomfort, maybe too much. I should have been watching more carefully, got him started on the codeine syrup sooner." Joe picked up the chart and scribbled a few lines.

"Dr. Stern," Mayme said, "you know these things just happen whether you're here twenty-four hours a day or not. You didn't put those bullets in him, and you didn't give him pneumonia."

"I know, Mayme," he said, talking to his lover now, not a nurse. "It's just, what if I hadn't been . . . " his voice trailed off, the question unasked. "Come on, let's get him cupped. It can't hurt."

"I can do this by myself," Mayme said. "Go talk to his family; they'll be here any minute." She watched him disappear through the doorway, her heart aching for him more than ever. She'd never known a doctor to care quite as deeply as he did for every patient he came in contact with.

Mayme moistened Freddy's chest with water, though it was already clammy with the sweat of his fever. She dropped three drops of alcohol into the glass cup, struck a match to ignite the alcohol, then inverted the flaming cup and pressed it into the moistened skin. The flame disappeared and a vacuum formed. She was careful not to burn Freddy as she applied six cups to the posterior region of his chest. Each cup would leave a perfect circle on his skin, but hopefully, some of the congestion in his lungs would be relieved so that he could breathe. As it was, he was drowning in his own fluids. After twenty minutes, she

231

removed the cups, just as Dr. Stern led his family up the stairs. Mayme pulled the sheet up over him so they would not be alarmed by the odd markings. In just twenty minutes, despite the cupping and other medications, his breathing had become more labored.

Freddy's wife, Ella, and his momma were red eyed and pale when they gathered around his bed. Neither one of them had slept a whole night through for the past month. After so many days of keeping vigil at the hospital, only leaving to take short naps and change clothes, they knew everybody's schedule, what they had for lunch, all the other patients and their visitors, too. Like all families that camp out in a hospital waiting room, Mayme knew they had started to think that life in the hospital was all that was going on anywhere, or at least it was all that mattered. They'd also come to believe that after this long, their Freddy would be coming home soon. This sudden turn for the worse was unexpected and unimaginable. They now could only brace themselves for the news that would shatter their hearts.

"Shouldn't we close that window?" Ella asked. "It's getting dark, and I don't want him to get a chill." She pulled the blanket up higher on his chest to just below his chin.

"No," Mayme said, her voice gentle and low. "We want to give him as much fresh air as we can right now. It makes the breathing easier." She picked up her box of glass bowls and took two steps away from the bed. "I'm just gonna put these things in the cupboard, then I'll be right back." There wasn't anything for her to do there with them, but she knew it helped for the family to know she was close by should anything happen.

Joe pulled his stethoscope from around his neck, inserted the earpieces, and bent over to listen yet again to Freddy's weakening heart and lungs. No cupping, fresh air or codeine syrup was going to save this man, not now. It was as if a thick veil of mucus had descended on him in one night, clogging his lungs and sending his heart into a relentless panic while he slowly drowned in his own fluids. Every breath was a struggle, a painful series of gurgles and moans, weakening with each respiration. His entire body was hot to touch and the color of chalk, a bluish white with touches of yellow here and there. He was dying.

Mayme was approaching the bed with plans to offer the women coffee and sympathetic understanding when Joe asked her to bring another dose of tincture of digitalis. "And," he added calmly, "bring a vial of Atropine as well and have it ready to go."

Mayme exchanged a knowing glance. They would want to have the Atropine on hand when he went into cardiac arrest. Apparently, Joe thought it was inevitable and there was no need to waste time running to a medicine cabinet or filling a syringe. They would be prepared to try to save him at the moment of crisis. Mayme had seen worse cases come around when she was sure they'd seen their last sunrise. If Freddy could make it to morning, he'd be okay. They just had to get him to morning. That was Mayme's goal for the night, nothing more, nothing less. She would drag that man to sunrise if she had to.

It was only an hour later, just as the first stars appeared in the Oklahoma sky, that the gurgling breathing paused and the once vibrant man lay open mouthed and gray, his body too tired to suck one more gulp of air. For a long second or two, everyone stood motionless, anticipating and praying for another rally, another strangled breath, but it didn't come. He stayed quiet.

Joe and Mayme went into action, moving expertly and with no hesitation or question of what should be done. Mayme took the prepared syringe from the nearby tray and injected the cardiac stimulant while Joe's hands moved automatically, pulling Freddy toward him, working desperately to draw air into the damaged lungs, using his own hands to press upward from the back, ignoring the surgical wounds, pressing and pulling on the ribs upward, pressing even after he knew his efforts were in vain. "Come on, Freddy, breathe."

233

At the foot of the bed stood the women who loved him most. "No, no, no, Freddy, don't do this, please," Ella prayed, her voice a desperate plea to her husband to work harder, to do what could not be done, to do what the doctor said. When those pleas failed, she tried for a miracle, praying louder now, her shyness forgotten. "Please, God, no. Don't take him from me, don't do this."

His mother stood quiet, one hand over her mouth, her tear-filled eyes fixed on the boy she'd brought into the world, her only son, her firstborn. She moved forward and took her boy's foot in her hand and his wife's hand in the other, her own fervent prayers racing through her brain, but silent all the same.

Mayme took a wrist and felt for a pulse, but there was none to feel. Joe paused to feel for a pulse in the carotid artery, his fingers moving gently along the frail neck. She waited for him to speak, for Joe to formally pronounce what they already knew. He was dead.

When he lay the lifeless man back on the bed, he turned first to Mrs. Edmondson, the wife, then Mrs. Edmondson, the mother. "I'm very sorry," he said, placing one hand on each of their forearms before stepping back. The two women wrapped their arms around each other and wept. They did not see what Mayme saw: Dr. Stern leaving the room, visibly shaken by the loss of a man he barely knew.

Peggy sat at the station desk, perched on the edge of her chair, looking like she was chomping at the bit for news from the isolation room. Dr. Stern marched past her without so much as a glance and then the wife and mother shuffled out arm in arm, weeping. No one said a word to her. She jumped to her feet at the sound of Mayme's footsteps headed her way.

"Did Officer Edmondson expire?" she asked, her voice dripping in curiosity as much as concern.

234

Mayme looked at the young woman in amazement. How could she not know? The two Mrs. Edmondsons had just left the hospital weeping; she had to have seen them.

"Yes," she answered calmly, ignoring her impulse to say something snippy to the foolish inquiry. "I'm going to call Reed right now, and they'll come get him shortly, so you really don't need to stay. Go on home."

"Oh, I don't mind staying a while longer, till you get everything under control." She nodded her head, urging her superior to keep her there working all night long. "Really."

As much as Mayme would have liked to have someone else to handle the bedpans and vital checks, she was in no mood for the chatterbox in a white dress - all that helpful energy just wore her out. Now that Freddy was gone, there was only a handful of patients on the floor, enough to keep her busy, but not so many to keep her from getting any rest at all. She'd find a spare minute or two to put her feet up and read the magazine she knew Peggy had tucked under the chart box.

"No, you go on home and get some rest. You already put in your time and then some."

She turned on her heels, not giving Peggy a chance to get in even one more word, not bothering to say good night or thank you for working the extra hours. Mayme needed to get downstairs and phone the funeral home. It was always better if they removed a body while the other patients slept so they wouldn't be reminded of their ultimate fate, regardless of what ailment sent them to a hospital bed. Mayme realized long ago that no matter how careful a man was, no matter how clean a person lived, he still died. Healthy ones died young and sickly ones lived beyond what they should. Nice folks died too soon and mean ones lived to see great grandchildren. If there was a God, he had a strange sense of timing.

As predicted, once Reed Culver removed Freddy's body, the night was quiet. After the 2:00 a.m. vitals check, Mayme put on a pot of coffee and took out the cheese sandwich she'd brought for her supper. She was enjoying a quiet moment, reading about a new motion picture with Greta Garbo and Joan Crawford when she heard the side door open downstairs. She knew before looking that it was Joe. She could sense his presence. She put the magazine down and hurried down the stairs to find him standing in the supply room, his hair a mess of curls, his wrinkled shirt untucked and only half buttoned.

"What are you doing here?" she asked.

"I couldn't sleep," he said, moving closer to her, slowly wrapping his arms around her waist to pull her in tight against his chest.

Mayme didn't remind him that someone could walk in on them, even in the middle of the night. Ernie could come racing in with somebody banged up or having a heart attack and ruin a quiet shift at any time. No matter how much they wanted to touch each other at the hospital, they were always hands off, even if they were the only two there other then a room full of sleeping patients. But now she recalled how he'd been that afternoon and knew better then he did himself why he was struggling with the death of Freddy more than any other patient who didn't make it. A little physical contact was what he needed, and she could give him at least that much.

"Come sit down a minute," she said, unwinding herself from his embrace and taking him by the arm. "I'll get you a cup of coffee."

He did as she said and, like an obedient child, took a seat in the sitting room where the nurses often took their short breaks. An ashtray with a smattering of half-smoked cigarette butts and the latest copy of the American Journal of Nursing sat on the small table. He pushed the ashtray away from him with his index finger, then studied the cover of the journal. By the time Mayme set the mug of coffee in front of him, he was deep in thought, his eyes focused on some scene that played in his own mind, not the words on the page before him.

"You're thinking about this too much," she said, knowing full well he was not interested in an article about nursing students in small hospitals. "Patients get pneumonia and die after surgery. It's sad and it hurts to lose someone like Freddy, but it just happens."

He turned his face to her, but there was no expression, no agreement, no denial, just a blank slate, his thoughts slowly returning to the moment at hand.

"You know that time I come to your house for the Protargol?" she asked, taking a seat in the chair next to him. "The night you told me you knew about me pinching the morphine?" She reached up to comb his messy hair with her fingers, moving a stray curl so that it headed in the right direction. It occurred to her that she hated it when O.C. did that very thing to her so she pulled her hand away, taking his long fingers into her small hands.

His face softened at her touch. "Of course I remember," he said, reaching up to draw his thumb along her jaw and then down her lips. "That's the night I knew I loved you. Even if I could never have you, I was going to want you secretly forever."

Mayme's smile was almost sad. If Charley hadn't shown up at her door with a bad case of the clap, she would never have gone to Joe for help, and who knows what would have happened between the two of them? They probably would have just gone on working together, sharing the occasional chicken sandwich over small talk. She was perplexed by the way things had progressed and overcome with how much this man had done for her, to be with her, to help her with all she did. He'd risked his whole career and reputation.

"Do you regret it?" she asked, half praying he would say no, but all the while knowing their lives would be easier if he said yes. If he said yes, she wouldn't have to decide anything, wouldn't have to go on gambling what she had on a notion of love and passion.

"Not for a moment," he said softly, his voice suffused with a tenderness few people ever knew. "I am torn,

237

though. I'm worried that I sacrificed my best care of a patient to be out there playing some exciting game, treating Leroy in my own house, taking you into my bed while he and Sarah were just downstairs, as if I controlled the strings of some magnificent puppet show." He shook his head in disbelief and squeezed her hand tightly. "But I do not regret one moment with you, Mayme."

"If I'd never gone to you, you would never have been messed up in all this. I told you it was dangerous, and you knew that, but it can also tear you to pieces when you're working both ends of the rope. What you need to remember is that Freddy got better care than Leroy. When we weren't here, others were. He was never without someone who knew what they were doing taking care of him, following your orders. Poor Leroy mostly just had Sarah to nurse him. And," she added, her voice raising a pitch as she made the connection as she spoke, "Leroy's wounds were more serious than Freddy's. God, Joe, you know more than I do how fickle death is."

He smiled at her, blinked slowly. "How'd you get so smart?" he asked. "You are absolutely charming, but also so wise. So, so wise."

"Thank you," she said. "Now, maybe you should head home and get a little rest before your day begins. You won't get but a couple hours now. It's almost morning."

"Only if you promise me something."

"Anything."

"Can we go hide away at that cabin for a few hours and just rest and be with each other? A short vacation."

"Of course we can, if I can figure out a way to sneak away for a bit. I'll figure something out soon as things calm down around here."

"Tomorrow. I know for a fact that you don't have work tomorrow night." He leaned back in his chair and let his hands hang loose at his sides. His voice was low and full of temptation.

"Oh, Joe, I don't know." Her eyes scanned the small room, searching for an answer to her own internal

238

struggle, already waivering on her promise to sneak out to Horseshoe Bend for a while. "I think we might be best off if we just minded our business for a few days, think about all this. I mean, what good is going to come of any of this sneaking around? You and me."

Her thoughts returned to the soft light of her little house, the sense of loss she had felt. It wasn't that she loved O.C.; it was just that she didn't want to cause more trouble. O.C. was a good man, and she had made a vow to herself just hours before to make an effort to be a better wife, to be a better woman.

"You're not breaking off with me right after you promised to go away with me, are you?" Joe was suddenly sitting taller, his spine a rigid line from neck to tailbone. "Come to the cabin. We can talk about our options. And for the record, dear, I'm not, as you say, just fooling around."

"I said sneaking around, but regardless." She paused, considered what he'd just said. "What options could we ever have?" Her eyes lowered from the face she loved downward to her own hands, her fingers reddened from the harsh scrub soap. "What options are there for someone like me? I'm married. This is a small town, the place I grew up. Everybody knows me. I can't just pack a little bag and move without creating a ruckus that would haunt me forever."

"We have options, Mayme." He scooted his chair an inch closed. "You don't have to stay in this town forever, and you don't have to stay married to someone you don't want to be with."

"Oh, Joe," she whispered, her heart nearly breaking with so much love she could hardly breathe. "That's easy for you to say. It's not your town and not your marriage." Her mind raced, imagining the anguish it would cause O.C., imagining the way his mama would scowl, how Wilma would turn away to hide her own disapproval. How could she leave the folks who had been there for her since her own mama died?

239

"Just come to the cabin tomorrow," he said. He was good at advising others on what to do to make their lives better. "You have your own truck. When you get off work in the morning, just head out there. No one will think anything of it if they see you headed out of town alone. They'll just think you're making a house call. I know how to get there on my own, so I'll meet you there."

And with that he rose to his feet, kissed the top of her head and left out the side door.

Mayme slowly climbed the stairs to the patient ward, wondering why she had suddenly discovered a guilty conscience that made her question her actions. Two weeks ago she would have arm wrestled a three hundred pound man and won for a chance to spend a few hours out in the woods with Joe. Don't go, she told herself. Just go home and go to bed. But even as she began her round of vital checks, she was planning on making a quick stop home for a quick bath and change of clothes, telling herself it was one last time. Just one more time.

17.

Mayme wasn't the least surprised to see Joe sitting out on the front porch waiting for her when the old truck bounced through the tangle of hickory oak and Virginia creeper into the small clearing around the cabin. No lights were on at his house when she'd passed it less than an hour before. He leisurely rose to his feet at the sight of her, but by the time the old truck rattled and stalled, his hand was already on the driver's door. He would not waste a single moment of their short respite together.

"I didn't think you'd ever get here," he said, taking her arm as she slipped out of the driver's seat.

She kissed him before saying anything, a soft chaste peck on his mouth. "I stopped by my house to freshen up."

"Too bad. I was going to give you a bath here, out in the open for all the birds and squirrels to see," he said, taking her fingers to his mouth, kissing them and smiling down at her.

"Ah, you found the tub," she said. "I've had more than one bath in that old washtub. It's no easy task filling it with hot water, so it's usually a cold one."

"Well, I will gladly heat the water and fill the tub for a chance to soak in there with you. It's big enough for two."

She stopped him at the porch railing and started to turn back. "I got a basket of goodies for us in the truck in case you're hungry."

"I'll get it, but don't go in. Wait right here." He kissed her again and sprinted back to the truck for the ham and cheese sandwiches and sweet tea she'd packed at home.

Mayme watched him cover the short distance in three quick strides and smiled, staying put where he'd left her. No one had ever been so attentive, not even when she and O.C. were just dating. But they were young and innocent, she reminded herself. Neither one of them had a clue about life after marriage, the disappointment of a comfortable life. What she and Joe had was like you see in the movies, but movies are just make believe, a slip of fantasy shown in the dark. All that illusion vanishes when you step outside the theater and back into your own daily drama.

Although she had promised O.C. she would be home early, he was already gone when she arrived. For the past hour, as she bathed, dressed, packed the basket and drove the winding road to Horseshoe Bend, she told herself again and again that this was the last time, that she would allow herself this one last lovely day with Joe and then change her ways, go back to what she had before him and just do as she had always done. After this, she would have plenty of days to go home early and make small talk with her husband, but life somehow owed her and Joe this one day, and they were taking it. She could live on the memory of this time with Joe and be glad she was lucky enough to have known such a love.

Joe sat the basket down on the porch and pulled a handkerchief from his pocket. "Turn around," he said, "I need to blindfold you."

"What in the world are you . . .?"

"Shhhh," he whispered in her ear, his breath like a warm breeze on her neck. "Trust me."

Mayme groaned and turned her back so that Joe could use his handkerchief to cover her eyes. "I'm almost afraid to see what you've done."

"I seem to recall being the one blindfolded the first time we came here," he said as he tied a loose knot in the handkerchief.

With Joe right behind her, a hand loosely holding each of her elbows to guide her, they moved slowly through the door. Joe moved around to the front of her and slowly unbuttoned her soft blue shirtmaker dress. He slipped the garment off her shoulders and let it drop to the floor. She stood there, happy to be wearing her pink and black lacey two-piece dance set, the special undergarments she'd ordered from the Sears catalogue. She'd hidden the package away in the bottom of a drawer, knowing the right occasion to wear them would present itself one day. Because she was convinced this was their final time together, this was that occasion. She had not bothered to wear stockings and the air felt cool against her bare legs and stomach.

"Oh, Mayme," he said. "I've never seen anything so lovely in all my life." He reached up and removed the makeshift blindfold to reveal his romantic handiwork.

Candles burned on the table, casting a soft flicker of dancing shadows and light. Mayme's eyes adjusted to the soft light, and she gasped at the scene before her. What had to be flower petals from half a dozen stops along the road from Tahlequah covered the floor, chairs, tabletops, and even the turned-down bed he'd made with clean white sheets from his own home. Yellow stars, fire pink, tickseed, chicory, wild roses, and red haw petals...everywhere. Mayme thought of her dream of long ago, the storm of petals after their first time together, the way they had fought their way through a windstorm to find a patch of blue sky. The threat of tears burned her eyes. It was all so beautiful, so sad. She didn't want to ever wake from this dream.

Joe had thought of everything, knowing they would need some food and drink during their brief escape from duties. Two glasses of his best "medicinal" Kentucky

243

bourbon sat beside a loaf of bread, a chunk of cheddar cheese, and a bowl of penny candy.

"For you, my dear, our most luxurious holiday suite."

"Joe," she said, taking in every detail, turning to see him watching her. "I can't believe you did all this."

"Darling, if I could, I would check us into the finest suite at the Carlisle and order room service three times a day so that we would not have to budge from our hideaway for at least a month."

"It's lovely right here," she said, eyeing the room she'd known for years transformed into their private love nest for a few hours. "And I think it's just as nice as any suite at, what hotel was that?"

"The Carlisle, my favorite place to stay in New York. I plan on taking you there one day."

And with that he scooped her up in both of his arms and carried her to the flower-covered bed.

"These day lilies will stain the sheets," she said, knowing he would not care.

"I hope so," he answered just before kissing her on the mouth. He then slipped one brown kid pump from her foot and kissed the inside of her ankle before removing the other shoe.

Mayme closed her eyes and breathed it all in, the scent of wild roses, burning candles, a hint of her own talc, and then the familiar smell of him, his soap, his sweat, his bare skin.

The day lay stretched out before them. They made love slowly, whispered words of love, kissed, giggled, and teased, until at last they lay quietly in each other's arms, quiet and content, their bodies satisfied.

"Wouldn't you like to sleep like this every night?" Joe asked, his fingers slowly tracing circles on Mayme's back, her head resting on his chest.

"Yes, but I don't want to sleep away even a second of today." She pressed her ear closer and listened again to his heart beating, a steady, even rhythm. She loved that sound and etched it to her memory.

244

"That's fine with me, but you've been up all night, so if you need a nap, I'll just lay here and listen to you snore."

She bit his chest playfully. "I don't snore."

"Don't worry; they're cute little snores."

They giggled like children for a moment, and he hugged her tighter. "I love you, Mayme Holloway. I know I'm not supposed to, but I do."

Mayme avoided the talk that would come from this, the options he claimed she had. "You know what I want to do," she said, raising up on one elbow to look down at his face. "I want to take you to my special place, my thinking spot."

"Is it close?"

"Just a short little walk from here. Wilma and I discovered it when we were kids, a flat rock, just big enough for two. Come on," she said, "it'll be fun."

Wearing only her thin dress and shoes, Mayme led Joe along the narrow path through the woods. The trail was marked by a string of moss-covered rocks she and Wilma had spent an entire day hauling up from the river more than fifteen years before. Tucked in a maze of grasses and vines, tall stalks of coneflowers loomed, their long graceful petals drooping like wilted ballerinas. "Don't touch the shiny leaves," she said, pointing to a long vine that stretched along the trail, "it's poison."

Joe laughed. "I do know a few things about botany," he laughed. "Remember, I went to summer camp when I was a boy."

"That's right, that's where you learned all about willies," she said, poking fun at at his self-deprecating attitude, knowing he'd been to one of the finest medical schools in the country and probably studied more about plant life then she knew there was to study.

Mayme scrambled up the small ledge using her hands to pull herself up the steep bank, then turned and offered a hand to Joe to pull him up. He smiled and let her lead the way. There, just as she'd promised, was a small ledge, a boulder seat jammed into a cliff of tangled vines.

245

"My thinking rock," she said, then lowered herself down to sit.

"We should have brought our lunch up here," Joe said. "It's beautiful."

Mayme didn't answer. This was where she let her imagination, hopes, and dreams have wings; she wasn't thinking of bread and cheese.

They sat quietly for a while, enjoying the view, the breeze of a warm October day, and the closeness of each other.

"I feel like there's something on your mind," Joe finally said.

Mayme looked at him, her lips stretching to a smile, but her eyes were filled with sadness.

"You know me too well," she said.

"I will never know you too well. What is it?"

"This. Us. It seems so right somehow." She shook her head slowly, then pulled her knees up close to her chest and hugged her legs tightly as she watched his face. "Still, it's wrong."

"I knew that was on your mind, but I wanted to be sure, before I convinced you otherwise." He stroked the side of her leg with the back of his hand. "This is not wrong, just complicated."

"Joe, I'm married to O.C., and that's more then complicated."

"You could get a divorce," he said. "Believe me, like I said, it's not so uncommon anymore."

"It's sure not common around here," she said, "least not in Tahlequah. I don't know anybody who's divorced."

"We don't have to stay in Tahlequah." He felt her body twitch at the suggestion, the involuntary flinch of shock or fear or both.

Mayme looked at him closely, as though she could see down inside him, make him see down inside her to places where words couldn't go. She tried to make him understand how she was rooted to this land, these hills, these people. "But this is my home, Joe. I'm the one that

246

made O.C. move here. I never wanted to live anywhere other then right here where I know everyone and his brother. I wouldn't be a nurse if it wasn't for Doc Moody and Mrs. Daniels."

"And I'd like to add that if you'd lived somewhere else, under different circumstances, you might have been a doctor. You're as much a doctor as half the fellows at Baptist General."

"Hold on there, Mister. Do you think there's something wrong with me being from Tahlequah? If I'd wanted to be a doctor, I would have been. For the record, I wanted to be a nurse. I wanted to be like Mrs. Daniels, tending to them after the doctor is gone." She took a breath and laughed at herself. "But, thank you for thinking I could be a doctor. Most men would never even imagine a lady doctor."

"They haven't seen you in action then."

"Even some of them that have seen me in action, like Luther or Leroy or," she paused, "I hate to say it, but even Doc Moody might have issue with it."

"Touche'."

"Yes, Touche'. So, I'm a smalltown girl who likes living in the town that raised her."

"That doesn't mean there isn't another place out there for you, Mayme. And in case you haven't noticed, people are leaving this state in droves. If it keeps going like this, all these people you want to stay close to will be gone. And they won't be thinking of you when they go. They won't have that luxury."

They sat silently for a time, their minds taken with the image of the loaded cars and trucks of destitute families headed west, their homes and farms now owned by some bank. It was worse west of them where the dust blew in thick clouds like smoke, but they saw enough to know the pain of the less fortunate.

Finally Joe broke the silence. "Tell me this much. Do you love O.C.?"

"Now that's complicated," she said. "I love him like, well, kinda like you love your favorite old shoes, but you don't want to wear them anymore, just hang onto 'em in case you do. But, no, I'm not in love with him, not like I feel about you."

Joe stretched his arm around her back and pulled her body closer to him. "You are too young to live for an old pair of shoes," he said. "This is 1932, Mayme. Times are changing and for the better. Shoot, in a few weeks, we're going to have a new president, at least I'm hoping we will, and then things will really change. I've done a little research, and I think you should at least consider this one option. You could go to Reno, stay there and get your divorce. It seems that's what other women do, so you won't be alone. Meanwhile, I'll find a position in another hospital in another place. When things are all settled, you can join me. It would work, and after a few weeks of tongue wagging around here, everyone will get over it, and you can visit all the ones you love and ignore the others."

"Oh, trust me, Mama Holloway, for one, will never get over it. The folks at O.C.'s church will never get over it. Mrs. Daniels will certainly never ever get over it. Shoot, she'll be looking to thrash you and me both. Most everyone I ever knew will never get over it."

"So, you want to stay miserable to please the members of the Baptist church and a cranky old woman who can make a good pie?"

Mayme laughed at the way he made it seem so simple. "You know it's bigger than that," she said. "I have to live with myself, and I don't want to go through life feeling like I did something unforgivable."

"I love your sense of morality, your goodness. You've made me a better man and shown me a bigger picture of right and wrong and duty. It's not always easy. Look, we both cared for two men, one a lawman with a family who loved him, the other one an outlaw who probably put the bullet in the lawman. Both deserved our care, but the law says we are criminals for saving Leroy's life. I don't think we're criminals no more than I think you finding love after marriage makes you a fallen woman."

Mayme freed her legs and reached behind Joe so that they sat arm in arm. Away from the windstorm of trouble she feared, surrounded by the blue patch of light they had fought for in her dream, her plans to return to the quiet life with O.C. slipped away. The impossible seemed just within her grasp if she could muster up the courage to reach for it.

"You really think I could do it? Just walk away from this town, all my friends?"

"I do."

Mayme stared out over the dense wall of green that stretched high over the narrow band of dark water that flowed steadily out into the Illinois River. She loved this place.

"Mayme, the people who love you will understand, even if it takes them a while to get used to the idea of you and me. Even some of my own family will balk at first. Not only are you married, though they don't need to know that, but you're not Jewish."

"You're Jewish?" Mayme leaned into him and laughed. "How did I not know that? And I brought you a ham sandwich more than once."

"Let's just say I'm Jewish by birth."

"Come to think of it," she said, "you're the only Jew I know. Guess that's why there's no Jewish church in Tahlequah."

"Synagogue. A Jewish church is a synagogue."

"I know that much, but we still don't have one."

Joe kissed the top of her head, amused. "So, will you at least give it some thought? Don't send me packing just yet. Give my option a chance to grow on you."

"We're crazy, you know that? For even thinking about running off together."

"I do."

"Right now, sitting here with you, I can't imagine spending a single day without you in it, no matter what other folks may say." She reached up and bit his earlobe gently, knowing how that made him stir and moan.

"Let's go back," Joe whispered.

At the porch rail, Joe whisked her up in both his arms. Mayme threw her head back, squealed and laughed out loud as he carried her over the threshold like a new bride. Just inside the door, the fun and laughter came to a quick end. Joe stopped short, still holding Mayme like a small child, her arms wrapped around his neck, holding on tight. Neither one of them even dared to breathe.

He sat at the table, his fedora pulled down low to shield part of his face, drinking the glasses of whiskey Joe had poured earlier that morning, imagining Mayme and him enjoying the warm glow of the drink. Charley lifted his machine gun but not to threaten shooting the lovers. From the barrel of the frightening weapon hung Mayme's fancy undergarments. "Welcome home, friends. Looks like y'all been having some kinda wild party in here." His tone and manner dripped with angry contempt.

Joe lowered Mayme to stand on her own two feet beside him, never taking his eye off the man with the gun. He kept one arm stretched in front of Mayme, as if it would keep her safe from a bullet at close range.

"Charley," Mayme pleaded, her voice trembling, "it's not, it's just . . . "

"Mayme, sweetheart, I know exactly what this is." He took his hat off and tossed it into the rocking chair. "When I saw your truck and the doc's car, I thought maybe some poor sucker was getting a dose of your medicine. I sat in the outhouse and looked out the window for a time, but there ain't no one here but you and a bunch of flowers and shit. For example, my good friend O.C. is nowhere around, is he?"

"Charley," Joe said, trying to sound confident, "you, of all people, should understand our situation. I love her. She loves me. We aren't out to hurt anybody."

"She's a married woman, Doc. You forget that?"

"No," he answered.

250

"Charley," Mayme tried again. "I'm the one that's doing wrong, the one who's married. Don't hurt Joe." She had no doubt that Charley Floyd could shoot the both of 'em dead and leave them to rot out there. "Let him go. Please."

Charley laughed at their fear. "Calm down, Mayme," he said, clearly enjoying his place of superiority. "Don't go gettin' your gut in an uproar. I ain't gonna shoot you cuz that would break my good friend's heart. Nah, I'm just gonna persuade you to change your ways, let you know how things are gonna be from now on."

He stood up and moved to within inches of the guilty pair, close enough for them to smell the whiskey he'd enjoyed and the underlying remnants of O.C.'s sweet-scented aftershave. "And if you don't change your ways, then I'll have to change them for you."

"What do you want?" Joe asked.

"First, I want your little whore here to forget she ever knew you and ask the Lord to forgive her adultering ways and go home to her husband where she will finally be the kind of wife he deserves."

He looked her straight in the eye when he said the word "whore," his grey eyes piercing her flesh as if he'd shot her. Mayme nodded. Deep down, she knew he was right, that this was God's way, if He existed, or at least Charley's way of making sure she did the right thing. Pretty Boy Floyd, a bank robber and killer, was saving her from making a dangerous decision. From this day forward, he would always have this to hold over her head, to get her to do his bidding, no matter the risk. At this point, she would do anything he asked just to save Joe from his anger, his punishment.

"Second thing," he said, moving back to his place at the table, "I need to borrow the doc's car. I had to ditch mine down the road a piece. I won't be keeping it forever, but I can't gurantee it won't suffer a scratch or two, the way those damn troopers keep shooting at me. And, Doc, I

251

need you to set me up with that place back east that you was tellin' me about. Your mama's place."

"That's fine," Joe agreed, knowing he really had no option other than to agree at this point. "I'll call my mother today, tell her a friend of mine is moving back there for a while. She won't recognize you," he added, suddenly concerned about his mother's welfare living in close proximity to dangerous men. "I'll write the address down for you."

"One last thing," Charley said. "For some reason, these hills is crawling with cops, so I'm gonna stay holed up here for a piece. I need you to bring Adam and Beulah out here. Mayme, you get hold of Beulah, and she'll take care of everything. She's a smart girl."

Mayme nodded.

"Now, put your drawers on." He tossed her underwear to her. "Doc, you make sure you bring those two out here, and you can load us up with some groceries while you're at it."

"When do you want me to bring them? Tonight?" Joe asked.

Mayme picked up her underwear and held them close to her chest as though he might rip them away from her again.

"Just do what I said. Mayme will get hold of Beulah; she'll let you know when they're ready. Probably tomorrow, I imagine before sunup."

"Why don't I bring them?" Mayme offered. "Leave Joe out of this."

Charley dipped his head to one side and grinned. "If I wanted you to be running out here, I'd have said for you to do it. I want the doctor to come in that fancy car a his. And bring me some more of this. A lot more." Charley downed the rest of the glass, then wiped his mouth with the back of his hand. "Now, why don't you two hit the road."

Mayme and Joe left the cabin without saying another word to Charley or each other. They drove slowly along the dirt road, Mayme following in Joe's cloud of dust. She drove, wiping tears from her face, and prayed that Charley would let Joe be when he returned the next day. Charley didn't normally hurt anyone unless he had to, but that was before. Now that he'd already killed a man, he might figure he had nothing to lose. But Joe would be setting them up back in New York, so she hung her hope on that. If Charley needed Joe, he would not hurt him.

Joe continued down Muskogee Avenue. Mayme saw him watching her from his rearview mirror as she turned down Chickasaw Street and into the driveway of the little white frame house on the corner. She raised her hand, a gesture of a wave good-bye.

Mayme wasn't worried when Peggy told her the next evening that Dr. Stern had called to say he was ill. She even let her prattle on about how he worked too hard, didn't get enough rest, how he could use someone to take care of him. She told the chatty nurse not to worry about the doctor, that he would no doubt be back to work the next day. Peggy gushed on about how happy she was to be there in Tahlequah, how she hoped that she would find herself needed more by Dr. Stern.

Mayme busied herself by double checking every patient's vitals, taking a few minutes extra with each one to cheer them up with bits of gossip and poking fun, reminding them of mishaps of the past, or asking about every child or cousin they had within a hundred miles. She just wanted the night to end, to hear that Joe was somehow safe at home, though she already knew it would be more than a day or two before he returned. Charley would take Joe along for a good distance as a potential hostage should the need arise. She'd read enough newspaper accounts of Charley's escapades to know how he worked. No doubt they'd head to some place like Kansas City, where he would either find another car and send Joe driving back, or he'd let Joe off to catch a train home. That was no doubt why it had to be Joe to go back for him.   She would know all the backroads as well as Charley, maybe even better, but he would not want to take O.C.'s wife as his hostage.

Worry set in on the third day.   No matter what happened, Joe should have found his way back to town by the third day.   With each passing hour, Mayme felt her anxiety increase.   When she felt the floor slip out from under her and the world seemed to spin her around, she attributed it to shattered nerves and lack of food.   Since the incident at the cabin, the very thought of food sent her hunting for a vomit basin.   Finally, on the fourth day, Joe appeared through the side door of the hospital looking like he'd been on a three-day drunk. He was wearing the same clothes he'd put on nearly a week before, his beard thick and dark, his hair a tangled mess of curls.

"Oh, thank God," she said, throwing her arms around his neck and burying her face in his chest. She didn't give a thought to who might see or hear her.   All she cared about was standing right in front of her.   "I was so worried."

"I was, too, for a while there."

"What happened?"

"Charley had me drive them to some little place in Missouri where I rented them a room in one of those motor parks. I ran errands for him and Adam with Beulah and her sister, brought them food and newspapers, cigarettes, whatever they needed. For a while I thought I was going to New York with him, but then this afternoon, he handed me the keys, gave me back my car, and told me to head on home."

"Really?   Just go home?" Mayme pulled him into the small break room away from the doorway so that she could have some privacy with him, even if it was only a few minutes.

"Well, he also told me to get the hell out of Tahlequah. He said if I was still here when he came back, he'd make sure I didn't go anywhere else ever again, and the worst thing is," he swallowed hard and continued, "he was

254

headed to my mother's place in New York. I mean if I stay here and he finds out, well, I hate to think . . ."

Joe dragged his dirty fingers through his tangled hair and rolled his eyes, feigning a disbelief they both knew was untrue. If Charley said it, he meant it. The dark circles under his eyes and disheveled appearance showed her that he'd been through more hell then he'd ever let on. He was scared. Really scared. For the first time he seemed to understand how dangerous their lives had been, how one slip up could cost them everything, even their lives.

"What are you going to do?" she asked.

He took her hand and simply sat and looked at her for a long while. He took her chin in his hand to hold her gaze as he spoke, not allowing her to look away. "I'm going to go find another hospital or set up my own and then I'm coming back for you."

"No, Joe, I can't," she said, pulling her head away, freeing herself from his grasp. "I thought about everything that happened and what Charley said. I'm going to stay with O.C., settle down. You have to find someone else to be with in your new place. You got to get out of here quick, though; you never know when Charley will show up, and even though he's really a good guy at heart, he did tell you to go away. He doesn't like to be ignored."

Joe didn't say anything right away, just sat quietly. "Let's not talk about it yet," he said. "There's plenty of time for you to think while I go get settled in somewhere."

"No, no matter what, I've made up my mind. I nearly died when Charley caught us. I know I can't let anybody else know what I've been doing. I'm sorry, but I can't do it. I'm just not strong enough."

"Just give it time, Mayme. Things will settle down. You'll see. You're the strongest person I've ever met."

"No, Joe, I know you don't understand, but I have to do what I think is right. I'm staying here with my husband, at this hospital, with the folks I know, the folks who need me."

She pulled him to his feet and hugged him tight. "This is good-bye to loving you. From now on, we are just doctor and nurse, friends and neighbors. That's it."

"But, . . ."

Mayme shook her head no. "Shhhh. Trust me on this. I'm right. Please, let me do the right thing by you and O.C. both. Please." Her voice was resolute and certain, leaving no room for doubt of the decision she had made. She squeezed him one last time, then stepped away from him. "Now you got to go."

Joe approached her one last time and kissed the top of her head. "Good-bye, Love. For now."

"Good-bye Joe."

When the side door closed with a faint rattle of glass, Mayme wiped her wet eyes and returned to her station. It seemed nearly impossible that her world was splitting apart while half a dozen patients slept soundly just upstairs. She reached into her bag and pulled out her small flask and wished she had some of Joe's good whiskey to calm her down. She took a long drink from the bottle and felt the burn down in her belly. She'd forget the taste of fine bourbon and get used to Luther's nasty shine again.

18.

A dry breeze scattered fallen leaves across the road, bits of orange, yellow, and red tumbling to rest and gather in the hollow slope in front of their house, like a string of wishes and dreams, beautiful and short lived.   Though her spirits were lower than a snake's belly, the changing season offered Mayme a whisper of hope that things would be better soon.   Joe had already told everybody he was moving away to work in a new hospital in the western part of the state, a hospital that was owned by the community, the one that they had talked about so long ago. It pleased Mayme that he would be a part of something so lovely, so sensible. Like him. Once he was gone, it would be easier to move on, to forget how happy she had been all those early mornings they shared, the first light of the sun peeking through the curtains.

Mayme moved away from the window, leaving the leaves to themselves, and poured O.C. a cup of fresh coffee, setting it at his place at the table alongside the plate of biscuits and eggs.   The biscuits were from Mama, but Mayme had warmed them in the oven while she fried up the eggs so they seemed almost fresh baked. She wished the man would hurry with his endless primping and get to the table, or all her efforts would be wasted.

Finally, the bathroom door opened and the meticulous O.C. stepped out, looking good enough to be starring in the movies, not simply the man who cut hair and shaved beards. "Well, would you lookee here," he said, surveying the spread that waited for him, smacking his thin lips.

Mayme forced her best smile, tucked a stray strand of hair back behind her ears. "Well, since Mrs. Daniels hired that Peggy girl full-time, I can leave a little earlier. She's always in before she needs to be, like an eager puppy or something. Anyway, I figured you'd like a treat for a change."

Mayme poured herself a cup of coffee and joined O.C. at the table. She spread a dab of mulberry jam on a biscuit and took a bite. It seemed like she hadn't been hungry for days, but suddenly she felt like she could eat the whole plate of the golden biscuits and the entire jar of preserves while she was at it.

"I was thinking I'd come down and let you cut my hair this afternoon," she said between bites.

O.C.'s mouth was chewing a mouthful so he nodded his head up and down. "Good, good," he finally said. "How about we give you a nice short bob so you don't have to do all that braiding, just a little curl here and there, and you'll be the prettiest girl in town."

"I'm going to get some sleep first, but I'll come in before I go to the hospital." She reached for a second biscuit.

"I hear tell a new doctor is coming to take Doc Stern's place. Chester Peters said he'd been over to see Old Doc, and he told him he was making room for the new fellow."

"That's right," she said, "it didn't take more'n a minute and a telegram for Dr. Stern to find a replacement. It's one of his friends from back east, I think." Mayme was reminded of her struggle to maintain her composure when Mrs. Daniels gave her the news, how she'd smiled and acted pleased to hear how accomplished the new man was, all while her heart filled with a sadness that made her legs almost too heavy to move. Joe was really leaving. In a few days, he would be only a beautiful memory that she tucked away in the deepest crevice of her heart.

258

O.C. swallowed the last bit of egg and wiped his plate with a biscuit. Finally, he picked up the checkered napkin, wiped the corners of his mouth, and pushed himself away from the table. "Thank you for breakfast, Darlin'." He patted her on the top of her head and left her sitting at the table where she would eat another biscuit covered in mulberry jam and drink a tall glass of buttermilk before tackling the greasy mess she'd created in the kitchen.

Mama Holloway's familiar knock knock knock on the door came just as Mayme was pouring the grease from the fry skillet into the coffee can she kept under the sink. She wiped her hands on her apron and went to see what would bring the old woman to their house when she knew O.C. was not there. Everyone knew better then to disturb Mayme during her sleeping hours, and this should be a sleeping hour as far as anyone knew.

Mama stood on the porch holding a brown paper bag in both hands, her face glowing with a smug certainty, as if she knew what you did an hour before when no one was looking. Mayme saw the bag and assumed her mother-in-law was delivering O.C. another batch of biscuits and chicken to keep him from living off of canned soup and cheese sandwiches, somehow knowing Mayme had just swallowed the last of the earlier batch she'd provided.

"Morning, Mama," Mayme said as cheerfully as she could muster. She stepped back to let the stout woman pass in front of her, then closed the door behind them and followed Mama straight to the kitchen. "I'm afraid O.C.'s done gone to the shop, but I'll have you know he left with a full stomach."

"I didn't come to see O.C. I come to bring you somethin'."

"I hope it's one of your pies. Everone knows you make the best pies in Oklahoma. And Arkansas, too."

Mama placed the brown bag on the kitchen table, smiled, and reached in to carefully retrieve the gift she had for her daughter-in-law. The baby doll wore a lace-trimmed, sheer organdy dress and matching bonnet. Her

259

cheeks were painted a rosey glow, and her plump rubber arms and legs were so heavy she had the weight of a real baby. Bright green eyes sparkled and shined like emeralds, and her eyelids could slide down to allow her to sleep. Mayme had never seen the doll outside of Mama Holloway's dresser drawer. This was her treasure, the prize saved for her future grandbaby. She invited children to peek at her but never let anyone touch her, let alone hold her.

Mayme felt the floor slip out from under her, and she nearly fainted as the old woman placed the baby doll in her arms. Suddenly it all came too clear. The loss of appetite and nausea one day, voracious eating the next, exhaustion. All symptoms of being love sick and scared, she'd thought. Now she knew for a fact she really was love sick. One thing she'd come to know, Mama Holloway's hunches were not to be ignored.

"It's time I be giving that to you," Mama said.

"But, Mama, I ain't pregnant."

"We'll see." And with that she turned and headed for the door. "You best get some sleep, Mayme dear. You look even paler'n usual. I'll bring you some liver'n onions for supper." She paused at the door and looked back. "You want cherry or custard?"

"What's that?" Mayme asked, staring at the doll cradled in her arms.

"I'll make you a pie whilst I'm at it."

"Oh. Custard sounds fine."

As soon as Mama left, Mayme carried the doll to the bedroom and tossed it gently on the bed. She tried to remember the last time she and O.C. had shared a bed and had relations. Lord, she thought, it's been so long I don't know when. Then she tried to remember the last time she'd had her menses, but she'd never been regular. It was always a surprise, a slight cramp her only warning. She wrapped her arms tight around her midsection and paced around the room. "What am I gonna do now?" she asked herself. "This just can't be happening now."

Mayme yanked the pins out of her hair and nearly tore the buttons from her uniform before burying herself in the unmade bed. She curled up into a tight ball and prayed that Mama was wrong, that she would feel that ache in her belly and that the cursed dark blood would appear. Somehow, her mind and body relaxed enough to allow her to be lost to fitful sleep and fractured dreams.

Crickets were screeching loudly and Wilma was yelling something to her, but the crickets were so loud she couldn't hear a word she said. She wanted to know if it was a boy or girl, but she didn't understand cricket screeches, and Wilma was too far away and the screeching bugs were so loud. Joe was dancing and laughing with Peggy in the operating room, and Mayme was pounding on the small glass window, praying that he would look and see her, that he would open the door.

When she finally woke, her legs were twisted in the sheet that she had yanked free from the mattress, a pillow hugged tight to her chest. Mayme looked at the small silver clock on the night stand. It was just after one; she'd slept only four hours, but it was enough. She had things to do.

Wilma was sitting on her front porch snapping the tail ends from a big bowl of green beans. Her oldest boy, Eldon, was laying on the grass, examining a string of ants while his baby brother slept in a big basket under a shady redbud tree. "Well, ain't this a surprise," she said when Mayme stepped out of her truck.

"Hey, Big Boy," she said to Eldon. "Remind me to show you what we can do to those critters with a magnifying glass."

He scrambled to his feet and let her give him a bear hug, but he didn't say anything. He was a quiet one and seldom said a word. Mayme told Wilma not to worry, that he'd talk when he was good and ready or when everbody quit talking for him. She rubbed the top of his buzzed head and said, "You musta been to see O.C."

261

"Yeah, I took him over to the shop yesterday, get him cleaned up before his birthday."

"That's right," Mayme said. "His big day is comin' up. How's it possible he's gonna be four?"

"I have no idea. Billy's nine months now, if you can believe it."

Mayme looked over at the sleeping baby, then reached over and touched her friend's arm gently.

"So why are you visiting me on your way to work?" She pointed to Mayme's spotless uniform. They both knew it would not look like that in a few hours, no matter how many aprons she wore.

"I got a problem," she said, taking a seat beside her friend. "And you're the only one I can talk to, so no matter what I tell you, you have to promise you'll forgive me cause I need a friend. Can you do that?"

Wilma studied her friend's face and set the bowl of beans down at her feet. "Sweetheart, I don't care if you killed Herbert Hoover, I'm gonna forgive you, you know that. We're blood sisters, and you can't get closer then that." She reached over and took Mayme's hand, a reminder of a day twenty years before when they'd poked needles in their fingers to make them bleed, then pressed the wounds together to allow their blood to mingle and pool together.

"I think I'm pregnant," she started, and put her hand off to stop the expected burst of joy from Wilma. "It ain't O.C.'s baby."

"What? Well, for heaven's sakes, Mayme, whose baby is it?"

"Joe Stern's." She watched Wilma's jaw drop in surprise, her brown eyes widen, her mouth open.

"Dr. Stern?"

"Yep." She looked away, out over the top of Eldon's ant parade to where the road turned out of sight.

"How did that happen? Mayme, are you two timing on O.C.?"

"Yep." She turned back to meet Wilma's gaze. "Well, I was, I'm not anymore. You know Joe is moving away this week."

"Does he know?"

"No, and I ain't gonna tell him. If he goes away, everything will just go back to how it was before. 'Cept now I'll have a baby to take care of."

"Does O.C. know about you and Joe?"

"Hell no," she said, shooting a look of daggers at her friend. "Are you crazy? If O.C. found out, he'd have a damn heart attack. O.C. can never find out."

"So you're just gonna let O.C. think it's his baby?"

"That's right, but there's one problem. Me and O.C. haven't done nothing together in weeks and weeks."

"Mayme," she cried. "Have you done lost your mind? Go home and sleep with O.C. today. Right this minute, if you can."

Mayme chuckled at her friend. "Well, that would sure draw attention, me hiking up my skirt at the Normal Club Barber Shop right there for everyone to see." They both laughed at the idea of Mayme seducing O.C. at the shop.

"Naw, I know that's what I got to do, but I just needed to share the truth with one other soul. It was too much for me to hold onto all by myself." And with those words, the lump in her chest rose to her throat and salty tears stung at her eyes, but she never let one spill.

"Wilma, I want you to know we love each other, me and Joe. I never knew what that was like. I'll have a permanent reminder of our time together with this baby."

"I'm sorry, Honey." And that was all she could say. There were no words to fix this problem, no Cherokee magic to make it better.

Mayme went on. "For a minute I thought about going to Reno and getting me a divorce, but then it all seemed so scary, and Charley Floyd caught us."

"What?"

"Charley caught us together in your cabin."

"In my...? Good lord, Mayme, you said it was to take care of Charley," she whispered as if someone might be around the corner, listening.

"It was. That was before. We snuck out there a couple of weeks back, and Charley happened on us. He's the one made Joe move on. If I don't make this work with O.C., I'm afraid of what might happen."

Wilma held her friend's hand, her lips pressed tight. "Did you consider not having the baby?"

Mayme looked at her sadly and admitted that it had crossed her mind, but she couldn't bear the thought of ending what she and Joe made together.

"I even thought of packing up and moving away somewhere on my own, something I never thought I'd do before."

"Don't do that."

"I know. I can always find work, but I'd be alone."

"And who would take care of the baby? Strangers?"

"I just thought about it for half a second, probably because I'd been imagining running off with Joe."

Wilma squeezed Mayme's hand a bit tighter, a small hug of assurance.

"What time do you go on duty?" Wilma asked.

"Not till six."

"Why don't you let me fix you a little something to eat then. You can take it to work with you, eat it later tonight. You're gonna have to take better care of yourself now, you know that."

"I love you, Wilma," she said, reaching up and sweeping a loose strand of her friend's long dark hair back behind her ear. Wilma always wore her hair in one long braid down her back, a thick rope that swung from hip to hip when she walked. "It will be like we planned when we were kids. Our babies will be best friends, even though mine will be a might younger then yours."

"Unless I have me another one soon," she laughed, "and with me you never now. Shoot, Matthew looks at me and I get pregnant."

264

"I never thought I could have kids," Mayme added whistfully, her thoughts far from the idea of Wilma making one more child. "I mean, I never got pregnant before."

"Maybe O.C. can't."

"Maybe so."

They sat and watched Eldon crawl around on his belly, then roll onto his back and holler at the sky. When Mayme stood up and said she had to get going, Wilma rose to her feet and put her arms around her friend. "I'd like to tell you off for being unfaithful, but I think I'll save that for another time. Right now, I just want you to know that nothing will make me hate you. Come back on your day off and spend the whole day with me. You haven't done that in a long time." She stepped back and smiled slyly. "Now I know why."

"I love you, Wilma Jean."

There wasn't a single parking spot in front of the barber shop. Mayme had to park around the corner, just outside of Conley's Market. Cora and Henry were sitting on the sidewalk outside the store, no doubt hoping for a bit of a handout from some kind neighbor.

"Hello, Cora, Henry," Mayme said. "What are you two up to out here?"

"We're gonna sweep," Cora said.

"Well, good, good for you."

Cora got up and pulled Henry up, too. They fell in step with Mayme, and Cora asked in her dull voice, "Do you have anything to eat?"

"Not on me, but if you're around when I come back, I'll get you something. I'm just gonna let O.C. give me a haircut right quick." She smiled at the odd pair and patted Henry's head. He'd had a bath within a week, but he sure needed another. "If I give you some supper, will you both go home and take a bath?"

Before Cora could promise, she spied somebody or some thing that sent her scurrying to try and hide behind

Mayme, tugging at her clean white skirt, pulling Henry along with her to scrunch down behind Mayme's legs.

"What's the matter?" Mayme asked, looking around to see what frightened the poor girl. And there he was, that darned Scotty Walker. Mayme never liked him, not even when he was a kid. She knew he was one of those fools that ran around in white sheets causing all manner of trouble at night, then parked his butt in the front pew on Sunday morning singing about grace and God's love. There was something about him that had always made her skin crawl, an extra dose of meanness. She glared at the lanky man as he passed, saw him curl his lip and smirk at the cowering woman and her boy. And with that passing, she knew. She felt it like she felt her own skin. He was the bastard that made Cora pregnant. It was his own boy he sneered at as he passed. Fool, she thought, he's probly too dumb to even notice the boy had his same flat-tipped nose. This is how Mama must feel all the time, just knowing stuff without being told. She shivered at the thought of Scotty Walker forcing himself on the poor girl. It must have near scared her to death.

"Don't worry about him, Cora. I'll take care of him. You won't have to worry about him anymore." One of the benefits of being a nurse was not just knowing how to make people feel better; she could also make 'em feel a whole lot worse. Sooner or later her chance would come.

Cora let go of Mayme's hem, leaving a long smudge of dirt and grime where she'd used the dress as a shield. "Go on and do your sweeping. I'll give you some supper when I get back over there." She took two steps and looked back to see the pair watching her. "Go on now, I'll be back."

O.C. was just brushing a soft dose of talc on a handsome boy's neck when Mayme walked through the door. For a moment he wondered what might be wrong for her to pay him a visit. He'd forgotten all about her announcement that she'd come in for a haircut, but she'd never know that. He wondered what had gotten into his wife, fixing him breakfast, now fixing her hair.

266

"Hello, Darlin'," he sang, his voice a lilting melody of sweetness.

"Well, I'm here," she said, "ready to get chopped." Mayme hadn't been in the shop for weeks, maybe even months, she thought, but nothing had changed. She was greeted with the familiar smell of Burma Shave and soap, the whirr of a slow fan that hung from the ceiling, and the shuffling of O.C.'s feet as he danced around his customers, snipping bits of hair, brushing their necks with talc. He lived in a safe world, a clean world.

O.C. released the apron from around the young man's neck and gave it a quick shake, sending bits of golden hair flying. "Leon," he said, "this pretty lady is my wife, Mayme. She's a nurse over at the hospital."

The boy stepped down from the chair and nodded to Mayme and muttered softly, "Nice to meet you." He dug fifty cents from his pocket and handed it to O.C., who immediately dropped it into his cash register.

"Thank you kindly," he said, then picked up a broom and started sweeping before the fellow even got his jacket on. "You keep up your studies and stay outta trouble and..."

"I'll see you when I see you," the young man said, beating O.C. to his favorite farewell, then ducked out the door with his freshly cut hair and velvet smooth face, smelling like he'd taken a bath in Burma Shave.

Mayme smiled and tossed a wave to the boy, then took her place in the barber's chair, resting her head back on the pillowed headrest and her feet up on the big silver footrest. She liked it when O.C. raised the chair higher; the gentle rocking with each pull on the hand lever felt a bit like being on one of the rocking horses she had when she was a kid.

"Why on earth did you ever bother doing all this to your hair?" he asked, nudging her head foreward while he carefully removed the row of hair pins that held her braids tight to the back of her head.

267

"Habit, I guess." She shrugged her shoulders and rotated her ankles, willing herself to relax completely while he changed her looks to his liking.

O.C. dropped the pins into his pocket, unraveled her yellow bun, and started combing her fine hair, first examining and planning his approach, pulling a lock up straight, then to the right. When he moved to the front of the chair, he noticed the dirty smudge on her white dress and paused before making a part down the middle of her head.

"What happened to you? You fall down or something? Your dress is all dirty and you haven't even set foot in the door to the hospital yet. Good gravy, Mayme."

Mayme lifted the edge of her skirt to examine the dirt. "Oh, that. I run into Cora and Henry on my way here, and she took a fright when that Scotty Walker walked by us. Poor thing grabbed my skirt to hide from him." Mayme pressed hard on the padded armrests and sat up straighter so that her face was only inches from her husband. "O.C., I think he done something to her, something bad."

O.C. draped a clean apron around her and snapped it around her neck. "Oh, now, Mayme, don't get excited. Scotty's just an old peckerwood, likes to strut and squawk, but he ain't dangerous. He probably just scared her with the way he looks, he scowls kinda meanlike sometimes."

"I'm telling you, O.C., I know he hurt her and what's more, I think Henry is his boy. Just look at their noses. It's plain as, well, it's plain as the nose on Henry's face."

That made him smile as he combed a lock of hair between his fingers, then snipped the whole lot of it off with his sharp shears.

"Lawsy, O.C., don't scalp me!" She gasped at the sight of her yellow hair scattered on the floor.

"You're in good hands, Darlin'."

"Well, I'm gonna fix that Scotty. Sooner or later I'll get my chance, and I'll let him know I know, or maybe he'll get a little extra dose of castor oil in some baked cookies. You know me, I'll find a way." She closed her eyes. After seeing another handful of blond hair fall to the floor, she decided it might be better not to look until he was done.

"Well, for what it's worth, Scotty Walker has his merits. He never misses Sunday service, even helped out with the clean-up day we had over at the church last month. If I recall, he repaired a broken door to the prayer room. He's good with a hammer and nail, that one."

O.C. didn't doubt for a minute what Mayme said. Scotty Walker was the biggest scoundrel to pass through his shop. He didn't tell Mayme, but if that Dr. Stern hadn't left town on his own, Walker and his boys was planning on sending him on on their terms. Mrs. Daniels had mentioned to someone that she wished there was a Jewish girl around for him to date. Those old boys didn't much care for the idea of a Jew doctor in their town, and they had plans to do something about it. O.C. was always amazed at what men would talk about in the safety of a barber's chair, knowing that whatever they said in those walls was sacred. And really, O.C. had to admit, he didn't much care for the way Mayme spent so much time in the doctor's house, no matter what the cause. There was just something unseemly about the whole mess.

He looked down at his wife, her eyes closed, sitting straight up in his chair, letting him have his way with her. He reached down and fumbled the hair pins he'd pulled from her hair and for the hundred and umpteenth time thought of the pins he'd picked up from the doctor's house, from that little room by the kitchen. He hadn't been able to get it out of his head, wondering why on earth she would have pulled those things out in that room. She put them in there snug so's they wouldn't fall out. He imagined her with that Jew doctor, the two of them naked and twisting like snakes in that little bed, their bony bodies bumping together. The thought of it made him want to retch.

With one hand he held the back of her head, as if he held it still, and with the other he held the sharpest shears he owned. He knew that soft vulnerable spot along the

269

neck where one jab would make her blood flow and spurt like a fountain. She would finally be washed in the blood and pay for her sins. Her white garment would be forever stained with her blood, and she would be redeemed. The Lord would take her into his open arms so it would be a favor, a work of goodness.

"O.C." she said, reaching up and touching his arm gently, sending a shudder through his mind and body that seemed to shatter his confounded nightmare. "I was thinking maybe I'll take the night off, and you and me could go home after this and spend the evening together." She met his gray eyes and tried to convey a desire she did not have, but needed. "What do you say?" She touched the side of his face, then let her fingers travel down his chest. "Like old times? We can celebrate my new look."

"You can just take the night off?"

"It's not that busy down there, and I'm sure that Peggy will be more than happy to work herself silly. And they know I ain't been feeling up to par. I'll tell them I'm sick."

O.C. put down the shears and picked up a black plastic comb and dragged it through her new short bob cut. He swallowed the bitter pain and studied his new wife in the mirror. Yes sir, he thought, the Lord moves in mysterious ways. "I think that's the best idea I heard in a long time," he said.

19.

It was unusually hot for the middle of October, as if Charley was saying farewell in a blaze of white hot glory. Mayme had never seen so many people in one place. As far as she could see, cars lined the small road to Akin, Oklahoma, a town so small you'd miss it if you blinked twice. The dust was thick from all the cars, trucks, and buggies traveling the dirt road that led to the country cemetery. There wasn't a flower left to be picked or bought within fifty miles.

O.C. cried buckets of tears when the news came that Charley had been shot and killed on a farm in Ohio. It was the heartbreak he'd always known was coming, no other way for it all to play out other than for his friend meeting a bad end, leaving his wife and boy, his own mama, brothers, sisters, and a host of friends who loved him like family. His grief was inconsolable until his Mama paid him a visit and reminded him that now Charley could rest in the arms of Jesus and not be running and hiding out all the time. For some reason, hearing it from his Mama made it believable. He never doubted anything his mama said. When she added that she had been thinking of taking him up on his offer to move in with his family, it gave him another reason to smile through his days of sorrow.

They stood near the family, close enough to hear the sobs of Ruby and Dempsey, to see her swollen eyes as she glared the short distance to Beulah and Rose, knowing her

271

husband had lived with his whore in New York for the last year of his life. Mamie Floyd cried loudly, screamed that her boy never hurt no one. A men's choir sang "Rock of Ages" and "Old Rugged Cross." Finally, the minister began his remarks about Jesus and Charley both finishing their work on earth and moving on to better things.

Mayme gently shifted Hannah from one shoulder to the other and wished she'd remembered the carriage. Holding a sleeping 18-month-old baby was like having a hot water bottle strapped to her chest. Any other day she would have asked O.C. to hold her, but not today. He needed to be free to weep and grieve without a little girl wriggling in his arms.

When the preacher finally finished talking and folks started walking past the coffin, Mayme made her way to a shady grave and took a seat on the grass, not caring that she sat on someone's final resting place and not needing to parade past another dead body. She'd been too close to death too many times to go out of her way to brush up against it.

Hannah began to whimper and stir awake. Her dark curls were stuck to the side of her face, and her pale pink dress was damp with sweat. "Hey, sweet girl," her mama said, stroking her little head, "you ready to get up and run a little bit?"

"She's beautiful. Like her mother."

Mayme felt her heart skip at the sound of his voice. She looked up into his face and smiled.

"Joe," was all she said. She looked at his face and then into the face of Hannah, the coffee-colored eyes they shared, eyes that seemed to baffle everyone who wondered how she and O.C. could make a baby with brown eyes like that. His hair was cut short, so the familiar curls that framed her daughter's face were no longer there. She had not seen him since he left Tahleguah two years before, both of them keeping their promise to leave the other alone, to move on with their lives. She had never told him she was carrying his child.

"What's her name?" he asked, dropping down to one knee for a closer look at the little girl.

"Hannah," she said softly, stroking the little girl's hair, avoiding his gaze. Hannah sat in front of her mother, silently eyeing the stranger.

"That's a beautiful name."

"Thank you," she said, knowing he knew full well that she had named her after his mother, the secret silently flowing between them.

"How old is she?"

And there was the question Mayme feared most. He would know now, if he didn't already. "Eighteen months yesterday." Hannah turned around and touched her mother's nose and giggled. "Go on, you can get up," Mayme said. Hannah squirmed and rose to her feet and moved to examine the engraved headstone of Elmer Conklin who died in 1922.

Joe looked from Hannah to Mayme, then out over the mass of mourners. "I didn't know there were this many people in the entire state," he finally said.

"I guess no matter what he did, they loved him."

Mayme was sure the world went silent for just a breath, as if the thousands of voices surrounding them somehow drifted to the heavens.

At the sight of Mayme and Joe Stern sitting together, O.C. left his Mama in the company of her old friends from Sallisaw, other women who knew Charley when he was just a boy who picked cotton with his daddy.

"Afternoon, Dr. Stern. I didn't expect to see you here."

"I was actually quite fond of Charley Floyd, despite some of our disagreements." He rose to his feet to meet O.C.'s gaze.

"Are you still living in our neck of the woods?"

"Not really. I joined a hospital west of here, a community hospital."

Mayme looked up at him and smiled, genuinely pleased to hear his news. "It all worked out there then? I

273

know how much you wanted to be a part of something like that."

"That's right," he said, returning her smile.

"I read somewheres, probably the journal, that there's all kinds of folks want it shut down."

"We have some struggles, but it's exciting, all the same."

Hannah trotted back and fell into her mother's arms. "Hannah," she said, "I want you to meet someone special. This here is Dr. Stern. Can you say hello?"

Joe reached his hand out and took the small hand in his own. "Enchante'," he said, and the little girl giggled at the funny word.

"Why don't I take her over to Mama," O.C. offered, already reaching his arms out to carry her away.

"No," Joe said, "Let her stay; I think she's delightful."

Mayme smiled. "She is," she said. "Now, I want to hear all about this socialist hospital from the horse's mouth."

Joe continued to stare at Hannah and held his hands out to hold her. Without a moment's hesitation, she let him pick her up and put her on his shoulders. "Hannah has the best seat in the house now," he said.

"O.C.," Mayme said, "why don't you go on and see some of the people that you and Charley knew as kids, maybe you can even talk to Ruby if you can get through that crowd. Tell her to come see me when things calm down."

O.C. turned and scanned the crowd of people that milled about the cemetery, the long line still waiting to pay their final respects, the masses of flowers, and the dust cloud that rose from the road where cars began to make their way home. He looked back at his wife, who seemed flushed, and the lanky doctor, who held his giggling daughter on his shoulders.

"Go on, O.C.," she said. "We'll be fine here."

O.C. looked over at Joe. "You ain't gonna run off with my girl, are you?"

Joe looked at Mayme and smiled. "If I recall, Mayme only goes where Mayme wants to go."

"I meant Hannah."

"I know that. I just assume that Hannah goes where Mayme goes."

"Lord knows that's right," Mayme said and rose to her feet. "Go on, O.C. We're gonna talk about things that won't interest you."

O.C. turned and walked away to join his mama. When he looked back, all he saw was the three of them, walking toward the dusty road. Mayme never looked back.

Acknowledgments:

There are many people to thank for their endless encouragement and support. First and foremost, I am grateful to my daughter, Mary Kate Monahan, who always believed in me. I want to thank Nelson Lowhim, my editor. Thank you Liza Wieland, Steve Yarbrough, Connie Hales, Debbie Wray, Amy Bartel, John Hales, Linnea Alexander, and Patti Ringo. I also want to thank the people of Tahlequah, Oklahoma who were so gracious when I visited, willing to sit and talk with me about the history of their town and the Cookson Hills. Thank you Beth Harrington, Deborah Duval, and Merv Jacobs for your kindness and generosity. And, a special thank you to the staff at the Northeastern University Library who gave me access to special collections and archives. It is also important to thank many friends, particularly Donna McCloskey, Kathy McKinney, Martin McIntire, Audrey Kirk, and Frank and Doreen Dunn, for all the encouragement, kindness, meals and good wine.

I also must acknowledge the following sources that fueled my own story telling: Pretty Boy by Michael Wallis; The Bad Boys of the Cookson Hills by R. D. Morgan; An Oral History of Tahlequah and the Cherokee Nation by Deborah Duvall; and my grandmother's medical textbooks saved from her nursing school days.

THE AUTHOR:

Tanya Nichols (born May 27, 1957) is the author of the novel, The Barber's Wife. Her work has appeared in North Carolina Literary Review, Sycamore Review, In the Grove, and San Joaquin Review.

Nichols received her MFA in fiction writing in 2004 at Fresno State University where she won creative writing awards in both fiction and creative non-fiction. For the past eleven years, Nichols has taught writing and literature at Fresno State. She also serves as the coordinator of the Young Writers' Conference and editor-in-chief of San Joaquin Review.

As a child, her family moved often, up and down the state of California. Frequent moves and new homes fueled her love for stories as constant companions. Tanya is also a musician who plays mandolin and sings in a folk band. As a writer, she is naturally drawn to music with lyrics that tell a story.

Tanya has one daughter, Mary Kate Monahan-Zolin, a video producer living in San Francisco with her husband, Maksim Zolin.